J. A. BOULET

THE
ORIGINS

Also by J. A. Boulet

The Strong Amongst Us

The Strong Within Us

The Wars Between Us

J. A. BOULET

THE ORIGINS

Published by J. A. Boulet

Book cover design: J. A. Boulet

ISBN: 978-1-7781999-1-2

This book is dedicated to my late mother, Maria.

Her memory helps me grow every day into a better human being.

Be strong, no matter what life has in store for you.

Note to Reader

This book is a work of historical fiction. I have attempted to be accurate with many of the historical events, although some details have been intentionally skewed to fit within the story. This is a fictional saga of strength, love, Icelandic culture and natural disasters. Even though many of the historical details are accurate, this book should be read as fiction.

J. A. Boulet May 2, 2022

PART ONE

1850

CHAPTER 1

Margret looked down at her mother's slim hand and grasped it within her tiny palms. The morning rays scattered beautifully into the room, highlighting the yellowish hues of the walls and the brownish tones of the blanket that covered her mom's body. Momma was barely awake, and Margret was worried.

Mother had been sick for the past few weeks. It had all happened so suddenly. Just a month ago, her momma was labouring with the animals in the fields with Pappa. Then the cold weather descended, and influenza snuck into their home like a devil in the night. First Margret was sick, then Pappa and then Momma.

But Momma wasn't improving as Margret and Pappa had. Momma always had a wheezy breath, and this terrible influenza just made it so much worse.

Mother coughed hard, and Margret could feel her convulsions rock the bed. The coughing fit shook her Momma's body, and Margret could do nothing but watch helplessly. She whispered a silent prayer and held her mother's hand tighter.

"Get her some water," Pappa said from the corner of the room, his eyes red from lack of sleep.

Margret rushed to the kitchen and poured a glass of water. She returned quickly to the bedroom, sitting down lightly and carefully tilted the glass to her mother's lips. Momma drank it sloppily, some water spilling onto her nightgown.

Margret adjusted the glass to a trickle so her mom could swallow better, but the cool liquid still spilled over. It was almost as if her mother couldn't swallow.

Mother coughed hard, and water spurted into the air as another coughing fit racked her body.

Margret looked at her father in alarm. "Pappa!"

He stood and tilted his head in distraught. "Let me take that water, Margret," he said. "I wish you'd call me pabbi like every other child in Iceland. Go in the kitchen and warm up some soup for dinner." Pappa laid his hand on his wife's forehead and was alarmed at the heat emanating from his wife's head.

Margret looked worriedly from her mother to her father but didn't budge. She had always called her pabbi and mamma by the English versions, much to the dismay of her parents. "You are Pappa to me," she said lightly for the millionth time. Margret curled over her momma and hugged her fiercely, trying to crawl into the bed with her.

Pappa squeezed his eyes shut, hoping to quell the tears threatening to escape. His daughter was a defiant child, but she was just as scared as he was. He could see it in her eyes.

After a few moments, Pappa laid his hand on Margret's small head. "Sweetheart," he said. "Go heat up the soup."

Her small 12-year-old body uncurled from the bed and stood as strongly as she could muster. "Alright," Margret said simply, then walked away into the hallway.

Pappa watched her retreating form and then laid another hand on his wife's forehead. He leaned over and hugged her warm body as another coughing fit shook her chest. Pappa fisted the sheets together and tightly grabbed his wife, rocking her back and forth. He knew it was serious, but he was hoping she would make it.

The doctor was going to be here tomorrow morning to save her, he hoped.

Margret stirred the soup slowly on the iron stove, worrying about her mother. She had always had a wheezy breath, and sometimes in the fields, she would start coughing hoarsely. In the middle of a harvest, she would take many breaks to catch her breath.

When influenza came into their home, Momma had nursed both her and her Pappa better with soups, hot drinks, blankets and loving care.

Now Momma was sick.

Some people had died from this nasty influenza. A few adults succumbed, and many babies died. Margret wrapped her momma's red shawl around her shoulders and shivered. She couldn't imagine a life without her momma. It was unfathomable. Momma would just simply have to survive. She must be here with them.

Margret would have to think positively. Such thoughts were like the devil trying to enter her brain. She had heard the pastor at the church say such things. That must be what it is, she thought.

She gazed through the kitchen window across the bleak frozen landscape. Iceland had some bad winters, but mostly it was bearable. Drift ice along the shores in the north brought cold weather along the eastern side of the island, and this past year was colder than usual. They lived on a sheep ranch near Horn. It was an expansive hilly countryside with beautiful views of the ocean to the east, and the mountainous regions rose to the west.

It was quite sunny today, and the weather was pleasant enough to lift her hopes. It was the start of spring and a new beginning. They had harvested all the weak animals before the last harsh winter, the neighbourhood community chipping in to help. Even Margret had been out in the fields tending to the vegetable crops and helping to build shelters for the remaining animals. The winter was typical, cool but pleasant with the ocean air, until January when the winter struck hard, with freezing temperatures and blowing winds. Sometimes the door would stick, the wooden frame swelling in the humidity, imprisoning them all in their home.

Margret sometimes wished she could fly away on a bird's wings to a different country, somewhere more pleasant, somewhere easier. Her eyes glazed over as the sun shone brightly into the kitchen, warming her hands.

She was only a child, but she had her share of life's tribulations. Her younger brother had died at birth, and her mother could not conceive again. The doctor said the blood in her uterus was no longer any good. Margret wondered if such talk was true or just a simple explanation for a complex problem.

The soup began to boil, and she grabbed the oven mittens. Margret lifted the pot to the side table, placing it on a large ceramic cooling pad. She ladled hot soup into three bowls. Hopefully, Momma would eat. She sat down and waited patiently for the bowls to cool enough to take one to Momma. Margret laid her chin in her hands and daydreamed across the bleak landscape. One day, she would grow up, fall in love with a handsome man and have many children of her own. She looked forward to that day. Margret always wanted a big family.

The longcase clock chimed at 2 o'clock in the afternoon. The sound awakened her out of the daydreaming.

She tested the soup with a small spoon and blew on it. It was cooled enough. She would feed her mother, and Momma would get better.

The sun slowly lost its shine when nobody was looking. Margret and her father tried everything to help Momma, but she wasn't getting any better. It was frustrating and heartbreaking. Margret cooked all the food and cleaned the house, trying to become the woman of the homestead while her mother was sick. Margret thought if she worked harder, then God might smile upon them, and good things would happen. Her father took care of Momma in bed, cleaning her delicate pale skin with a wet cloth. Margret fed her and made sure Momma always had water. But Momma wasn't getting any better.

The clouds had turned grey today, and the skies were bleak. Spring was not bringing the new beginning she had hoped for.

Margret tried to stop the shaking in her hands, but it was futile. She was too upset. Her father stood beside her smoothing her hair slowly, almost absentmindedly. The old blankets were laid straight over the bed, covering her Momma's body and face.

"She's gone, my dear," Father said, his voice shaking and cracking with emotion.

"No!" Margret shouted, looking at her Pappa like he somehow had lied, and this was all a dream.

"Your Momma has died, sweetheart," Father replied sadly. "The doctor tried what he could, we all tried what we could, but it didn't work. She was too sick."

Margret opened her mouth to speak and closed it. She tried again and lost her words. There were no words she could speak that would make anything better. The worst had happened. The very thing she had prayed for never to happen had just destroyed her life. She suddenly felt faint, like the floor was light beneath her feet.

Her mother had died.

She fell towards the floor as her father caught her falling body from hitting the hardwood.

Pappa picked up her petite body, cradling Margret in his arms and wept for himself and their future.

CHAPTER 2

The next few months inched by slowly. It seemed like she was trapped in a strange slow-motion play, and somehow everything wasn't real. Margret cried in her bed for weeks before Pappa started teaching her numbers and reading again. She was always interested in numbers, and she had begged her father to teach her when she was young. He complied grudgingly, noting that girls had little use for such knowledge, although Margret was a quick learner and absorbed every little thing.

She read and completed her numerical questions for the day. Margret looked up and exhaled wearily. She knew her father was worried about her. Margret was becoming more and more withdrawn. Some days, it felt like she was only living to make others think she was okay. But, when the day ended, and her head hit the pillow, she knew that nothing was alright.

Uncles, aunts and cousins had visited. They helped around the house, cooking and cleaning. They always looked at her with this pitiful look in their eyes. It made her emotional when they looked at her like that. She wished they wouldn't. Her relatives always apologized and expressed their condolences.

Life went on. The relatives filtered out, and the neighbours helped out in the fields. Several boys from surrounding farms would help with the sheep farm. Her father paid them with dinner or frozen fish. One boy, Einar, lived in the neighbouring homestead. He was a teenager, and Pappa paid him regularly to help out.

He was at the dinner table tonight. Einar chewed with his mouth open, and Margret thought that was disgusting. He was a hardworking boy, though, Margret mused; maybe that was why.

"Sorry about your Momma," Einar said, a mouthful of food in his cheeks.

Margret froze with her fork to her lips. She placed the fork back onto her plate and stared at him. She became upset when people said such things. It made her feel uncomfortable. "How do you think I'm supposed to respond to that?" she said impulsively. "Am I supposed to say it's alright? I can't say that because nothing's alright anymore. I lost my mother. Nothing will ever be okay again."

"Now, sweetheart!" her father chastised. "The boy was just trying to be polite."

"No, Mr. Petersson," Einar said softly. "It is my fault. I'm not so good at expressing my concern for your family and your hardships. My parents always said that I am too brash."

Margret looked across the table at Einar. Yes, he was brash, but he cared enough to say something. Margret continued eating in silence as the conversation turned to the weather and the sheep. She listened but didn't contribute. She had little to say since her mother passed away. Life was full of greys now like it somehow was missing its colours.

She stood when everyone was finished and gathered the dishes. She would be turning thirteen next month. Her life was still a slow-moving play.

PART TWO

1855

CHAPTER 3

The fields were lush and green, with dew resting on every blade, it seemed. Margret rushed across the fields to get home from her friend's house. They had giggled at the boys and laughed all night until she fell asleep on the sofa. Her Pappa would be mad that she didn't come home last night, although she was eighteen now and growing into an adult. Her breasts were getting larger, and her face was elongated with a womanly curve. She looked a lot like her mother, her relatives said.

A boy at her friend's house had asked her on a date, and she had said yes. She was thrilled with the possibilities. Her heart lifted impossibly higher. Could it possibly be? Finally, she could marry and have a family? The boy was quite handsome and charming. She felt her confidence soar. He made her feel attractive and alluring whenever she was around him. His name was Magnus. He was tall, blue-eyed and slim. His eyes had a dreamy way of undressing her, she thought. Her body would immediately respond without the consent of her mind, it seemed.

There was one problem. Magnus was twenty years old. Her Pappa wouldn't like that.

She had grown very close to her Pappa. After the first rough year of losing Momma, they had developed a routine. He would go outside and work with the animals; Margret would take care of the house, cleaning and cooking. She had become an amazing cook. There was an abundance of sheep meat, so she learned how to maximize the bounties, balancing them with the other scarcities of living in Iceland.

Margret made wonderful sheep stews with plenty of potatoes and vegetables. She had developed a knack for spices and herbs that made her stews taste like heaven. Grains were scarce, so she used rye for all the baking, often making flatkaka, an unleavened bread. Potatoes were more common, so she added potatoes to everything, often mashing them to hide them in the recipes.

On weekends, her father would take her out fishing on the boat. They would bring in large nets of fish, then spend almost the entire weekend gutting and slicing the fish into portions. It was a pleasant change from the constant staple of eating sheep meat.

It was a hard life, but they had each other, which is what mattered. Einar and the other neighbours helped out occasionally. Their sheep flock had grown to forty animals. They were finally prospering after those early tough years.

Margret opened the front door slowly, trying not to make the hinges squeak. She held the door open and listened to the early morning household. She didn't know if Pappa was sleeping or tending to the herd outside.

She carefully closed the door behind her, and just as the door reached halfway to the jam, it squeaked loudly.

Damn, those loud hinges, she thought.

She braced herself for her dad's questions. Nothing, the house was quiet.

She closed the door firmly and then jumped in surprise.

"Where have you been, sweetie?" Pappa said, his large form filling the doorway towards the back hallway.

Margret swallowed. "I was at my friend's house," she said, pulling her coat off and hanging it on a hook. "I'm sorry, I fell asleep on her sofa. It was getting too dark to come home anyways. I hope you didn't worry."

"I did worry," Father said. "But I trust your judgement. I know you'll always make the right decisions."

"Thank you, Pappa," she responded. "I try."

Father walked into the early morning sun shining in the kitchen. "Today is a special day," he said, pausing momentarily.

"It is?" she asked.

"You forget," he chastised. "It would have been your mother's birthday today, if she would have lived."

"Oh, yes," she said softly. "I didn't forget that. I never could. It is burned into my memory."

"You remembered?"

"Yes," Margret said, lifting her shoulder-length hair from her back and smoothing it onto her shoulder. "I try to forget how much it hurts, but it never works."

Pappa looked at her and smiled weakly. "We can do something special tonight," he offered. "Let's bake some flatkaka, just like your mom would have done."

"Ok, let's do that."

Her father tilted his head suspiciously. She never readily agreed to everything. Something was wrong. "Are you okay? Is there anything you need to tell me?"

Margret shuffled her feet. "Well, sort of."

"What is it?"

"I agreed to go on a date with a boy," she responded swiftly, as if getting the words out quicker would make the uncomfortable subject go away.

"Oh, I knew this day would come soon," Pappa said, scratching his beard. "You are becoming a beautiful young woman. Soon every boy will notice."

"No, it's not like that," she said hastily. "He's nice."

"How old is he?"

Margret looked down at her shoes and thought briefly of a good answer. She could lie and say that she didn't know or some other excuse. "He's my age," she blatantly lied. "Magnus is eighteen."

"Oh, I must be happy for you then," Pappa said slowly. "But please be careful. I would like to meet this gentleman. When did you agree on the date?"

"No specific time," she replied. "He was planning on asking you first."

"Well, I approve," he said. "You have had nothing normal in your life lately, so you deserve to socialize with friends your own age."

Margret nodded, the words sinking in and the lie sinking deeper. She shuffled her feet out of her clogs and ran down the hall to her room. "Thank you, Pappa. I'll make sure he talks to you!" She closed her bedroom door and fell against it breathing heavily. How was she supposed to tell her father that Magnus was really twenty and that he hadn't even attempted to ask for her father's permission? Boys were so confusing. One minute they were showering a girl with attention, and the next minute doing things that were against her standards of upbringing. She could never understand why boys did things like that.

But she liked him. She liked him a lot. As she thought about Magnus, her body felt hot and on fire from within. Her face became flushed, and her breathing grew heavy. These sensations were so new to her. Margret didn't know what to make of these new feelings.

But she liked feeling this way. It made her glow.

They were meeting secretly at the secluded beach. Magnus stood confidently with his hands shoved deep into his pockets. He had darkish hair, which was odd in Iceland. It made him even more mysterious. He was also quite tall, higher than six feet. His face was in the wind, and his shoulder-length hair flapped near his ears.

He was a handsome devil, Margret thought. A fleeting idea floated into her mind. Maybe he knows how attractive he is. Perhaps she wasn't the first girl to notice his looks and fall for his charm.

"Margret," Magnus said smoothly, his hand outstretched to hers.

She continued walking happily towards him until she reached him. Margret clasped his hand easily, and they turned to walk along the beach, relishing in the warm summer evening. The beach was still blessed with the sun even though it was close to bedtime. Iceland in July had a glorious twenty-one hours of daylight. The midnight sun graces the land in the short summer months. Margret smiled as they swung their hands and started skipping along the shoreline.

He laughed and pulled her hand playfully. Margret ran to keep up. Soon, they were running and laughing at the same time, the wind in their hair. They ran along the sandy shore at full speed, their hands still joined, laughing joyfully. Margret glanced at Magnus and could feel the spirit of playfulness radiate from him into her. It was the most exquisite feeling in the world.

Finally, they stopped, winded and breathing hard. Magnus had his hands on his knees, and his breath came out forcefully. Margret was the same, her breathing was fast, and they could barely talk.

"So fun!" Margret said between heavy gusts of breath. She curled an errant strand of hair from her eyes and closed her skirt between her knees.

"Yes! Thrilling!" Magnus shouted, gulping in oxygen. His eyes gazed down at her skirt.

"I love this," Margret said, her breathing slowing enough to talk now.

Magnus grasped her other hand and held her closer, his face looking directly at hers. She smiled coyly and accepted his embrace. He hugged her firmly, bringing her into his warmth. Her breathing increased again as if on cue. She looked down, and Magnus kissed her forehead. Her skin became hot, and she felt pleasant tingles from where his lips had touched her forehead.

Margret looked up. Suddenly, Magnus took the opportunity and kissed her lips. A full-body sensation immediately overtook Margret. Shards of electricity spread all over her body, from her head to her toes. She had never felt like this before. It was a wondrous feeling. Her legs quivered, and her hands briefly shook. His tongue was hot, and it poked into her mouth, parting her lips. She opened her mouth to accept him, and he took control. She melted in his arms from the overwhelming bodily sensations.

Magnus lifted his hands underneath her armpits and lifted her effortlessly to a rocky outcrop, placing her firmly against the rock wall. He continued kissing her, and it fuelled her reactions even further. She involuntarily groaned.

The little noises she made filled him with an intense desire that he could no longer control. It was as if her body was holding a conversation with him. Magnus just followed his instincts. His hands slowly slid up her skirt, inch by inch, until finally, he felt her soaked undergarments. His penis hardened like a rock, and his brain stopped working.

His hands rummaged in her undergarments until he found the spot. He tugged, and the fabric wouldn't budge. He tugged again, and it still wouldn't budge, so he rubbed her vagina through her undergarments hard, pressing his urgent fingers against her hidden lady parts.

Margret felt her mind wander off, and her legs started vibrating. She was extremely wet between her legs, as if she had peed herself, but somehow she knew that she had not. Her entire groin felt like it was on fire.

Magnus kissed her roughly, his tongue probing deeper into her mouth. Margret kissed him back with a surprising urgency. He wound one hand into her hair and tilted her head to kiss her more deeply. Her hair knotted in his fingers, and she relished in the slight pull. She was no longer thinking; her brain had shut down. Her physical body had taken complete control. Her urges were just as strong as his, and together they floated on a precarious cliff of desire. Their physical needs for each other threatened to wash them away into the ocean with no return.

Margret felt his fingers poking and rubbing at her vagina urgently. Her legs melted into his expert hands as if they weren't attached to her body. His fingers became more and more insistent. Her brain only focused on his fingers now. Nothing else mattered, not his kisses, not his hands in her hair, only those daring fingers at her entrance.

Her vagina quivered, and she groaned again.

Magnus tugged hard at her undergarments, and something ripped. A thick hot finger slipped into her vagina expertly. Margret gasped in shock, her entire body stiffening. A gush of liquid coated his hands, slippery with the wetness of her sex.

He poked his finger roughly into her, probing urgently, not even thinking about what he was doing, his primal urge taking complete control of his mind.

He felt her move uncomfortably and froze.

"No," she said weakly.

Magnus stopped. His breath was coming out in heavy gusts similar to when they were running. He panted on her neck and told himself to let her down from the position he had her in. Gently he eased the pressure of his hips on hers. He hadn't even realized that he had been grinding his hips against hers.

"I'm sorry," he said breathlessly. "You make me lose all control."

Margret exhaled rapidly. What was she thinking? She had just met this man! He was older than her and hadn't even met her father yet! "I don't know what happened," she said dumbly. "One minute we were laughing and running, then the next, we were clawing at each other." She giggled softly.

"You are so incredibly alluring, Margret," Magnus responded. "You reduced me to a puddle at your feet."

"I think it was the other way around," she said, her voice coated thickly with desire.

"I want to see you again," Magnus said, swiping a strand of hair from her face and curling it around her ear. He kissed her gently on the cheek. "Will you come on another date with me tomorrow?"

Margret thought about it briefly. "Yes," she lied. Her body was beginning to panic as if something had set off her danger response. Magnus had stopped when she told him to, but she was confused. Her body sent hundreds of mixed messages everywhere. She didn't know which responses to believe.

"Okay," he said. "Let's get you back home before your dad worries about you."

"Thank you," she said, linking her hand into his. The instant memory of her vagina spilling fluid onto his hand made her cringe, but it gave her a strangely happy glow. She felt like a grown woman, although it scared her at the same time.

Magnus walked with Margret calmly along the sand. He slipped an arm around her waist to steady her. They walked like this together across the expanse of sand they had previously run across. It took a long time to cross the sand in this slow, unsteady intimate walk. Finally, they teetered out of balance, and Margret almost fell. Magnus caught her in time.

Then they both felt the earth move.

Margret looked up at him in alarm.

"It's just a small earthquake," he said calmly. "It happens so often here."

The earth moved again under their feet as they both stood rooted to the spot. It wasn't a huge earthquake, but it was alarming enough to have the earth move below your feet.

"I guess," she said calmly, even though her heart skipped a beat.

"It's alright," Magnus said reassuringly. "I'll walk you home."

The earth shook again slightly, weaker than before, and the panic in her throat calmed somewhat. Magnus held her tight, impossibly protecting her from the moving earth. She chuckled. It felt good to be held by a handsome man, especially when he was so obviously attracted to her.

"I wish we didn't have to live on such a volatile island," she said softly. "Earthquakes and volcanoes are all around us. I think Pappa told me there were two hundred volcanoes here!"

"True, I think it's a bit higher than two hundred," Magnus said, squinting against the midnight sun. "Where else would you live if you could choose?" he asked.

"I don't know," she said noncommittally. "Just somewhere that has a stable earth." She chuckled.

Magnus laughed. "You're funny," he said as they walked across the sand.

The midnight sun settled on the horizon, shining brightly over the volcanic peaks and valleys. They both stopped in wonderment to watch the midnight sun setting over the mountainous regions. Magnus hugged her from behind as they stood gazing at the setting sun. Rays of gold, purple and blue streaked across the sky, taking their breath away. The scenery was still, but the sun moved ever so slowly, setting late in the evening as it always did in July. It was earlier than midnight, of course, because the mountains were higher than the ocean. They would soon not be able to see the sun.

"It's so beautiful," Margret said, awestruck.

"The south side of the island is beautiful too," he replied. "You can see the sun setting right on the ocean."

"I'd love to see that," she said softly.

"Maybe one day," he replied vaguely, dreaming of the future. Magnus released her from behind and stood beside her, holding her hand.

Margret gazed at his handsome face and then glanced back at the setting sun as it dipped below the horizon, basking the opposite eastern shores in a purple bluish darkening sky.

"Maybe one day you'll never want to leave," he said smugly as they began walking again, stepping off the sand and onto the grassy fields.

She chuckled. "Maybe you're right," she replied, walking beside him, her hand firmly in his.

They strolled an extra hundred yards until they reached her house. At the bushes leading to her home, he kissed her gently. "I'm sorry I lost control earlier; please forgive me," Magnus asked genuinely.

Margret smiled. "I forgive you," she said, her heart hesitantly agreeing with her words. Watching the sunset with him was a wonderful feeling, and it had dulled the previous misgivings she had.

"I will see you tomorrow evening on the beach," he said softly, kissing her hand.

"Yes," she replied.

Magnus walked away, waving, then drifted into the fields as dusk finally began to descend.

Margret waved and turned to walk up the pathway to her house. She ran her hands through her knotted hair, worrying about her dad seeing her hair so messy. He would interrogate her about where she had been. She licked her hand and slicked her hair down, praying that he wasn't awake.

She opened the front door quietly and stepped in. As luck would have it, Pappa was fast asleep in his room, his snores filling the house. Margret padded gently to her room, sat down on her bed, removed her clothes quickly and masturbated herself to sleep.

CHAPTER 4

"When did you come home?" Pappa asked, standing by the stove as he spooned porridge into two bowls.

"I don't know," Margret said shyly. "I didn't look at the clock."

Pappa placed the bowls on the table and sat down. "Did you have a good time?" he asked.

"I did, yes," she replied, stuttering. "I went walking along the beach with some friends."

Pappa ate his porridge in silence. His daughter was growing up. He had to fight down the instinct to kill any boy that got too close to his daughter. Instead, Pappa had to trust that she would make good decisions. The values he had instilled in her had moulded her into the good woman she was today.

Margret exhaled a sigh of relief that her father had not asked too many questions. She was a terrible liar. Her face often turned pink, and she would jumble her words. Margret spooned the porridge into her mouth and added some more cream. She hungrily devoured the entire bowl and stood to clear the table.

"You were hungry," her father stated, chuckling.

"No, you just didn't eat fast enough," she retorted, smiling.

Pappa laughed heartily and finished his porridge, helping clear the dishes. "Did you want to go fishing today?" he asked. "Maybe we can catch a large cod."

"I would love that, Pappa," Margret replied immediately. It gave her the perfect excuse not to be home when Magnus called.

She had mused over the past evening with Magnus and had concluded that he was not the kind of boy she should be spending time with late at night. The alarms he had set off in her heart had been loud enough of a warning. She could not dismiss such reactions. Watching the midnight sun was delightful, and being with Magnus was fun, but something about the man worried her deeply. Margret was too young to understand it all, so she simply chose to ignore it.

She would spend time with Pappa instead.

Magnus arrived early at 9 pm, and the house lights were out. He wasn't brave enough to knock on the door, so he waited several minutes. He could hear some faraway voices at the dock.

Margret's voice lilted in the air. "We caught a big one! Just like you said, Pappa!"

"We will have a good dinner!" Pappa exclaimed. "But it is so very late. We will put some of these fish fillets in the pan right away. The rest we will salt."

Together, they stumbled out of the bushes into the clearing hauling all the fishing materials onto the deck. Margret held the net proudly with the large cod in it. They fumbled with the door and slammed it behind them, laughing loudly about their fishing trip.

Margret immediately began slicing the large fish into fillets and preparing the rest for salting. Pappa shuffled around the house, putting things away and changing his wet clothes. Margret sensed something strange but didn't know what it was. She had forgotten about her plans with Magnus quite easily. Margret finished preparing the fish happily and slapped four large fillets on the cast iron pan. It sizzled as it hit the lard. She was glad she had spent the time with her father, her only family. It meant so much to her.

"You were always a good cook, my sweet," Pappa said, kissing her cheek. "I'll get the dishes on the table. Then we can have a delicious feast."

Margret smiled and looked out the front window at the darkening landscape.

Magnus swallowed and walked slowly away. She had forgotten about their planned rendezvous today, he thought. Margret was enjoying time with her family. Magnus never had any family; he was always a loner. He would love to have a father again.

He stepped onto the dirt road and walked back to the friend's house where he was staying nearby. Magnus was only visiting friends in Horn for a short time. He would have to return back home soon.

Magnus hiked down the large hill with sadness creeping into his heart. Maybe she didn't like him anymore because of his dogged persistence. He would try to see her again. If she avoided him again, then he would just disappear. She was just another woman, after all.

～

"Mr. Petersson," Einar said, his hands moving around the sheep's body while shearing the wool from the animal's skin. He looked up and paused. "Could I get my pay today? I have been supporting my entire household now. My parents have grown old, and my brother has left for Reykjavik. Our property is small, with only a quarter-acre useable; the rest is mountain ash rock. We only have a few horses, nothing like the sheep herd you have."

"Yes, I can do that," Pappa Petersson replied. "I will give you some coins to buy essentials for your family. I can also give you some sheep meat."

"That would be perfect," Einar said gratefully. "I appreciate it."

Margret came bouncing out of the house, her skirt flowing behind her gaily. Einar watched her dance lightly across the fields. He thought she looked like an angel. Her skirt was light pink with a dark grey overcoat, and it billowed behind her. Her legs were skinny but muscular, and her hair was darkish blonde.

"Pappa!" Margret shrieked.

"Oh my Lord," Pappa exclaimed. "What is it, my sweet? You look so excited!"

"Aunt Helga and Uncle Sig have come to visit!" she shouted gleefully. "You must return to the house! They just arrived."

Pappa looked at Margret, then glanced back at Einar. A funny look was on the younger man's face. A wave of fierce anger boiled in his veins as he noticed his farm helper ogling his daughter. "Einar!" Pappa shouted, snapping the boy out of his funk. "I have to go. Make sure those sheep are all sheered tonight. I will pay you when you're done."

"Yes, sir," Einar responded.

Margret glanced at Einar. "You can join us for dinner!"

"Sweetie," Pappa interjected. "Einar is busy with his family too."

"I can stay for a quick meal," Einar replied. "My parents will be okay tonight."

"Fine then," Pappa shouted back as they crossed the field. "But finish that shearing! I need to sell that wool to a neighbour this weekend."

Margret looked curiously at her dad. "Why are you being so strict with Einar?" she asked innocently. "You are never that way with him."

"He needs some boundaries," Pappa responded stonily. "That man will start thinking he's part of our family otherwise."

Margret glanced at her father strangely. "Alright, Pappa, whatever you think is best," she said. "Come on, let's help Auntie and Uncle with their things. They can stay in the third bedroom. I will make the bed while you help them in."

"Good idea," Pappa said.

After settling the relatives in, Margret and Pappa began cooking dinner when Einar knocked on the back door. Margret opened it joyfully. "Come in, Einar," she said. "Go wash up in the basin over there."

Einar dutifully obeyed and returned to the dining area to be introduced to the sparse family. Aunt Helga and Uncle Sig never had children. There were rumours that her uncle had contracted a virus when he was young, and it had stolen his ability to have babies. They didn't know if it was a true story or not.

Regardless, Margret was thrilled to have relatives over. She had always wanted a larger family, although she was content with the people that she had. Some cousins lived on the north side of the island, and they would visit periodically when travelling was safe.

"You must eat more, my dear," Helga insisted. "You are too slim, Margret!"

Margret chuckled. "I eat plenty," she smiled. "Don't worry about me." She stuffed the meat mixture into the sausage lining, forming slátur, a blood sausage made out of the heart, lungs and blood of the sheep mixed with oatmeal, seasoning and onions. Her father had brought everything she needed to make the sausages. Pappa supported Margret with her keen interest in cooking. She turned to Helga. "I will give you some slátur to take home with you. We will have too much."

"That would be wonderful, Margret," Helga replied, patting Margret's forearm. "You have become a good cook like your mother was."

Margret's eyes clouded over as if a dark cloud had abruptly stopped over her head. She looked at Helga blankly and continued stuffing the large sausages. She decided to change the subject. "Dad is selling a small amount of wool to a neighbour this weekend," Margret said. "Einar was shearing the last sheep today. He had sheared most of the flock in May, but a few sheep were left over. I hope he gets good money for the raw wool. We could use the extra money." Margret turned to the wood stove and stirred the contents in a pot. There was a large solid hunk of meat and water filled over the top with just enough room to cover the mutton. This delicacy would need to boil for some time, she knew.

"Your dad is doing a good job raising you on his own," Helga said admiringly. "I am sure you'll learn everything about farming. I am sure that he will get a good price. His wool is high quality." Helga picked up a sausage and sewed the ends with a needle and thread.

"He bought me a sausage maker for my last birthday," Margret said proudly, returning to the wooden preparation table. "I have yet to figure it out. This one has a handle that turns!" Margret stuffed the next large sausage by hand with an old wooden club.

Helga smiled. "Yes, I will have to help you one day. We can figure out the machine together."

"It's not really a machine," Pappa said. "The tool equipment are more like machines, not sausage makers."

"But they are machines," Einar said boldly. "They turn like some of the tools and force the sausage to grind and fill into the intestines."

Margret eyed Einar. Why would he dispute Pappa? She mused over this, wondering why they seemed to have had a strained relationship lately.

Pappa smiled politely. "You may be right that the kitchen tool turns, but it is far from any relation to farm tools."

Einar opened his mouth, then thought better of it. He closed his mouth in silence and sipped the Icelandic brennivin, a clear, strong alcohol with caraway. He enjoyed its taste but wasn't keen on drinking it too often as it made him act silly.

Einar's stomach growled as he plucked a tiny piece of the pickled herring from the serving platter on the kitchen table. He stuffed it hungrily into his mouth as Margret satisfyingly nodded. At least they all appreciated her cooking. She had pickled the herring the prior season. It was one of the last jars.

"Mmm," Einar mumbled, chewing the herring appreciatively. "You are a good cook, Margret."

"Thank you, Einar," she replied happily, checking on the strange hunk of meat boiling and steaming into the air.

Helga brought out the plates, and the rest of the family helped, bringing a wide assortment of food to the table, including potatoes, turnips and fried fish. Margret cooked the blood sausage in a frying pan as it sizzled deliciously, billowing a heavy aroma throughout the house.

They talked and celebrated the comforting family bonds they had. Einar laughed with them.

When the sausages were finished cooking, Margret sliced them onto a serving plate and proudly set the platter on the table. Everyone took their seats as she kept the last item of food as the main meat delicacy. She went back to the kitchen and removed the boiling water from the pot, and placed the large piece of meat onto a serving platter. The sheep's head slid eerily onto the plate, one eye staring out, glazed over and browned like the rest of the head. Margret didn't make sheep's head or svið often; it was always a special treat when rare guests were in their home. Svið was an Icelandic favourite, originally developed from the lean years and bad winters when no part of the sheep was wasted.

"Enjoy!" Margret announced gleefully and sat down at the table as everyone devoured the delicious array of meats, vegetables, fish and sausage. The eyeball of the sheep's head was always Pappa's favourite. He would be the one popping it into his mouth. Margret never had a chance to taste the delicacy, maybe one day when she was older.

Magnus watched from across the gravel pathway as the house lights were all on and laughter floated out into the warm summer evening. He was disappointed that she didn't seem interested in seeing him again. He had really liked her.

Magnus must have done something wrong. He wasn't sure what.

He had come again to see her, and she was busy entertaining guests now. He would try one more time tomorrow. If she was too busy to see him, he mused, then he would leave and never see her again. Magnus sulked with his shoulders bent into his chest. He thought she was a wonderful young woman.

Magnus wanted her to come live with him on the other side of Iceland in his house. He would never tell her that, of course. He had scared her away with his strong sexuality already. It was too much for her to process. Magnus really liked her, but he wasn't sure how to tell her that.

He would woo her properly, he decided.

Chapter 5

The next day was a beautiful day. The summer sun was warm and comforting on Margret's shoulders as she hung the clean clothes on the line. Margret had woken up early, scrubbing the clothes on the washing board. Finally, after an exhausting hour, she was done and wrang out every last piece of clothing. She had five more to hang then she was done with the arduous chore.

The meal was a success last night. All the food was devoured with not a single morsel left over. Helga and her uncle had stayed overnight. They mentioned they could stay for a few more days to help out, and Pappa happily agreed. It was early morning when Margret had started the wash, so her aunt and uncle were still asleep. Pappa had unusually slept in, and Einar went back home.

She pulled one of her favourite dresses onto the hanging line. It was the dress she had worn with Magnus. She thought about him often. The sheer magnetic attraction between them scared her. Margret wasn't sure how to explain it all in her head.

She had never felt so aroused in her life before. It was like he had some magic over her or something.

She missed his touch and his energy. He smelled so virile, she remembered. His slick fingers in her hand as they walked home remained stuck in her mind. She wanted that again, but she was confused about the overpowering physical feelings.

As she reached and hung one of her dad's shirts up, a familiar voice spoke softly on the other side of the clothesline.

"Good morning, Margret," Magnus said softly. "I feel that I need to apologize. I don't know what I did wrong, but please give me a chance to make things right. I really like you, Margret. I shouldn't have let things get carried away. It seems like when we kiss I lose all control."

She was surprised but happy it was him. "Yes," Margret said, straightening the shirt on the line thoughtfully. "I think we both lost control somehow." She smiled as he poked his head around the shirt.

"You look beautiful today," he said smoothly.

Margret smiled shyly. "Thank you," she replied.

Silence filled the space between their bodies. The wind blew the clothing, billowing the articles of fabric on the line. Magnus stared at Margret as if she was an apparition.

"What do you see when you look at me?" Margret asked.

"I see the best woman I could ever hope to meet," Magnus replied instantly.

She smiled.

"What do you see when you look at me, Margret?" he asked.

She looked up at the skies thoughtfully, conjuring up a caring but honest answer. "I see an experienced adult man two years older than me. That scares me." She paused, pondering her next words. "But, I think what scares me the most is how my body and mind responds so quickly to you. You must have a certain magic over me."

Magnus looked down at her words. "I am only two years older than you," Magnus said, running his hands through his dark hair. "I apologize for that. I wish I were the same age as you."

"Don't wish that!" she said abruptly. "You would then be an eighteen-year-old child."

"You don't act like an eighteen-year-old, Margret," he said. "Nor do you look like a child."

"My momma died when I was young," she said slowly, her eyes becoming level with his. "I was forced to grow up quickly. Sometimes our lives don't give us any choices."

"I'm so sorry, Margret," Magnus said sincerely.

"It was five years ago last February."

Magnus immediately hugged her warmly as Margret's arms hesitantly curled around his tall frame. They hugged for an eternity, it seemed. The wind swirled around their bodies as if they were made for each other. Margret snuggled her nose into his shoulder as they embraced. She could smell his manly scent, which aroused her, despite her resolve not to be physical with him.

"Come for a walk with me," Magnus offered. "I found a spot that you'll love. The sun is so warm there."

She glanced at the house and followed his gaze along the beach. "I have my aunt and uncle visiting," she said.

"We won't be long," he said. "Walk with me, please. I've missed you."

She tilted her head back and pulled entirely out of his embrace. "I missed you too."

"Then come with me," Magnus said convincingly. "We can search for a hot spring."

Margret smiled broadly. "Are you serious?"

"Yes, definitely," he said confidently. "We are in southeast Iceland. It is so beautiful here. I saw some hot springs nearby. It's a little hike up towards that scenic mountain range behind us, but it's well worth the trip."

"That mountain?" she pointed behind her incredulously.

"We won't be climbing the mountain, silly!" Magnus said excitedly. "It is just a short little walk. I could get you back before lunchtime."

Margret grinned mischievously. "But I would need to be back here before lunch for sure. Do you think we could make it?"

"I know we can," Magnus smiled proudly, outstretching his hand. "Come. I promise I will behave."

Margret laughed gayly and clasped his offered hand. "Let's go!" she said, unknowingly leaving a few shirts unhung on the dried washboard.

Margret walked quickly with Magnus towards the majestic mountain. Its peak was whitish and the sides grey. The ocean was now behind them as they ventured towards the island's center. They wouldn't get far, of course, because the center was filled with volcanoes, some rumbling and some like Hekla in the south, flowing with lava without a moment's notice. The last time Hekla erupted was in 1845, before her momma's death. They had travelled as a family to the site as far away as they could for safety and saw some of the lava flows. Living in the path of these volcanoes was everyday life for Icelanders. It was the risk they all took to live here. It was harsh but beautiful at the same time. It was home.

They travelled hand in hand for almost five hundred feet before she saw the grassy area mixed with rocks.

Their feet crunched onto the rough ground as they approached the hot spring. The earth trembled slightly here, and Margret glanced worriedly at Magnus. He held her hand protectively. The ground tremored again as Margret gazed up the hill. Steam rose over an isolated area in the distance.

"Is that the hot spring?" Margret asked, her hand shielding her blue eyes from the sun.

"Yes, that's the one," Magnus said gleefully, tightening his grip on her hand.

Margret walked faster, becoming oblivious to the ground tremors. She was excited to find a hidden paradise so close to home. Why had she never learned about this spot all these years? She almost pulled Magnus along with her curious energy.

Magnus held her hand firmly and negotiated the rock outcroppings. "Slow down," he said sincerely. "Let's be careful here. I don't want you to fall."

Margret slowed her pace to parallel his. They stepped around several outcroppings of rocks in the grassy fields as the ground tremors faded back into the depths of the earth. He had a firm grip on her hand, and she felt protected by this man.

The steam became wider and wider until they were inside the fogginess. Margret's eyes widened as the water came into view. It was a small natural hot pool, not larger than three feet across, shaped similar to a long egg. The hidden, hot spring clung to the side of the hilly area, overlooking the ocean.

"It's so beautiful!" Margret exclaimed. She dipped her toes in the hot water. It was very warm but not scalding.

"How's the temperature?" he asked. "Sometimes, these springs can be too hot."

"It's perfect!" she shouted happily. She immediately let go of his hand, unbuttoned her dress, and pulled it down hastily, discarding the clothing. She removed her undergarments too and laid them in the same pile of clothes. Margret dipped her toe in again and then took some hesitant steps into the natural hot waters. Finally, she slipped into the hot springs fully, allowing the water to pool around her. Margret looked up and realized that Magnus was still standing there in shock. "Come in! What are you waiting for?" she chuckled.

Magnus tried to focus on something other than seeing her naked body so abruptly and realized it was futile. He unclasped his pants, pulled them down around his feet and removed every other article of clothing until he was completely naked also.

Margret's eyes combed over his body. His chest was narrow but well defined, with his muscles forming hard ridges near his ribs. He was slim, tall and fit. But his penis is what interested her the most. It was semi-hard and pointed to the side. He had dark pubic hair like the hair on his head. As his slim muscular legs moved out of his pants, his penis jumped to the side again. She realized that she had been staring and averted her eyes abruptly. Hopefully, he had not noticed.

Magnus saw her hungry eyes, making his penis twitch with excitement. He was not going to repeat the last date, he told himself. Magnus was going to play it cool. He slipped into the hot water next to her.

"I didn't want to get my undergarments wet," Margret offered as an explanation, feeling a bit embarrassed now at her brazenness. "I've never been in a hot spring. I hope you don't mind."

"I don't mind at all, Margret," he said smoothly. "I love your body, and I will respect your limits, no matter how much it drives me crazy."

Margret sank into the warm pool until her chin touched the surface. Her breasts bobbed upwards in the water. It felt good. Her breasts were sensitive lately, and she yearned for Magnus to notice them. Margret slid slightly out of the water to allow her breasts to float in front of her.

Magnus watched her, his eyes entranced by her unabashed beauty. No words were coming from his throat. He was mesmerized, watching her breasts bob beautifully on the water. The water was very warm, almost hot. He stretched his legs out, trying to remain a gentleman and averted his eyes to the landscape. They were on an incline. A cliff was to their left, and bushes dotted here and there, mostly grass and pasture land surrounding them. The sun was high in the sky. The morning was promising a hot summer day.

Margret shifted closer to him. She felt drawn to him but fearful at the same time, almost like the intensity was too much for her mind to unravel.

Magnus accepted her closeness and wound an arm around her shoulders, relaxing backwards against the wet rock wall. Suddenly, she leaned over and kissed him on the cheek. He smiled. She was being flirtatious.

He kissed her on the forehead lightly. "This is such a beautiful spot!" he said, wetting his hair. "So serene and beautiful."

"It's so close to my home too!" Margret said exuberantly. Her knee touched his, and she melted back against his arm. Her vagina was feeling funny, and her breasts were tender. It was confusing and bewildering. She wanted his hands on her body, she realized. Her skin was aching for his touch. She didn't want it to go too far, but she didn't want him not to touch her at all either.

Magnus fought with his control. He was motionless in the hot springs with beautiful Margret naked beside him. He feared if he touched her, he would lose all control again. His fingers and penis would be entering her so quickly that she wouldn't have time to blink.

"Can we kiss again?" Margret asked. "Only kiss."

Magnus thought about how he could kiss her and not go crazy touching her everywhere. She was completely naked after all! "Yes, we can kiss," he replied, turning to kiss her wet lips. Their mouths connected, and the fire inside them roared back to life as if time had not even passed since the last date. His tongue entered her mouth, and she sucked on it briefly, dancing with it in her mouth. He kissed her back passionately and felt his penis stiffen. Magnus instinctively grabbed one of her floating breasts with his large hand. He plumped it and massaged her beautiful breast. Magnus pulled away briefly and found the other one, grasping it in his other hand. Her body mesmerized him as he played with her breasts, squeezing them together and kissing them lightly.

Margret felt her body go limp in his arms. She moaned heavily. The sensations were too much. It felt so good. His touch, her breasts in his hands and the water surrounding them melted her senses. She closed her eyes, stretched her head back and floated on a cloud of pleasure.

Magnus continued massaging her breasts, one and then the other. He was enthralled by her responses to his touch. It was like her body wanted him badly, but her mind would only allow him to go so far. He had never met a woman that entranced him as she did. The chemistry was undeniably strong. So strong, in fact, that they were both powerless to stop the chain of events when they were together. He bent down and kissed her right nipple.

She moaned and closed her eyes.

He sucked the nipple right into his mouth. Magnus rolled his tongue along the tender tip until the entire nipple was in his mouth, milking the rest of her breast with his hand. The effect it had on her was marvellous. Her neck stretched out, and she pushed her chest into his face. He grabbed the left one and sucked on it as well, plumping her right breast. "So beautiful," he mumbled.

Margret cranked her head forward and was greeted by the sun's rays shining on her breasts as his tongue swirled deliciously around her left nipple. She was devoid of normal thought. All she wanted was for him to devour her.

Magnus squeezed both her breasts together and sucked on them both together. His lips wrapped around both areolas and suckled hard, pulling the tender nipples entirely into his mouth.

She groaned as a wave of pleasure engulfed her. He immediately wrapped his arms around her waist and lifted her floating body to the surface. Magnus kissed her shoulders, then peppered her with kisses along her stomach, then slid his mouth to the apex of her thighs.

She stiffened, pulling her hips back slightly.

He understood her body language and returned to her breasts, fondling them lovingly. He sucked and plumped them wildly, unleashing his sexual tension on her breasts.

"Oh my Lord, Magnus," Margret said. Her breathing was coming out in heavy gasps, and she started panting. "Yes," she cried.

Magnus kissed her on the lips devouring her mouth, grasping the back of her head and entering her mouth as deeply as his tongue would go. She sucked on his tongue hard. His hands slid into the water and touched her body everywhere, her buttocks, legs and thighs. He grabbed one buttock and squeezed it into her body, pulling her slightly up.

She groaned like an animal.

He squeezed it again and watched her face stretch back in ecstasy. She loves this, he thought.

"Magnus," she said. "That feels so good."

He grasped a breast and plumped it at the same time as her buttocks. She panted passionately. He wished to go further but knew in the back of his mind that he might be reaching her limits again.

His erection was throbbing. Magnus moved his hand away from her breast and squeezed her buttocks together, lifting her slightly up again. Her vagina lifted up, and he could smell her sex. His hands couldn't stop, and they travelled to her vagina. The spot that so achingly needed his attention.

He hesitated briefly at her entrance and then couldn't control himself. He slid one finger over her folds and slipped a finger inside smoothly, her wetness grasping his finger.

Margret moaned heavily.

Magnus removed his finger and circled his fingertip on the top of her vagina, massaging the sensitive spot until he felt her shudder in his grasp. He slowly slid his finger into her vagina again, then slid it out. She bit his shoulder. Magnus gazed appreciatively at her body stretched out before him. Her pink breasts bobbed, the swollen nipples pointing at him, and her face was stretched out beautifully, carving the outline of her neck and her perfect jaw.

"We have to stop," she breathed between pants. "I don't want to go any further."

Magnus slowed his rhythm and tried to slow his breathing. He didn't realize it, but he was panting as well. Magnus tried clearing his mind, but his fingers didn't obey. He wanted her so badly. His fingertips circled around the top of her vagina, swiftly rubbing the sensitive area. Margret squirmed, but he held her tight and continued with the relentless circling movements. He was going to satisfy this woman.

Margret lost herself again. She couldn't stop. Margret felt her desire rise high, and her heart started beating wildly. She couldn't think of anything else except his fingers on her vagina. It felt so exquisite, and her body tingled all over; tiny impulses started firing from her breasts to her vagina.

Magnus circled faster and faster as a current of wetness covered his hands. He felt her legs vibrate and shake. He circled faster and held her legs tight with his thighs, pinning her against the rock wall of the natural pool.

"Magnus!" she cried breathlessly. Margret moaned crazily, stretching out her entire body; her legs, arms and neck were tense. Then like a river that had finally breached its dam, her whole body convulsed into an ocean of pleasure.

He slowed the movements until she pulled lightly back. He left his fingers floating in the water between her legs and gripped her buttocks with the other hand. Magnus laid his head on her shoulder, breathing heavily in her ear. "You are so beautiful," he whispered.

She melted in his arms and instantly regretted orgasming in his hands. Her vagina throbbed and convulsed repeatedly; her body happily satisfied. Margret grasped his penis underneath the water. It was smooth and incredibly hard. She wrapped her delicate fingers around the base and moved her hands up slightly, then back down.

Magnus grunted and exhaled in her ear. "Yes," he breathed.

She didn't know what she was doing, but his groans told her he liked it, so she couldn't stop. Her fingertips slid to the tip of his penis as she cupped the end and vigorously massaged it. Her fingertips continued the movement until she felt a sudden gush of slippery fluid in her hands.

Magnus grunted heavily, and his penis pulsed in Margret's hands. He panted in her ear as his legs shook involuntarily. "Margret," he murmured as he slid his hands down her curves and then kissed her lips softly. They stayed like this, kissing softly in the sunlight, half-submerged in the natural hot pool.

Margret kissed him back languidly, feeling his tongue move inside her mouth gently as they both felt the intense sexual energy drain from their bodies.

Magnus pulled away slowly and cupped her chin. "Thank you, my sweet," he said, his voice thick with lingering desire. "You make me feel so happy inside."

Margret looked into his dark blue eyes. "Do I really make you happy?" she said, pausing momentarily. "Any other girl would probably do the same."

Magnus frowned, "But you are not like other women."

"I suppose," she said. "But women must fall all over you."

"They do, sometimes," he said slowly. "But that doesn't mean I think differently about you."

"Are you sure?" Margret said. "I'm not like all the other women?"

"Far from it," he said, a devilish smile creasing his cheeks.

She wrapped her arms around him and held him tight. Maybe he was sincere, she thought.

They dressed and walked back to her house in the late morning sun, kissing and holding each other. He dropped her off at the bottom of the hill and parted ways so she could go back to her family without having to introduce a strange man to her relatives. She agreed to see him again at the end of the week. A joyful giggle rose inside her heart and lightened her steps.

She bounced happily up the pathway until she reached the door, swinging it open.

"Where have you been, Margret?" Pappa asked, a stern look on his face as he struggled to make a lamb stew. "It's already lunch, and I was worried. You disappeared."

"I just went for a walk," Margret mumbled, looking down at the floor. "I found a natural hot spring nearby," she said, deciding to tell a partial truth. "It was beautiful. I had no idea that there was a pool in the rock side so close by."

Pappa eyed her suspiciously, wondering whether that rotten Einar had taken advantage of his girl. He exhaled deeply and finished cutting turnips, plopping them into the water. "Yes," he said finally. "There is a hot spring nearby up the hill. I used to take your mother there."

"You did?" Margret asked, astonished that she had never known of these springs.

"It was our secret spot," he said solemnly.

"I'm sorry, Pappa," she said gloomily.

Pappa sighed and put down the chopping knife. "It's alright, sweetheart," he said slowly. "I'm glad you found it."

"Here, let me finish the stew," Margret said, taking the wood cutting board out and chopping the potatoes.

Pappa watched his little girl and was astonished that she was growing into a woman. How could this be? Pappa thought. She was so small when they had both lost her mother. Now, she looked like her beautiful momma so much that, some days, it pained him to be reminded of his loss.

"Are you okay, Pappa?" Margret asked just as Helga walked into the kitchen, interrupting.

"Good morning, my brother; that stew smells amazing," Helga stated cheerfully.

"Thank you," Pappa Jon replied, smiling. "I'm alright, sweetheart," he said to Margret, hugging her shoulder. "Don't you worry about me. I'm tough as nails."

"He is! Trust me!" Helga said, patting him on the shoulder.

Margret smiled and felt a glow emanate from deep inside her belly. She was worried about her Pappa, but she knew he would be alright. Margret felt happy. She mused that her feelings were not so happy during the past five years. She was often gloomy and sad. The years right after the loss of her mother had been rough for both Pappa and herself. She went through many years feeling like she had lost her belief in the universe, as if the world had somehow failed her. Some days, Margret had felt bitter and rejected by the world. How could a young girl mature into a woman without her momma?

Pappa was often withdrawn and suffered from deep sadness quietly. He sometimes would accidentally mention Momma like she was still alive. It disturbed Margret, and she wanted to fix her father. But she learned that the broken could not fix the broken; they can only offer solace in the sharing of common pain. It was neither healthy nor unhealthy. It was stagnant. There was no growth with staying broken.

Margret had continued studying with her pappa and began to excel. So much so that she had become insistent on learning more. She had a strange mathematical ability. Margret could figure out the solutions to problems with formulas.

Pappa said it must be a Petersson family trait. He was always good at mechanical math, often finding the solution to every problem and sometimes constructing his very own tools from the sheer power of his brain and his hands. He was good with his hands and measuring things out.

Margret smiled at her Pappa. He meant everything to her. She pondered what had changed her mood to feeling light and happy.

It was Magnus, of course.

He had singlehandedly turned her outlook in life to a much more positive one. He made her feel beautiful inside, desirable and light as if she was floating without a care in the world. She enjoyed sharing special moments with him and exploring the beauty of the land that surrounded them.

She was slowly becoming more relaxed with him and trusting him more and more.

"Grab the bowls," Pappa instructed.

"Oh," Margret said, pulling herself out of her wandering thoughts. "Yes, I will set the table."

Pappa looked curiously at his daughter.

Helga grabbed some spoons and cloth napkins, spreading them out before each spot. "It smells so good!" Helga exclaimed.

"Yes, it is!" Margret said loudly. "My pappa is the best at lamb stew." She smiled and brought the large pot to the table. "Let's eat!"

Chapter 6

He watched his friends around the fire. They all laughed as the brennivin passed around. One took a sip, then another, until it came full circle.

He didn't want to drink tonight. Magnus felt high with love tonight. Even though Margret had not physically had intercourse with him, he felt weightless, like he had finally met the perfect girl. For the longest time, his friends were all he had. Magnus was an only child, and both his parents had perished on a fishing boat when he was only twelve. He had learned to fend for himself, working odd jobs and making ends meet. He still lived in the house he inherited from his parents in the city of Reykjavik in southwestern Iceland. Magnus had come to the eastern part of the island to visit with some old friends. He spent most of his time fishing and drinking with friends, but he was steadily feeling bored with the same routine. Something inside of him yearned for more.

He laid back and looked up at the stars, wondering how things would work out with Margret. He hadn't told her yet that he lived on the opposite side of the island. He didn't want to lose her. He really liked her.

He hadn't really told her anything about himself at all, he mused. Maybe he should start opening up to her.

Magnus scratched the back of his head and rehearsed what he would say to her when the time came.

"Hey, Magnus," said Georg, one of his fishing friends. "You look like you're deep in thought! What's going on inside that brain of yours? Is it that woman you've been seeing? What's her name?"

"Margret," Magnus responded. "Her name is Margret."

"Well, whatever her name is," Georg said, chuckling. "Forget about her. Come join us for another round of drinks. She's just another pet."

Magnus frowned. "She's not my pet."

"All the other women are!" Georg shouted, laughing hysterically.

Magnus shook his head in disgust. They were drunk. He was blocking out their comments; it was just drunk talk. He would make Margret his girl soon enough. Then they would marry and move to Reykjavik.

"Please stay another few days, Auntie," Margret begged as she cleared the dinner dishes and cleaned up the kitchen from the large family dinner. "I enjoyed having you here. It is so lonely, just the two of us out here."

"You have Einar too!" Uncle Sig interjected. "He's a hard-working ranch hand!"

"He's not family," Margret countered.

"He's here all the time!" Uncle Sig argued.

"Yes," Margret said. "But he's not family. He's just a paid farmhand."

"Don't let him hear you say that," Aunt Helga responded.

"It's true," Pappa agreed.

"Well, he is here a lot," Helga said.

"There's a lot to do around the farm," Pappa said finally.

"I guess you're right," Helga said.

At that moment, the back door opened loudly, and Einar stood in the kitchen surrounded by shocked faces. "Mr. Petersson!" Einar shouted, clearly agitated. "Come urgently! The fat young sheep is giving birth! I didn't even know she was pregnant! She is very young to be a mother, and it's late in the lambing season. I'm worried; come quick!"

Pappa grabbed his sheepskin gloves and took two large strides towards the door. "Let's go," Pappa said decisively. "Let's save her."

Einar kept the door open as they both rushed out, the door slamming behind them.

Helga looked at Margret. "He was right," she said. "You both really need Einar around."

"Yes, we do," Margret replied. "We probably need three farmhands but can only afford the one."

"He looks at you with love in his eyes," Helga said.

"Who?" Margret asked surprised. She was sure they hadn't met Magnus yet. Maybe they saw him that morning folding laundry?

"Einar," Helga replied.

Margret laughed. "Oh no," she said. "You are mistaken. Einar has been here with us since I was twelve years old. He's like family."

"So he is like family!" Helga said, chuckling.

"Sort of, I guess," Margret responded, laughing.

"He does look at you differently than others," Helga said. "Maybe I'm wrong, but I think that man would do anything for you."

Margret smiled. She knew Einar would always be here for them. It was a comforting feeling, she mused. But it was preposterous to think Einar loved her. She loved Magnus!

The thought was so random and unexpected, she realized. It took her by surprise. Was she falling in love with Magnus so soon? She would need to distance herself from him again. She needed to guard her heart; it was too fragile.

Helga and Margret finished eating, then cleared the dishes with Uncle Sig, awaiting the return of Pappa and Einar. An hour had passed, and Margret was becoming increasingly concerned that something bad had happened.

"I'm going to check on Pappa and Einar," Margret said, grabbing her mother's old red shawl. "Please wait here before leaving so we can all say goodbye properly." Margret rushed out the back door and ran up the hill. At first, she thought the ground beneath her feet felt funny; then, she felt the ground tremor. Fear flitted in her throat. She was alone in the middle of the field. Margret ran faster towards the barn as the ground shook again. Earthquakes were becoming increasingly common in this area. They would sometimes have five small earth tremors in just one week, but this one felt stronger.

She reached the barn and found Pappa with blood up to his elbows and splattered on his shirt. He looked up at his daughter with a solemn face. "We lost her," he said simply.

Margret looked down at the massacre of blood that was once the young sheep. The ewe's belly was split open with a crude farmer's knife. She was dead, her whitish wool body covered half in blood. A tiny lamb struggled in Einar's arms. He held a crude homemade bottle of milk to the small baby's mouth; the lamb sucked eagerly on it. "How old was the mother?" Margret asked, her eyes tearing up at the bloody sight.

"She was only ten months old," Pappa said.

"She was still a lamb herself," Einar said, wiping the sweat from his brow.

Margret thought she saw a tear of sadness in his eyes.

"We tried to save her," Pappa said quietly. "The baby was stuck in the birth canal. Both the mother and baby were suffering. I had to make a choice."

Margret burst into tears and turned her head away, holding on to the door frame.

Einar stood up, still holding the baby lamb. He walked towards Margret to console her just as the earth shook again.

Margret's eyes flashed with fear.

"It's okay, sweetheart," Pappa reassured. "It is just another minor earth tremor. It'll be alright. We just need to wait it out."

The ground shook the structure, causing several loose boards to fall from the barn's ceiling. Einar grabbed Margret and shuffled her outside protectively. The barn creaked back and forth for a terrifying few minutes. Pappa came running out of the barn with his arms empty. "We will clean up the mother later today," he said.

Margret looked at the blood all over her father's hands and arms. "That's so much blood," she said. "Is giving birth always so bloody?"

"Sometimes it is," Pappa said.

Margret blinked hard and closed her eyes briefly. Childbirth was so dangerous and frightening, she thought. The earth trembled again, a bit softer now. She could feel the tremors fading back into the depths of the earth.

"We have a healthy baby lamb, though," Pappa announced. "And she's a girl!" Pappa walked towards the house and shouted back. "Einar, take care of that baby lamb. I'm going to wash up and say goodbye to Helga and Sig. I'll be back." He wound his bloody arm around his daughter's shoulder and squeezed. "It'll be alright," he whispered.

Margret blinked away another tear and nodded as they walked back down the hill towards their house.

Pappa and Margret helped Helga with her luggage, securing it to the boat. They bid Helga and Sig farewell, hugging and kissing their cheeks. Immediately afterwards, Margret and Pappa went back to the barn.

"Why did the young ewe have to die?" Margret asked innocently, her heart still shocked from seeing the young mother sheep dead.

"Because everyone has their time," Pappa said wisely.

"Momma had her time then too?" Margret asked.

Pappa rubbed his face in grief. "I suppose," he said.

"I wish Momma didn't have to die," Margret said solemnly.

"I wish the same, dear," Pappa said, nodding in sadness. "I wish the same."

Magnus couldn't wait to see her again. The morning fog separated in billows as he walked across the field to her home. Magnus was thrilled to see her again. It had been a few days since their last date, and he was excited. He will tell her about his home in Reykjavik and his plans for their future. Unfortunately, Magnus had to leave to go back home soon. He prayed that she would understand. Magnus walked up to the hanging clothesline and searched for her pretty face.

Nothing.

He searched among the freshly washed sheets. Margret was nowhere to be found. They had agreed to meet on Friday morning, he thought. Maybe she was late?

He would wait. Magnus sat down easily on a rocky outcropping, looking at his worn shoes. He wondered what it would be like to have Margret as his wife. The mornings would be bright, and he would kiss her on the shoulder as he plunged deep inside her wetness from behind. She would be his, and he would be hers.

The door slammed open, and Magnus jumped up happily, pulling a billowing sheet to the side to see her pretty face.

It was not Margret. It was her father, Mr. Jon Petersson.

Magnus looked nervously at the larger muscular man. "Who are you?" Pappa Jon asked.

"My name is Magnus," he said smoothly. "I am a friend of Margret's. She was supposed to meet me this morning for a walk." Magnus shifted nervously from foot to foot.

"She is still sleeping," Jon lied. "She didn't tell me about you."

"I'm sorry, Mr. Petersson," Magnus replied. "I should have introduced myself earlier."

"How does she know you?" Pappa asked intrusively.

"She agreed to go on a date with me," Magnus said hesitantly. "We met from mutual friends. She was afraid of introducing me to the family right away."

Pappa Jon felt his blood boil and his blood pressure rose in his throat. This was the man that she had talked about! He was a handsome devil, and Pappa instinctively didn't like him. A small voice in his head told him that he most likely wouldn't like any man that was interested in his daughter. He instantly abolished the thought as heresy. "So you're the man she talked about?" Pappa said almost to himself.

"She talked about me?" Magnus said, his hopes soaring.

"She mentioned that she was going on a date," Pappa said, satisfyingly bursting the man's hopes.

Magnus smiled weakly, disappointment crossing his face. "I'm here to take her for a walk along the beach."

"I told you," Pappa said stubbornly. "She's asleep. We had a late night with a surprise lambing."

Magnus shifted anxiously from one foot to the other, not sure if he should go or wait. He looked at Mr. Petersson's aggressive stance and decided the man wanted Magnus to leave. "I'll be on my way then," Magnus said. He turned to leave and took ten quick paces down the hill. Magnus thought it was unfair to be dejected like this. He turned his head back. Pappa Jon stood defiantly beside the billowing sheets watching him leave the property. "Tell her I'll be back at lunchtime," Magnus shouted back, then skipped down the hill.

"You chased him away!" Margret shouted, her dress flowing behind her as she angrily cleared the morning dishes. "You have no right!"

"I have every right!" Pappa shouted back. "You are my daughter, and it's my duty to protect you. I don't like that man. He's too smooth. He'll break your heart."

"That's my decision to make!" Margret retorted. "If I get my heart broken, at least I will have loved!"

Pappa glowered at her from across the table.

Margret busily washed the dishes seething in silence. She banged pots around and then finally burst into an emotional tirade. "Do you think it's been easy on me these past years?" she cried. "Have you ever stopped to think once about how I feel?" Her eyes flashed angrily. "I have been so sad and lonely, Pappa. I even stopped believing that the world was a kind place. For many years, I walked in and out of a dark dream; every day was the same veil of sadness. The world had lost colour for me, father!" She swallowed, her emotions bubbling up to the surface as tears threatened to escape her eyes. Her voice wavered. "Magnus made me feel valued and happy again. I felt joy with him for the first time since Momma's death."

The room fell silent. Pappa's face fell.

Margret felt the tears escape from her eyes. It was as if one rain cloud had formed, and instantly a rainstorm came rushing from her eyes. The hot tears ran down her cheeks, and she sobbed into her hands, running to her bedroom.

"My sweet daughter," Pappa said, his voice cracking with emotion. But it was too late; she couldn't hear him anymore. She was already in her bed, crying on her pillow. "I don't want to lose you," he said softly to himself as he sat down heavily on the hard sofa.

Chapter 7

Magnus came back at lunch like promised and fully expected to be disappointed yet again. But to his delighted surprise, Margret was sitting on the step wearing a dark wool dress with a tail-cap on her head. He felt elated. She was there waiting for him! He was almost certain that her father would have forbade them from ever seeing each other again. Pappa Jon's defensive speech this morning was not something he ever wanted to repeat.

Magnus ran across the field and up the hill. She looked up, and her face brightened. He reached her in seconds and scooped her up in his arms. She joyously laughed as he carried her lithe body down the hill. He slipped unsteadily on the slope, and they tumbled to the ground, giggling crazily. Magnus hugged her, and she kissed him back, laughing. Margret pushed him playfully, and he rolled slightly down the hill. She imitated and rolled after him. It became a game until he hugged her, and they rolled down the remainder of the hill in each other's arms. Margret was surprised when they reached the bottom near the sand. Magnus landed on top of her, laughing. It was so fun and spontaneous.

He looked into her eyes and felt his heart thump heavily in his chest. Magnus kissed her soft lips, and she kissed him back, moaning with desire. Her honey lips wrapped around his tongue, and he sucked on it. He felt his penis harden uncomfortably. His hands ventured into her top, unbuttoning the clasps clumsily.

Margret inhaled sharply as his hand found one of her breasts, plumping it. She grunted softly as Magnus felt her body brazenly on the open grass. Her skin felt electrified and alive. Margret's legs felt strangely weak and flopped open on either side of his legs. Magnus slipped comfortably in between her legs. They both looked into each other's eyes for a split moment and felt something important happen between them like an event was close to happening.

They kissed slower this time, a long sensual deep kiss. Margret could feel his hard erection poking against her pelvis. Her vagina felt hot, and she had an urge to take off her undergarments, which was ridiculous, she thought. She hadn't even discussed marriage yet!

Magnus fumbled with his belt.

"No," Margret said weakly. Her breath came out in gasps, the sexual heat intoxicating her entire body. "I want to wait."

Magnus stopped immediately. His hand rested on her pelvis. "Okay," he said, breathing hard. "It is wrong to get so carried away with you. I can't help myself around you. You have cast a magic spell on me." He adjusted his pants.

"I am no witch," Margret replied stonily.

"I know, my sweet," Magnus said. "It just feels like magic when I'm with you."

She smiled. They kissed again, more softly this time.

He wanted her to know that he was hers. "I want you to come back home with me," he said confidently. "Then we can marry and do this every day."

Margret was satisfied that he had finally mentioned marriage. She didn't know where he lived but assumed it was somewhere close. Margret was happy that he was finally talking to her frankly. "You have your own house?" she asked, raising an eyebrow.

"Yes," he replied. "My parents passed away, and I took over the family home."

"I'm so sorry," she said sincerely. "When did they die?"

"I was only twelve," he replied.

"That's the age I was when my momma died," Margret said, looking down.

"It's tough living your life without parents," Magnus responded.

"Yes," Margret looked into his eyes. She blinked, wondering how much to tell him about her feelings. "Magnus, I talked to my father. I told him how much you've helped me feel alive again. For years after my momma's death, I felt dead inside."

"I was the same," he said. "It took me many years to see the world as it really is again." Magnus hugged her fiercely, wrapping his strong arms around her lithe body. He buried his face in her hair and kissed her ear. "You've made me feel alive too," he whispered in her ear.

Margret felt her soul melt into him as they exchanged grief and loss with each other. They talked for a long time about the process of death, what they both went through and how it affected them at such a young age. She truly felt like someone in this world finally understood her. It was the most important thing that had happened to her since her mother's death. She wondered if she might be falling in love with Magnus.

"Come live with me, Margret," he said, feelings of love thumping in his chest.

She wondered if she could leave her Pappa. If Magnus's house was close, she could always come back home to Pappa every day. "Where is your house?" she asked thoughtfully.

"It's in Reykjavik," he answered. "It's a big old house. It needs some repairs, but I will fix it any way you want it to look."

Margret went silent. "Oh," she said numbly, her heart falling into her stomach.

"We could have many children," he said. "It's a bigger house than your father's." Magnus paused, thinking. "I have to go back soon, and I want you to come back with me."

Margret closed her eyes slowly, then opened them again, looking into Magnus's tender eyes. "We can talk about it at another time. When will you be going?"

"Tomorrow," he said. "If you cannot come with me this time, I will come back for you."

"That sounds like the best," she said simply.

Magnus frowned. "Is there something wrong?"

"No," she lied. "There is nothing wrong. It is just a lot to comprehend in a few short weeks."

Magnus leaned over her, kissing her deeply. He would make her his wife. She would soon agree and come live with him. "I will come tomorrow morning before I leave then," he said confidently.

Margret curled into her pillow and cried, the tears streaming down her cheeks. She peered out of her window at the night sky. It was still light outside, but the daylight would soon be growing shorter.

They had walked all night, and finally, Magnus had walked her back home, shaking Pappa's hand at the door and bidding them all goodnight.

Margret felt her heart shatter into pieces when she saw the fear in her father's eyes. She could tell that he was terrified of losing her. She was part of momma, the only piece of his wife he had left. When the door closed, Margret hugged Pappa. "Don't worry, Pappa," she said quietly. "I will never leave you. I am here, and I always will be."

She had barely slept. Her mind and her thoughts swirled around in her brain, begging for a resolution, something to make everyone happy. Margret crawled out of bed before the sunrise and prayed. She wanted to please everyone but was there any happiness left for her?

She quietly knelt upon her bed, her elbows on the mattress and clasped her hands together in prayer.

Margret wondered if true happiness was achievable. Did it exist at all? Everyone in the world dies sooner or later, she knew. Whatever peace and love she is blessed to have are only in those moments. Margret cherished the moments that she was allowed to live with enthusiasm. These little etches in time meant so much to her. But sometimes, things weren't meant to be, she thought. The people she cherished were more important than any man. Her family meant everything to her. Margret would die before she would allow anything bad to happen to her father. Her selfish mind argued that she should be allowed her own happiness too. Margret grimaced and finished her prayer.

Margret stood, nodding to herself, her mind intent on a decision.

She would tell Magnus this morning.

Margret walked into the hallway and quietly padded into the kitchen for breakfast. She spooned some skyr, an Icelandic yogurt, into a bowl and sat down. Margret ate slowly and looked at her bowl blankly. Her appetite was not good, but Margret knew that she needed to eat. She was already quite slim, and the summer would be over soon, with the long dark winter coming soon.

Margret finished her small breakfast and looked up at the ceiling, exhaling heavily.

A slight knock on the door interrupted her thoughts. She stood up intently and walked to the door. Her Pappa was still asleep and would be sleeping in his bedroom for another hour.

She opened the door.

Magnus hugged her warmly and buried his face in her neck. "Good morning, my love," he murmured.

Margret hugged him warmly back, enjoying the moment. "Good morning, Magnus," she replied, wrapping her hands around his waist, feeling an instant rush of emotions.

He kissed her neck and squeezed her into his chest as if he wanted to somehow merge their bodies into one. Magnus was convinced, beyond any doubt, that he wanted to marry Margret now. There was no other woman for him. He would propose to her properly, he thought, and then she'd know he was serious.

"My sweet man," she said slowly.

"My sweet woman, Margret," he said, pulling her away slightly so he could look into her blue eyes. He cleared his throat and let the words stumble out. "I want you in my life every day. We can be happy together. We can build a new life in Reykjavik. I have my wagon packed and a horse ready outside.

You can bring whatever you like." Magnus stopped short of a formal proposal. He would buy her a ring in Reykjavik if she said yes today.

Margret smiled and swallowed hard. "Magnus," she said softly. Her stomach dropped, and her throat felt constricted. She kissed him on the cheek as her eyes moistened with emotion. "I am staying here with my Pappa. I'm sorry. I cannot leave him. He's the only family I have." Margret closed her eyes painfully and opened them to see his face. His smile had disappeared and a slight quiver formed on his lips. His eyes dropped down into a sad frown, and she felt his disappointment rush through her body. She began to cry. "I'm so sorry, Magnus. If you lived across the street, I would live with you in a heartbeat. I would marry you in an instant. But Reykjavik is too far away. I could never desert my father like that." Margret grasped his hand and looked into his moist eyes. "I know you understand. If your father were still alive, you'd do the same."

Magnus slipped his hand out of hers. He looked down at his shoes, not wanting her to see his tears. He rubbed his eyes and motioned to turn away.

"Say something," Margret pleaded, grasping his arm. "Please, Magnus."

A veil of stone settled over his face, and he grimaced momentarily. Magnus shifted his feet and turned completely, walking away to his horse. He turned back once briefly, not wanting her to see the tears now coursing down his face. "There's nothing to say, Margret," he said, his voice cracking with emotion. "Nothing at all. But goodbye."

Margret stood with her shoulders back and her forehead to the sky, inhaling sharply at his words. It was the right thing to do, she knew. She had to be strong. Margret watched Magnus mount the horse and trot away without another glance back at her.

She felt utterly deserted and alone.

Margret stood there for hours, it seemed, until he was completely out of sight. He never turned back once. He didn't wave or anything. He just left with that stone look on his face.

The landscape glowed in the early morning sunrise, leaving no trace of the man who stole her heart.

Margret crumbled then, her body falling down to the ground in a crouch, hugging her knees and crying heavily into her dress. "Why?" she asked the universe, sobbing into her hands. "Why can't I be happy?" she shouted as she sat in the dirt, praying for forgiveness.

CHAPTER 8

"You've barely eaten," Pappa said softly. "Please, Margret, eat some dinner. I cooked your favourite sausage."

Margret looked up numbly. "My tummy feels sick, Pappa."

"Are you sick?" he asked, concern washing over his face. "Do you have a runny nose? You've been sniffling."

"I'm a bit sick, I think," she replied.

"Did anything happen?" Pappa asked.

Margret paused, wondering if she should tell him but then thought otherwise. She would never want him to feel guilty for her unhappiness. She chose her father instead of her lover, and it was her decision to make. Pappa didn't need to know the details. "Nothing really," she said. "Just a bit sad."

"Sad about what?" he asked. "Does this have anything to do with Magnus? Did he do something to you?" Pappa's face turned an odd red colour as his emotions of protective parental anger showed.

"No, nothing like that, Pappa," she replied. "Magnus is a good man. But I did tell him that it was over between me and him."

Pappa looked down at his plate and thoughtfully cut the sausage, placing a piece in his mouth. A ground tremor shook the table slightly, and he placed his palms on the table, trying to stop the table from moving. Margret held the table also as the house creaked. They both watched the house trembling for several minutes until it subsided. After a few moments of calm, they both resumed eating.

Pappa cut another piece of sausage and placed it in his mouth. He chewed the morsel entirely before responding. He knew the feeling of a broken heart, and he cared deeply for his daughter. "I'm sorry, sweetheart," he said. "I know how much you liked Magnus. Sometimes love is like that; it hurts badly, and it feels like a piece has been torn from you. But it is not true. We are all strong people. We heal with time." Pappa chewed another morsel and swallowed. "If you want to talk about it, Margret, I am here for you."

"Thanks, Pappa," she smiled weakly. "There's not much to talk about. It is what it is."

They both ate in silence. Margret pushed the food around her plate, and Pappa ate heartily. He stood and gathered the dishes as a smaller tremor shook the house again. He paused, then resumed clearing the table, gently patting her on the shoulder.

She looked down with teary eyes.

Pappa cleaned up the kitchen, washing plates and putting away things. He looked back, and Margret was still sitting in the same spot. She hadn't moved one bit.

Pappa grunted to himself as he remembered something. "I need to go to the other side of the island soon to trade the annual wool at the market. I have to go before the winter comes. I want you to come. We can leave in late August." Pappa replaced the few pots they had in the small cupboards. "We will get some more pots too. They are so hard to find here."

Margret barely heard him. She nodded and went to her room.

Einar corralled the sheep into the enclosed stone fence. He would have to pick a young male to slaughter for meat. He analyzed the herd, looking for a suitable animal. They all seemed relatively healthy and robust. Some were even growing fat, Einar mused.

He jumped off his horse and closed the gate. There were almost fifty sheep now, including the twenty lambs born this year. Mr. Petersson was doing better this year than last. Pappa Jon had promised to pay him with a slaughtered sheep for his family to eat. There were many jobs Einar had been taking on to reduce the burden on the Petersson family. Einar had been working hard, sometimes even past dinner time. He was a muscular, robust fellow with a barrel of a chest but a kind face and ice-blue eyes. He had been working so hard lately that he had no time to spend finding a wife. There were not too many women his age nearby, so he just had to do without at least until he figured out where this life was leading him.

A lithe figure walked across the field with a veil flowing over her legs. It looked like an angel. He stood with his herding staff and gazed at the figure walking toward him. He wondered if his eyes were playing tricks on him and the apparition wasn't real.

But as the figure neared, he could make out that it was Margret. Her dress billowed, flowing behind her and to the side from the strong winds.

It was a windy day as many of the days often were in eastern Iceland.

"Einar," Margret spoke in a sad monotone voice. "Pappa wants you to gather all the wool. He needs it for the market trip he's planning."

Einar frowned, his eyebrows pinching together. It was not like her to be so withdrawn. "No problem," he said. "I can do that." Einar paused, placing the staff point into the ground aimlessly. "You seem sad and withdrawn lately. You have barely left the house. Are you alright?"

Margret paused momentarily and wondered how it showed so obviously that she was in such emotional pain. "I had some difficulties, but it is getting somewhat better," she said. "There's no use in boring people with the details." She sat down on a large rock jutting out near the fenced-in sheep. "Just tired."

"You know, I'm here for you always, Margret," Einar said empathically. "I'm always here for you and your family. Never doubt that."

"I know you are, Einar," she replied honestly. "You've always been there for us, and I wholeheartedly appreciate you being in our lives. Who knows what would have happened without you after my Momma's death?"

"You would have survived," Einar said softly. "Icelanders are strong people. I didn't do much during that time. I did my daily jobs as your father asked me to do."

Margret looked into his blue eyes, then diverted her gaze to the side. "It was a tough period for us to go through. You helped us more than you know." She suddenly reached out and hugged him. He smelled like hay and animal dander, but it felt good to show him appreciation. The hay and animals were part of his job. This was who he was, she knew.

Einar accepted the random hug from Margret and enjoyed it immensely. He wondered if she ever thought more of him in a different way, a sexual way. He banished the thought and hugged her back. It felt so good to wrap his arms around a woman. She smelled like flowers and baking. "Did you bake today? I can smell it," he said, laughing. "It smells wonderful."

She chuckled. "Yes, I was baking skyr cake and some flat-kaka," she responded, smiling. "I made lots of flatkaka to keep us fed for a while. I only made one skyr cake, but that doesn't need baking except for the crust; actually, neither does the flatkaka. I make those in our old iron pans." She paused and then thought about something she needed. "Actually, I need to pick some wild berries for the skyr cake." She swung the small wooden pail she held in her hand. "Would you like to pick some berries with me?"

"Definitely," Einar said, rubbing his hands on his pants. "I don't know where to find the berries, but I'll come."

"They grow everywhere," she said, feeling a bit happier. "I will show you." She turned and began walking up the mountainside with Einar following.

"Wait for me," he said, laughing and running to catch up.

They swiftly climbed the countryside until they arrived at a meadow. Einar could smell the sweetness in the air. The meadow was dotted with blue bilberries and wild strawberries. She showed him which ones to pick and which ones to leave. A few they popped into their mouths, chewing happily. After a while of picking berries, they had the small bucket filled.

"You're welcome to stop by for dessert," she said politely as a gentle rain began to fall.

"I cannot come tonight, unfortunately," Einar said quietly, wiping the moisture from his forehead. "My parents are expecting me back early to fix the leaking turf roof. It's becoming a problem that I need to address properly."

"Okay," she said, her face falling in disappointment. She knew the disadvantages of Icelandic green turf roofs. They provided sorely needed insulation in this harsh climate but often needed repairs. "Maybe another day."

"I will definitely do that!" he exclaimed, watching her demeanour change. "I need to taste this skyr cake!"

"Okay," she said. "I will make it for you one day."

Einar waved goodbye and sauntered towards his home across the field.

Margret walked back home feeling alone. When she reached the door, she broke out into sudden tears and wondered why. It was just berries. She looked back, but Einar was already gone, somewhere on the other side of the barn.

It had been another long day with the sheep, and the barn also needed roof repairs. The grass roofs in Iceland were troublesome but provided them with excellent insulation. Wood was scarce on this harsh island, so the Icelandic people used what they could and made a life for themselves in any way possible. The house foundations were built with blocks of flat stones and then framed with wood, limiting the use of wood as much as possible. Turf was laid upon the roof, and grass naturally grew on the roof year after year.

The Petersson's turf home was built firmly into the side of the mountain, reducing the impact that the wind had on the structure. Pappa Jon had fixed the roof leaks on the home many years ago, but now the barn was leaking. The barn was also built into the mountainside but much farther from the family home.

The roof had started leaking, and some wind erosion was appearing on the north side. Jon Petersson worked hard all day on it. Finally, Einar showed up to help in the afternoon, and they had fixed the leak.

"I started fixing my parents' house the same yesterday," Einar said. "It's a more extensive repair than the barn, but a little mud, stone and turf is all it needs. It'll be good for another twenty years."

"Let's hope so!" Pappa Jon said exuberantly. He was impressed with Einar's evolving knowledge and his ability to learn quickly. The boy had grown into a capable man. "I need your help, Einar," Pappa said, washing his dirty field hands in the water pump near the barn.

"I'm here for whatever you need," Einar replied.

Pappa Jon wiped his hands on his pants and put the tools away. "My daughter and I are going to load up the wool and sell it at the market this year, and I need your help," Jon said. "I would appreciate it if you could come with us."

"Will you be going to Reykjavik this year?" Einar asked.

"Yes," Pappa Jon replied. "It's the best trading market in Iceland. We can get the most money for our wool there. We need to trade for tools and pots. I need to get rid of this wool and trade some live sheep as well. My daughter will come. We will stay in an inn while we are there. Will you come?"

"That's a five-day trip by horseback," Einar replied, pointing out the length of the journey. "Some difficult terrain."

"I will pay you," Pappa Jon countered convincingly. "I have hired guides, but I will still need your assistance. We have a large amount of wool this year. It will be worth the trip."

"Who will take care of the farm while we're gone?" Einar asked.

"I have asked young Petr and his brother Stephan from Horn to take care of the farm," Jon replied. "They will be arriving here in the next few days. They are good honest workers."

Einar gathered the extra tools and put them away with Pappa Jon. They both stood admiring their handiwork on the roof. "I will come," Einar said firmly. "I'm sure Petr and Stephan will be able to manage the flock. I have heard of them before. They are good men." Einar looked down at his callused hands. "My brother, Olafur, lives in Reykjavik. His wife just gave birth to a baby boy. I'd like to have the chance to meet my new nephew; they named him Aron. He was born almost six months ago, and I haven't had a chance to meet him yet. This trip works perfectly for both of us." Einar nodded firmly. "You can just pay me the regular pay. I will make sure you both get there and back safely. Your safety means a lot to me."

"Thank you, Einar," Pappa Jon said. "Don't tell Margret. I will tell her myself."

"Sure, Jon," Einar said. "You just tell me the weeks you are planning to go. I'll be ready."

CHAPTER 9

"How much further, Pappa?" Margret shouted as the caravan proceeded across the windy fields. She tucked her hair in the back of her coat and pulled up the hood as the winds buffeted her back.

"It's a few more days, darling," Pappa answered, shouting into the winds.

"What?" Margret exclaimed. She patted her small horse's neck, whispering into the animal's ear, chuckling. "Pappa has lost his mind."

"We should be there by Friday, just in time for the market," Pappa replied.

They had been travelling all day, and it was soon time for an overnight camp rest. The small caravan included two guides, Einar and five more horses. The guides motioned to an area ahead as they rode up the slope on the Icelandic horses. Several other horses carried sacks and sleighs full of wool. The entire group was tired, and everyone needed a rest. One of the guides pointed to an outcropping of sheltered rocks. It was most likely a homestead at one time. The land had a way of claiming things back after time. "Let's stop over there," he said, pointing.

The group trotted to the outcropping and dismounted, pulling backpacks out and setting up for a fire. Pappa Jon bent down to start the fire with used hay in the fields to start it. The warm flames shot to life as Margret and Einar huddled closer to the fire.

"We will be passing by Mount Hekla tomorrow," Pappa said. "You haven't seen the volcano since you were little."

"I barely remember it, Pappa," Margret said.

"Yes, you were small when I took you and your momma there," Pappa said, his eyes clouding over with memories. "We had a beautiful time together as a family when you were young."

"I still miss Momma," Margret said.

"So do I, sweetheart," Pappa agreed.

Einar pulled out a small cooking rack and placed it on the fire. He rummaged in his travel pouches and pulled out salted fish and potatoes as the guides set up blankets and crude dishes. The fish seared as it hit the heated rack, and the potatoes hissed on the open fire. Einar glanced at Margret as she hugged herself. He wanted to comfort her, but she became prickly and sensitive every time they talked about her mother. Einar didn't want to feel her wrath again, so he stayed quiet.

"The fish smells good," Margret said softly.

"We need nourishment," Einar responded. "It's a long journey."

"Thank you for coming with us," she said sincerely.

"No need to thank me," Einar replied. "I would have come even if Pappa Jon didn't pay me. My nephew was born six months ago, and I'd like to meet the little guy."

"Oh, I didn't know you had a nephew," Margret replied.

"Yes, my brother left Horn a year ago to be with his wife's family," Einar said. "They just recently had a baby. It's been difficult here without his help." He flipped the potatoes with a stick and looked at Margret over the fire. "I would have still come on this journey with you and your father. I want you both to travel safely. It's the least I can do for all your years of keeping me employed."

"You're more than just an employee," Pappa Jon said, sitting down to join the conversation.

"Thank you," Einar replied. "I appreciate that."

Several moments passed in silence, only the sizzling of fish and the wind whistling around them. Margret pulled her coat tighter around her body and stared into the fire. The flames danced with shades of blue, yellow and orange. Her mind drifted to thoughts of Magnus. She missed him. Her heart, mind and body ached for him. She wondered why she had thrown him away so readily. In her heart, Margret knew it was the right thing to do. She could never abandon her father that way. But her happiness was less important? She mused with millions of contradicting thoughts swirling through her brain. Maybe this is what it's like growing up. The adult world was harsh and filled with difficult decisions. Nothing was black and white; it was all different shades of colours and feelings. Some decisions were more difficult than others, she told herself. She had made the right choice, but her body still ached for Magnus. Her breasts felt neglected, and her vagina had a special kind of ache that she had never experienced before.

"Here," Einar said, handing her a plate of fish and potatoes. "Enjoy. I hope you like it."

Margret looked up and accepted the plate on her lap. Einar glanced down twice and then looked away. She was always perplexed when he did that. She never knew what Einar was thinking. He was always so withdrawn and private, the opposite of Magnus. Einar was physically strong and robust, too; Magnus was slim and tall. Einar was a pleasant-looking man with blonde hair; Magnus was dark and devilishly handsome. The two men were complete opposites. She chewed her fish and wondered why she was even comparing the two men.

"We will wake up early and journey to Hekla in the morning," Pappa said between mouthfuls. "I'd like to spend some time at Mount Hekla then continue our travels, getting in as much distance as possible before the night comes again."

Margret glanced at her father. He was a good man, she thought. She would be blessed to find a husband similar to her Pappa. "Okay, Pappa," she replied as the night began turning to dusk. "I am looking forward to seeing Mount Hekla."

The volcano had a high cap of snow and was looming in the distance. It was shaped strangely, sloping on the sides gradually, indicating that the prior lava flows had recreated the mountain over time. They didn't venture too close because it could be dangerous. Margret felt a mixture of fear and awe. It was such a sight to see!

"Does the lava always flow?" she asked.

It was Einar that answered this time. "No," he said. "Hekla is one of those volcanoes that only spew hot lava during an eruption. Not all volcanoes are alike. It's the dormant volcanoes that are more dangerous, I believe."

"The dormant ones?" she asked. "Why would you think that? Hekla just had an unexpected eruption in 1845. This mountain destroys anything in its path. That's why there are no farms left here."

"Yes, active volcanoes are dangerous," he said. "But it's somewhat more predictable. The dormant volcanoes are not. They build up and build up, until one day, they blow, and everyone has to run for their lives."

"I think Mount Hekla looks pretty dangerous to me right now," Margret argued.

"Yes, it's dangerous," Einar said. "Don't ever get too close; you would never have enough time to run if an eruption started." Einar watched in fascination at the large sloping mountain in the distance. "It has a certain beauty to it."

"I was just going to say the same," Margret said, chuckling.

They all stared as the mountain trembled slightly, vibrating the ground underneath their feet marginally. Margret shivered in fear.

"Is it erupting right now?" she asked fearfully.

"No, this is just an earth tremor," Einar said, grabbing her arm protectively. "We are close enough to feel its power." Einar mused thoughtfully as they all stared at the powerful beast in the distance. "I think Mount Askja is more dangerous than any of them. We live too close to that sleeping monster."

"Mount Askja!" Pappa Jon exclaimed. "That mountain hasn't erupted in hundreds of years!"

"Those are the worst kind of volcanoes," Einar said. "Too much pressure builds up. I looked at it from afar; it even looks like the base is somehow sinking."

Margret looked at Einar, wondering if what he said could be true. They lived within 90 miles of Mount Askja. She always thought the southeastern side of the island was the safest. She blinked heavily and sighed. "What if he's right, Pappa?" she asked.

"I suppose any of the volcanoes could erupt at any time," Pappa said reasonably. "But that doesn't mean they're going to erupt in our lifetime."

Margret shivered and pulled the coat around her body tighter. "But what if it does?" she asked, her voice pitching. "What if the mountain nearest to us explodes? What do we do?"

"I don't think it will, dear," Pappa said. "But I suppose we could make some emergency arrangements just in case."

Einar nodded thoughtfully. "I could build an emergency escape route and boat for our two families."

"That's a good idea," Margret said admiringly.

Pappa Jon nodded his chin rapidly in agreement. "That is an excellent idea, Einar!" Jon said. "Could you get started on the boat when we get back?"

"I sure can," Einar said as they all began walking away from the active volcano behind them. "It's getting hot. Let's continue onto the city and find another place to stay overnight. I don't want to sleep with Hekla tonight."

Pappa Jon chuckled and followed the guides along the countryside, waving his daughter to stay behind him.

Margret followed the caravan and watched Einar's arms strut out confidently. She appraised his form and decided that he was a good man. He had been in her life ever since she was a child. He knew more than the guides, Margret realized with astonishment. She had always grown up thinking that he was a farm hand and that's all. Now Margret saw him in a different light. Like her aunt had mentioned, Einar was becoming important to them, and she liked the feeling.

The sun was setting earlier than in July. The caravan had travelled for three and a half days now, and they were all growing weary. The midnight sun was fading away quickly, an indicator of the coming winter. It was 8:30 pm, and the sun was glowing like a bright orange ball against the horizon. The windy fields and rolling hills blew at their faces as they set up camp, stopping for their last night of travelling. They should arrive in Reykjavík tomorrow afternoon.

"Tie those two sheep, Margret, to keep them from straying while we sleep," Pappa Jon said while he rummaged in his sack. "There are some bushes nearby; you can tie them there." Pappa stopped and surveyed the area. "On second thought, we will maybe set up camp a bit closer." He returned his items to his pack and pulled the horses' reins towards the bushes.

As they neared the bushes, the horses began fussing. Margret walked with the two sheep as her father handled both horses. Einar and the guides were in the back with the rest of the caravan.

"The horses must be tired," Einar said, urging his horse to move closer. "They are putting up a fuss."

Margret's horse whinnied and nodded her head repeatedly, prompting the other animals to do the same. Even the young sheep noticed and began pulling away from her in the opposite direction.

"I don't know what has gotten into them," Jon said, yanking the reins to control the animals.

Margret eyed the bushes and thought she saw something move. "Maybe there is something in the bushes," she said.

Pappa pulled the horses strongly just as a small stealthy animal scurried from the bushes. It had dense grey fur speckled with light brown. Its ears were rounded and attentive. The poor animal was frightened.

"It's an artic fox!" Margret exclaimed, pointing.

The fox darted, attempting to escape the horses approaching him and mistakenly smashed into Margret's feet. Margret squealed and grabbed the small animal. It squirmed but affectionately licked her hand. "He's just a baby!" Margret shouted excitedly. The animal squawked loudly. Margret hugged the baby fox and rubbed the small animal's fur, whispering reassuring words to it.

"Put the fox down!" Pappa said loudly. "If it's a baby from June, then its parents aren't far away."

"It's probably an orphan, Pappa," Margret responded. "The poor thing is starving."

"Those foxes are sly," Einar added. "I wouldn't assume anything."

Margret looked to Einar and then over to her dad. "Alright," she said, bending over to release the small fuzzy baby fox. "But if he comes back, I will feed it something to help the little guy survive."

"You will do nothing of the sort," Pappa said firmly. "The last thing we need is a family of foxes stealing our sheep."

"The sheep are big enough," Margret countered. "They are young but are not lambs. They are too large for a fox."

"You would be surprised, my dear," Pappa said.

"He's right," Einar added. "Those foxes are stronger than you think."

The cute baby fox scurried away across the countryside, its bushy tail bouncing with every leap. Margret smiled warmly. "He's so cute!" she exclaimed.

"He won't be so cute in six months!" Pappa said. "He'll be stealing baby lambs then!"

"Oh, Pappa!" she retorted.

"The foxes are terrible!" Pappa complained. "If I could kill every one of them, I would."

"No!" Margret said passionately. "I'm going to name him Fuzzy, just in case he comes back."

"If he comes back, we'll be eating him for dinner," Pappa replied enthusiastically.

"Pappa!"

Einar chuckled at the exchange. "Foxes don't taste too good."

"Einar!" Margret grinned. "Nobody is eating Fuzzy!"

"Okay, okay," Pappa said. "I was only trying to make you understand how much of a nuisance those animals are to us."

"Let's set up camp," Einar said, throwing down his pack and sitting down to rub two sticks together for a fire. Once the fire started, he threw hay over the flames. It sizzled and cracked as Margret, Pappa, and the guides secured the sheep and horses, setting up for the camp.

As the night grew darker, Margret felt herself growing weary, and she laid down with her clothing bag as her pillow. She was surprised at how quickly she felt tired after stopping on the journey. She closed her eyes for just a moment.

The scratching sounds were bothering her. She kept hearing the odd noises. It was faint, but it was definitely there.

Margret opened her eyes. It was dark outside. She must have slept a long while. It surprised her because she normally didn't sleep so soundly.

Another scratch.

She turned instinctively towards the sound and saw a shadow move.

"Pappa!" she shouted. "Wake up!"

Pappa Jon groaned and rolled over. "What is it?"

"There's something at our campsite," she whispered.

"The foxes!" Pappa Jon shouted as he sat up from his sleeping position. He grabbed a knife from his boot and searched for his pack. "Where is my pack? I put it right here."

Margret allowed her eyes to adjust and surveyed the small campsite in the bluish night. She could see her dad's pack being dragged away by something. It was moving! Another pack had been split open, and all its contents were littered everywhere. "It's the foxes!" she hollered. "Over there, Pappa!" Margret pointed into the darkness.

Pappa Jon rushed out into the darkness to salvage his pack. A small squeal sounded, and then the foxes were scurrying away. Pappa stomped back to the campsite with the torn pack. "They stole the last of our dried meat and salted fish," he stated despondently.

"Is it all gone?" Einar asked, awakening from the disturbance.

"I think so," one of the guides spoke roughly, joining the commotion. "Our packs are torn too!" He threw the pack down in frustration.

"We'll have to starve tomorrow and buy something when we arrive in Reykjavik," Pappa said.

Margret frowned. "You were right about those little foxes. I hope the young sheep are alright."

"We'll know in the morning, but it seems they are all still with the horses," Pappa responded.

They had travelled for a long time and were ravenously hungry the entire day. Thankfully they had water, but everything else was gone, a fine meal for the foxes. Margret's stomach rumbled with hunger. They hadn't eaten anything all day, and it was late afternoon. The sheep were fine. They had a few bloody scratches on their thickening wool coat. Margret assumed they had gotten into a skirmish with the foxes, and the horses and sheep had won. Only the smaller lambs could be dragged away by the foxes.

The caravan continued over the hilly landscape throughout the afternoon until finally, they saw the city dotted over the rolling hills and shoreline. The guides collected their pay from Pappa and left the family, waving goodbye.

Margret gazed over the landscape at the large town. It was a port trading capital, the only city in Iceland. Across the horizon, fog from the numerous hot springs settled over the city, creating the illusion of a smoky dome, hence the name Reykjavik, which meant smoky city in Icelandic.

Margret was so happy to see the city. "I'm so hungry, Pappa," she said.

"I know, my dear," he replied. "So am I."

"We'll be there soon!" Einar shouted from up ahead. "Hurry!"

Margret and Pappa Jon urged their horses into a canter, the length of the journey too tiring for the horses to gallop. Margret snapped the reins gently as her riding horse led the way into the city.

Soon, the streets were teeming with life. They had arrived later than expected. The late afternoon crowds were settling in. There were more people than she had ever seen in her life. Thousands of citizens filled every alleyway, every street, some crowding over market stalls. Margret found it fascinating! She remembered Magnus lived here, and she began to peer at each man's face hoping that she might catch sight of him. After scanning hundreds of faces, she gave up. The city was too big with too many residents to be able to find one person in such congestion.

"We need to go to the central market," Pappa said. "This is where we will sell our wool and sheep tomorrow. But today, we will find some food." Pappa disembarked from his horse and walked up to a vendor selling blood sausage and fish. He paid the man with the Danish currency, one rigsdaler.

"What inn has vacancy tonight?" Pappa asked the sausage man.

The vendor looked at him like he had grown two heads and laughed. "There is no vacancy on market nights like this," the vendor replied hastily. "Everyone is selling their goods from the summer and buying everything they need before the coming winter. You will need to sleep in the streets, I'm afraid."

"But I'm a vendor myself," Pappa said.

"Then I suggest you get your stall set up tonight and sleep beside it."

Pappa nodded and waved his daughter and Einar over to an empty stall on the north side of the market. They tied the sheep and horses, then collapsed onto the ground, exhausted from malnourishment. They sat with their backs against a stone wall and hungrily ate the precooked blood sausage.

Margret was so hungry she was afraid she might bite her fingers. They had travelled so much distance today, running on nothing but water for fuel. She felt light-headed and shaky. She devoured the blood sausage, and her father passed her another one.

"You're hungry," he said.

She nodded and chomped the rest of the second sausage without uttering another word. She saw Einar devouring his sausage as well. They were all famished. Travelling all day was hard on the body, she thought.

"We'll sleep here for tonight," Pappa said quietly.

Margret nodded, drinking a full cup of water. "Where is the inn?" she asked, wiping her dainty mouth.

"There are no vacancies," Pappa replied. "This is the biggest market of the year."

"What?" Margret exclaimed, her voice a little too loud. "Where will we sleep?"

"Right here," Pappa Jon said uncomfortably. "We'll stay at our stall."

"We can't just sleep in the streets!" Margret shouted.

Pappa frowned. "Now that'll be enough, Margret!" he said commandingly. "Does it look like I have any choice, my daughter? If I did, I would pay for a room at an inn. But there are none left. So this is what we have. Take it or leave it. You must stay with us for your own safety. Pretty girls may be stolen just like the sheep."

Margret opened her mouth to protest and closed it firmly. She could not believe what her father was saying. They had to sleep in the dirty streets for the night? Camping in the fields was even better than sleeping in the streets. She pursed her lips and laid back onto her rolled sleeping blanket, crossing her arms. There must be another way! Her father was just not thinking. How could a girl be stolen in the streets? That's blasphemy! No one would steal her.

Einar watched the exchange between father and daughter, interrupting quietly. "My brother, Olafur, is in Reykjavik with his wife and baby," Einar said slowly. "We could visit him. I am sure he'll be accommodating."

"Not tonight," Pappa said firmly. "We can ask tomorrow if we cannot find another place to stay. I don't want to be an intrusion in your brother's life, especially with a newborn baby."

"Okay, I understand, Mr. Petersson," Einar relented quietly.

"We have to spend the next few hours setting up the stall display," Pappa Jon said. "We have arrived late and have much to do. Saturday morning will be upon us before we know it."

Einar nodded and stood, disappearing to the back. He located a large wooden table from the back of the market stalls and began pulling it. Pappa guzzled a large amount of water, then helped move the table as they all prepared for the busy Saturday morning. They retied the sacks of wool onto the horses and positioned the horses to pull the heavier sleds closer to the stall. Once they had one horse in, they returned for another and another. The arduous task took longer than expected. Margret tied the sheep closer to the stall, gathered some hay and found buckets of water for the animals, settling in for the night.

As the sun began to lower on the horizon, Margret went into the crowds with Einar to fetch more food.

"Hold my hand," Einar said protectively. "I don't want to lose you."

"Nobody is going to steal me!" Margret refuted.

"Maybe not," Einar replied. "But still, I'd like to make sure we don't lose each other in the crowd."

Einar held her hand firmly as they negotiated the crowds. Margret followed obediently. She had never been in such large crowds before. They purchased more blood sausages, a bag of dried sheep meat and flatkaka. They stopped to fill their water canteens in a public well and returned to the stall. Einar opened up the bags and spread them out on the blanket that Pappa had laid out. It was enough to last for an evening meal and one more day of food.

Pappa chewed the meat hungrily and drank more water. Margret ate until her stomach ached from overeating. Einar ate the last remaining bits of food. He shuffled closer to Margret, protectively placing his larger body beside hers.

"Watch over my Margret tonight, Einar," Pappa Jon said, unrolling his blanket on the ground. "I'm feeling quite weary from the journey."

"I'll keep an eye on her, Mr. Petersson," Einar replied, washing down the meat with water and finishing the last piece of flatkaka.

Pappa nodded but narrowed his eyes at Einar with a threatening frown, an unspoken male territorial warning. Einar understood completely, straightened his shoulders and looked down.

Margret shook her head, watching her father lie down in his makeshift bed. She shuffled and unrolled her blanket, slipping under the warm wool and curled up in it, edging closer to Einar. She was extremely fatigued from the journey, and her legs felt rubbery. Several thoughts raced through her mind of how they could find more suitable accommodations. She remembered her aunt and uncle lived in the northern part of the island, although they must have some distant relatives in such a big city. She ran through her childhood memories, trying to remember a piece of long-forgotten information. It tugged at her and annoyed her. She suddenly felt tired, and her weariness fought with her senses as her eyelids closed. A strong male arm wrapped around her shoulders as her mind drifted into oblivion. The only thought she remembered was that Magnus lived in this city.

Einar watched her sleep. She was a beautiful girl. Her thick darkish blonde hair swirled around her temples and down her neck, stopping at her shoulders. She had cut it shorter recently, and he just noticed. He liked how it looked. The waves bobbed when she walked. The night air was cooler than usual, so he wrapped his muscular arms more tightly around her shoulders and soon fell asleep with her, the weariness of the journey taking over.

CHAPTER 10

Margret awoke with the sun in her eyes. She groaned and tried to roll over but realized she couldn't. Her mind came up with all sorts of hazy, dreamlike conclusions, all of which she discarded. Margret peered down and noticed a hairy arm across her abdomen, holding her tight. She inhaled and smelled a sweet musky male scent. It was pleasant. Margret tried moving again, and the arm tightened protectively around her.

She was confused and elated at the same time. Margret was awash with gratefulness and relished in the feeling of this man's arms around her. She relaxed and melted into his embrace as the market teemed with early morning dawn activity. It was very early, so only a few vendors began setting up. The sheep were beginning to make noises, and the horses were hungry. It was so warm in her blanket. Margret closed her eyes and imagined Magnus's arms around her. Somehow she knew that he would never be the one who held her at night. Margret knew this, as clear as day, but her heart would not listen. She yearned for

Magnus. Some mornings, her body screamed for him, and she pleasured herself quickly so the terrible yearning would pass.

But today, right now, Margret felt so protected and loved. Yes, she felt loved! Then her senses began awakening. Who was it that held her? Margret guessed, and she knew the answer right away. The only man in her life that has stood steadfastly by her side. Margret hadn't even noticed him all these years. He had become so comfortably engrained into her life that she hardly realized the contribution he made.

A bell sounded from the market stall closest to them, awakening the nearby chickens. Einar jerked awake while holding Margret entangled within their blankets. Her head was resting on his curled arm, and her hair smelled wonderful. The street began awakening with vigour as a light rain began to fall. Pappa Jon was stirring, and Einar feared the man's wrath upon catching his farm hand holding Margret, his only daughter. He looked down onto Margret's shoulders and noticed that she was partially awake and quite enjoying the protective snuggle. Einar smiled. She was content in his arms!

Pappa Jon groaned and turned over, facing them.

Einar jumped out of his grasp with Margret and stood up, almost dropping the woman onto the ground.

"Ouch," she groaned, disgruntled that her warm place was disturbed.

"Good morning Pappa Jon!" Einar shouted, a bit too excitedly. "It is a busy day today! Let's get the stall set up so we can sell all this wool! Rise and shine!"

"Good Lord, Einar!" Pappa Jon exclaimed wearily. "It is too early in the morning to have so much vigour."

Margret sat up, ran her fingers through her messy hair and looked around bewilderedly. She saw her father rustling himself out of his blanket. A certain understanding dawned on her.

Einar must be afraid of crossing her father. Margret thought this was silly. Einar had no such thing to fear! But a part of her understood. Pappa could be overbearing, she thought. Margret rubbed her shoulder that had hit the ground when Einar dropped her. She looked over and grimaced at him.

Einar looked back at her with a mixture of adoration and apprehension. He stepped from one foot to the other in a gesture of suspended liveliness. His heart raced, and his groin was completely stiff. He tried to hide his erection by stepping from one side to the other, willing it to go away.

Margret wasn't quite sure what to think of Einar at the moment. He had been so sweet just a few moments ago, and now he looked quite foolish dancing about from foot to foot. She shook her head and ran her hands through her dark blonde hair. Margret didn't understand men; they baffled her with their mood swings. She straightened her plain dress and stood up. "Pappa," she shouted. "Einar is right. Get up. We need to set up before the customers start coming." She walked over to Pappa and shook his shoulder. "Get up!"

"Okay, okay!" Pappa growled back. "I'm awake." Pappa Jon ran his hands along his face and rubbed his beard. "Grab some hay for those horses and sheep, Einar. They're hungry." He looked at his dishevelled daughter and instructed her as well. "My dear, you can help me get the wool onto those barn tables." He gestured towards the roughly cut half-log tables Einar and himself had hauled to the stall last night. The tables were sturdy enough to handle the weight of the bales of wool. "Let's stack some of these fleeces on the table. There are fifty of them in total. We may only be able to fit ten on the tables."

Margret started grabbing the wool fleeces and was astonished at the weight. They weighed more than she did! Margret struggled to move a bale, and it wouldn't budge. She pushed at it with all her weight, and it finally moved. Margret pulled on it mightily, and it started moving, then she began to drag it inch by inch. Pappa Jon moved several fleeces as she struggled with one. It moved a few feet to the table, and Margret began perspiring. She grunted and tried lifting it like her Pappa, but she couldn't. Margret shifted her weight, turned to drag it across again and faltered. She teetered, her balance tilted, and Margret fell to the ground, the wool fleece bale opening up and spilling partially into the mud.

Pappa Jon shouted fiercely, "Margret! That fleece is not even saleable now! You dropped it in the mud!"

"Pappa!" she cried. "I'm not strong enough. I'm trying!"

Suddenly, Einar grabbed her side, lifting her from the mud and then hefted the wool fleece onto the ground near the table. "I will clean the wool, Pappa Jon, don't you worry. Let's get the rest of these fleeces out."

Pappa wiped his brow. "Thank God you came, Einar."

Margret sunk to her knees as she watched the men. She felt insignificant and disappointed in herself. Why couldn't she be as strong as a man? If she was, then Margret could help her father with the sheep farm more, and he wouldn't have to pay Einar as much. She tried many times to help, but it always ended the same way. Margret was too thin and clumsy.

She looked up at the sky, watching the clouds part. The day was clearing up, and it looked like they might have sunshine for the Saturday market. This was good. Nice weather meant more customers, and more customers meant more price haggling. They would have a better chance of getting a higher price.

Margret stood and smoothed her filthy dress in a futile gesture of feminism. She grimaced at her muddy state and walked over to the animals. She patted one of the sheep and spoke softly to her.

Einar laid the last fleece on the long table as Margret tied the sheep to the table to display the young, healthy sheep to prospective buyers. Einar paused, watching her every movement; then, as if he realized he was staring, he looked to the side and busied himself with the coin box and chairs.

Margret returned to the remaining sheep and brought him to the table too. The male sheep was the younger of the two. He most likely would be slaughtered for meat. She patted him along the head. He bleated. She spoke softly to him to calm him.

"You're good with the animals," Einar said, standing behind her.

She turned and faced him, smiling demurely. "I always think they can somehow understand me," she said.

"Maybe they can," Einar said. "They can understand tone, and your voice is very soothing."

"You think so?"

"Of course," he said. "You have a very sweet feminine voice."

Margret blushed. "Thank you," she said, looking at her toes. She looked up but couldn't make eye contact with Einar, so she fixed her gaze at the street teaming with life. Several stalls were opening up, and customers began filtering into the streets.

"Here comes some buyers now," Pappa Jon said abruptly.

Three large men on Icelandic horses with several cow bells rode slowly towards them. They each were pulling an empty cargo sleigh. One stopped and dismounted. "How much for twenty fleece?"

Pappa frowned. This was almost half of the wool he owned. He didn't want to part with so much so early in the day, although it would be nice to sell everything he had quickly. "Each fleece is fifteen rigsdalers, so twenty would be," Pappa paused, briefly calculating the amount in his mind. "Three hundred rigsdalers."

The large man scoffed. "Three hundred! That's too much. I'll give you three hundred for forty fleece."

Pappa stopped to think about it. That would be selling his entire fleece with only ten left. "If you were to take forty, I would give you the second twenty fleece for half price." Pappa paused to calculate. "So that would come to four hundred and fifty rigsdalers."

"No deal," the burly man pivoted and climbed upon his horses. "I'll come back at the end of the day and see if you've changed your mind."

"Depending on the market and demand, it may go up in price by day's end," Pappa said loudly, nodding the men farewell politely.

The burly man stood on his horse rooted to the spot, encapsulated in thought. "I will come back," he said and rode off, the cowbells clanging behind them.

Pappa Jon nodded and began bartering with a sheep farmer for the young female. The price went up and down until finally, they agreed on a satisfactory price and the farmer took the female sheep.

As the day wore on, they sold several fleeces at high prices, even higher than the fifteen rigsdalers he was initially asking for per fleece. Margret was pleased that the market was going so well, but they still had a lot of wool left. No one had wanted to buy in bulk like the first three burly men.

They had sold the young male sheep for an inflated price with several customers bidding on the same sheep. Pappa was a tough businessman and held his ground until the best possible price. Margret was proud of her father. His abilities went far beyond sheep farming.

By late morning, the crowd was thickening, and the prices for fleece were climbing higher. They had sold twenty-five fleeces and were hopeful that the remaining twenty-five would be sold by the end of the day.

Pappa was happy, although he worried that they would be left with residual fleece and be forced to sell at bargain prices or, worse, take it back with them.

Jon heard familiar cow bells and looked up as the three burly men returned with anxious looks on their faces. "Hello, men! You're back!" Pappa Jon was elated. He was hoping they'd come back and purchase all the remaining fleece.

The largest burly man disembarked from his horse. "How much fleece do you have left?" he asked.

Pappa Jon looked at the other fleece market stalls and noticed they were half empty like his stall. He assessed the burly men trio. Their cargo sleighs were only a quarter full. The men's prices were too low, and few farmers were taking the bait. "Twenty-five fleece left," Pappa Jon replied.

"I will give you fifteen rigsdalers each for the remaining twenty-five fleece," the burly man offered loudly.

Pappa Jon knew the competitor vendors could overhear the price. He knew that if he said no, the men would simply go to the next vendor and next until they got their price. "The prices for fleece have almost doubled," Pappa Jon said thoughtfully. "But I can negotiate a price with you."

"Fifteen rigsdalers each," the man said overconfidently. "That's three hundred and seventy-five for all twenty-five fleece."

"I doubt many fleece vendors would sell for this price since all my fleeces sold for over twenty rigsdalers each." Pappa Jon evaluated the men and noticed a strange young man disembarking from his horse. The man was familiar; he had dark hair and a handsome, chiselled face.

"I'll buy fifteen of those fleece for twenty rigsdalers each!" the young man shouted over the burly men's heads.

The lead burly man looked back and straightened. "He's not prepared to buy the lot!" he argued, pointing out the obvious.

Pappa Jon stretched his neck to see the new bidder. "He's offering to buy fifteen bales!" Pappa shouted, waving at the new bidder in the back.

The burly man stood taller, obstructing his view, extending his hand in surrender. "Alright, alright! I will buy all the remaining fleece at twenty rigsdalers each. That's my final offer."

"Sold!" Pappa Jon shouted happily.

Margret and Einar beamed as the men exchanged money.

Pappa was clearly elated. They had managed to sell everything before noon. They could now find pots, tools, and food. Hopefully, they will find some accommodations for the night once all the customers leave.

Margret was pleased, and she hugged her father. "We can go eat, then find those pots," she said cheerily.

"Give me a few minutes to unload the fleece, pack up and clear our stall," Pappa said as he hurried about helping Einar load the fleece onto the burly men's sleighs.

Margret stepped back and watched the men load up the sleighs. The dark, handsome stranger that had bid the higher price was looking at her. She squinted. Her eyesight wasn't the greatest. The man nodded at her. She was confused. Who was the man? Margret squinted again. She still couldn't make out who it was in the back of the crowd.

Once Pappa was done loading up the fleece, the crowd began to move again. The burly men left with their goods, and the crowd started dispersing. The strange dark-haired man moved with the throng of people. As he came closer and closer, Margret realized with a chill who it was.

"Margret," he said, stopping in front of her. "You look as beautiful as ever."

"Magnus," she replied. Her heart melting at the sight of him. "Do you come to the market often?"

"This is the biggest market of the year in Reykjavik," Magnus answered. "I never miss it."

"Oh," she said dumbly. Her body was on fire; every nerve, every muscle was responding to being in close proximity of this man.

"Come for a walk with me," he said, outstretching his palm. "Do you have a place to stay? I heard there were no vacancies at the inns."

Einar was suddenly by her side. "We will find accommodations once all the customers leave today," he said aggressively.

Margret peered curiously at Einar. She couldn't understand the man. One minute he was hugging her, then dropping her and ignoring her, then acting defensively. Margret shifted her gaze to Pappa Jon. He was finishing up, putting all the money securely into his money belt.

"Pappa, is it alright if I go find those pots with Magnus?" she asked.

Pappa looked across at Magnus and felt an instant streak of protectiveness cross his emotions. He shook the feelings away, remembering how deeply his daughter felt about Magnus. It was evident in her glossy eyes. She adored the man. "Yes, go," he said, pushing several rigsdalers into her hands. "Keep the money safe and buy sturdy pots. Hurry before they are all gone."

Einar watched with frustration as Pappa Jon allowed his daughter to leave with that womanizer. He could see right through Magnus. If only Margret could see the same thing. "I can go with them," Einar said a bit too loudly.

"No," Margret stated firmly. "I will go with Magnus and be back shortly."

Einar opened his mouth to object and then closed it firmly. There was no arguing with Margret when she had made a decision. He turned and walked away angrily. "I'm going for a walk!" Einar shouted back, stomping away.

Margret frowned and shook her head, clearly not understanding. She looked up at Magnus. "Let's go find some pots," she said. "Einar is probably just weary from the journey and sleeping in the streets."

"You slept in the streets?" Magnus asked incredulously.

"Yes," she answered as they walked into the throng of people. "We had no choice. There were no vacancies."

"You could have been kidnapped!"

"That's what Pappa said, too," Margret replied. "You men worry too much. Einar watched over me. I was safe."

"He likes you," Magnus said matter-of-factly.

"No!" Margret shouted back. "He does not! He's been like a brother my entire life."

"But he's not blood-related to you," Magnus said, gently slipping his hand into hers. "Please hold onto me; I don't want to lose you in this crowd."

Margret wound her fingers into his and held his hand firmly, wondering if Magnus was right and Einar had developed a romantic interest in her. She felt so naive and inexperienced around men. They baffled her and jumbled her thoughts. One minute they were saying and doing things so practically, then the next minute, they were expressing the most sincere emotions. It was as if men existed solely to confuse women. Margret wondered if men felt the same about women.

She followed Magnus through the crowd as she stared at his head full of dark hair. Margret wondered why Magnus didn't react as strongly as Einar had. Was she missing something about Magnus? Was there something about the man that Margret should have picked up on before? Maybe he knew that she adored him, and there was no need to be overly protective.

"Come this way!" Magnus said, shouting over the din of multiple conversations in the throng. "I know where some of the best pots are to be found!"

Margret followed obediently, afraid that she would get lost in the dense crowd. It was much thicker than yesterday. She immediately regretted not allowing Einar to join them. She followed her eyes to a stall with several iron pots as Magnus pulled her in closer and hugged her waist. She liked his touch and how he smelled. Margret enjoyed it a bit too much. She absorbed every single smell, word and touch of the man.

"Here we are," he said smoothly into her ear. He leaned down even further and whispered. "I missed you, my beautiful."

The words shot through her body, tingling her skin, her heart and her lips. Her vagina instantly ached, and it made her feel uncomfortable because the stall owner was staring at her.

"Are you here to buy a pot, young lady?" the older stall owner asked.

"Yes, she is," Magnus answered. "How much for the red earthen pot?"

Margret shook her head. "I want the cast iron pot," she said. "How much for that one?" She pointed across the stall over to the left.

"Twenty rigsdalers," the old man said firmly.

"What?" Magnus said in shock. "That's robbery! I'll give you eight rigsdalers, and that's all!"

Margret looked at Magnus. "I want that pot," she whispered.

"We will haggle for it," Magnus whispered. "Please let me handle this."

"Pots are extremely hard to find in Iceland," she said. "I don't want to lose it to someone else's bid."

"You won't," he said, pulling her chin up to look at his face closely. "Trust me, okay?"

She stared into his handsome blue eyes. "Okay," she said, relenting.

She watched as Magnus bartered with the stall owner until finally, they settled at a price far below what she was willing to pay. She was delighted and proud of Magnus. He had helped them sell all the fleece for a good price, and now the pot was hers for way less than she had expected. She opened her pocket money pouch and handed the stall owner twelve rigsdalers for the cast iron pot. She smiled as the stall owner handed the pot to her. "Thank you," she said to the old man, smiling.

Magnus curled his arm around her waist and motioned with her into the crowd again. "Are you hungry?" he asked.

"Yes, very much," she said eagerly. "We only had a small breakfast. Our food was all stolen by foxes on the last day of our journey."

"Oh my!" Magnus said. "Those foxes are terrible around here." He gently guided her through the crowd, clearly knowing his way around the market. "There are some delicious sausages over here." Magnus wrapped his arm tighter around her waist and lightly brushed against the side of her right breast.

A tingle rose up to her arm, and the entire side of her body felt warm. She felt her face flush as the sensual sensations coursed through her veins. Her vagina ached with a longing so intense it was all she could think about. Just the slightest touch from his hands felt like magic, and she yearned to feel his body against hers again.

"Two blood sausages!" Magnus shouted. "And two flat-kaka." Magnus let go of her waist as he paid for the food.

Margret felt a cold rush of air where his hands used to be. She hugged herself to keep warm as Magnus gestured for her to follow him to a patch of grass on a knobby hill. He held the food in his hands and nodded to a spot amongst many other picnickers.

"Let's sit here," Magnus said smoothly, picking out a spot.

Margret sat on the grass and accepted the small meal, eating voraciously. She didn't realize how hungry she was until the food was in her hands. Without another word, she chewed the sausage and bread until it was all gone.

"You were hungry," Magnus said softly.

"I was," she said simply, feeling his closeness jumbling with her thoughts again.

He leaned into her and hugged her body closer to his.

She moulded into him so easily. "I missed you so much," she mumbled into his shirt.

Magnus patted her hair. "I missed you too," he said, kissing the top of her head.

Margret looked up, and he met her lips, kissing them very slowly. The moment felt exquisitely frozen in time as if all that existed was only this kiss, only their scents with each other and the touch of their hands.

Margret's desire rose sharply, wanting Magnus more than ever. Her body lurched towards him, yearning for him with an incredible force that made her dizzy.

Magnus stopped abruptly and held her chin, looking into her eyes. "Let's go sit farther back," he said, standing up and extending his hand.

Margret stood up and followed him aimlessly. Her lips felt swollen, and she yearned for more of his kisses. She would follow him anywhere.

Magnus turned right and sat down behind a small bush, pulling her down with him.

Margret giggled and lost her balance, falling right into his lap. They both laughed and cuddled together, kissing.

The heat rose between their bodies immediately. A chemical fire of combined attraction, fuelled by longing, blossomed out of control. Magnus swirled his tongue inside her mouth and squeezed her right breast through her clothes.

Margret moaned heavily, her body absorbing every touch, satisfying a deep longing. She involuntarily pressed her hips into his knee urgently. She rocked on his knee, moving sensually to the soundless musical rhythm they were creating. Her senses were on fire. Every touch sent electric waves throughout her body and aching shards to her vagina. His smell intoxicated her so much that Margret felt like she was melting away in his arms.

Magnus moved on top of her, kissing her deeply, unable to stop himself again. He touched her everywhere. His hands ran freely over her breast, her stomach, and her legs, finally stopping at the apex of her thighs. It was moist through her dress. He could feel the heat emanating through her clothing. He wrestled with his clothes and undid his belt.

Margret groaned as his full weight pressed on top of her. She kissed him even more passionately, doing nothing to stop him this time. She wanted Magnus so badly, and no amount of overthinking would hamper her mind.

Magnus kissed her swollen lips and unzipped his pants. He fumbled with her dress hastily, pulling it up to her waist.

Margret kissed him back urgently, running her hands along his slim muscular body, trying to feel him through his clothes until finally, she felt something. A smooth, rigid naked piece of his body miraculously landed in her hand. She relished in the feel of this private body part. It was so smooth, Margret thought wondrously. His penis was average but thick, much thicker than she thought a penis would be. Margret wrapped her small hand around it, with her fingers barely circling around his penis. It was very warm, and she marvelled at how much she wanted it inside of her. Every single cell in her body wanted Magnus's penis inside her vagina. She had little control. Her sex drive was ruling her mind. No other thoughts remained but this one urgent necessity.

Magnus curled over her, fumbling with the layers of clothing until he finally slid her panties to the side.

She groaned heavily as his fingers lightly danced along her moist labia.

Magnus was enraptured by her urgency and felt no hesitation as he guided his penis inside her vagina.

Margret gasped as the head of his swollen penis nudged her entrance.

Magnus pushed with his hips and slid his penis into her entrance farther as she gasped again. Her vagina walls were extremely tight, almost painful. He stopped with his throbbing penis halfway inside her vagina. He looked into her eyes. At that moment, she looked up at him, and their wild eyes met.

"Yes," she mumbled. "I've dreamt of this moment for so long."

He glided gently with his hips then he felt a resistance inside her. He kissed her lips and rocked gently inside her back and forth, every movement sending his penis deeper and deeper inside her until finally, he breached her wall of resistance. Magnus breathed heavily as her vagina gripped him fiercely. The smell of grass wafted up to his nostrils. He briefly remembered in the back of his mind that they were on a very public hill behind a bush.

"Is this what you want, Margret?" he asked. "Tell me."

"Yes," she answered breathlessly. "I want you now, all of you."

Magnus lost all control. He pumped madly inside of her vagina, pulling out then back in, his testosterone fuelling a maniacal surge of desire that had been building up like a volcano. Magnus slid once more deeply into her vagina and held himself firmly, pausing his thrusts.

Margret could feel him throbbing and pulsating inside of her. The effect it had on her was exquisite. Her entire body was flat, her legs splayed, and her arms laced tightly around his back. She bit his shoulder lightly, offsetting the pain. It felt both painful and intensely pleasurable at the same time. Margret felt like someone had picked her up and deposited her in heaven. She mumbled her feelings of love into his shoulder as he began in earnest again, pumping wildly into her.

She groaned heavily and stretched her neck upwards as his thrusts went impossibly deep inside her. Then suddenly, he grunted softly and ground his hips into her, pushing her up the hill slightly. A gush of fluid released inside of her, the hot stream of semen sending sensations throughout her body, purer than anything she had ever felt before. It shot inside of her in three streams of hot liquid. Margret gasped, her mouth wide open as the sensations threatened to rob her mind. She quivered. First, her legs trembled, then her torso and arms until her entire body was shaking with sexual gratification.

Magnus attempted to stop the quivering by soothing her arms lightly, but he was suddenly exhausted, laying his full weight on her petite body. He exhaled heavily into her shoulder and collapsed on top of her.

Margret kissed his neck lightly as the quivers began to subside. Her body finally started to relax as his flaccid penis slipped out of her.

"I love you, Margret," he said softly into her shoulder. "I missed you so much."

She kissed him on the neck again. Those words were exactly what she needed to hear. "I love you too, Magnus," she replied breathlessly.

They had laid together on the grass for a long while before either of them moved. Then gradually, Margret's mind started to come back to reality. "We need to go back and find Pappa," she said. "He will be worrying about me."

"Yes," Magnus said, pulling his belt back on and zippering up his pants. He stood and pulled her up. "How do you feel?"

"It hurts a bit," she said. "And my legs feel wobbly."

"There will be a little blood," he said. "Don't be afraid. This is normal for the first time."

She nodded. "I know," Margret said. "My closest friend, Anna, told me this too."

Magnus held her waist tightly and walked back with her, ensuring every step she took was supported by him. It took a while before they found Pappa and Einar. They had travelled quite a distance away, farther than she had thought.

Einar eyed Magnus suspiciously.

Magnus shook hands with Pappa. "I wanted to invite you all to my house for the night. Margret said you didn't have any accommodations last night."

"That would be very kind of you," Pappa said. "But I have bumped into my late wife's sister here at the market, and we will be staying with her."

Margret's eyes widened. "Johanna!" she cried. "Yes, that's who I was thinking about last night. I couldn't remember because I was so tired, but I knew we had some relatives here in this city."

Magnus let his arms fall by his side. Margret curled her hand into his. "It's alright, Magnus," she said happily. "We will stay at Johanna's, but you can visit with us, and I will go see your house tomorrow."

Magnus brightened. "Okay, that sounds acceptable."

"Let's go!" Margret said hastily. "I want to see my aunt again!"

CHAPTER 11

Johanna's house was tastefully decorated with artistic paintings and drawings on the walls, along with warm woollen rugs on the floor. She was a pleasant, inviting woman, and she looked like Margret's mom in many ways. Her nose was long, and her hair was wavy and blonde. She had the same smile as her mom. Margret was fascinated by her aunt and wanted to spend as much time as possible with her, almost ignoring Magnus.

Einar and his brother's small family were also invited to dinner. Olafur, his wife and the tiny infant boy were a joy. Margret couldn't get enough of the cute baby. She held him and rocked the baby, cooing and speaking to him in a gayly high-pitched voice. Einar thought it was quite lovely how Margret held his nephew, even when the boy began fussing. Several times, he patted the small baby's head and kissed the baby while Margret cuddled the adorable boy. Einar felt Magnus's hot glare on his back but didn't care. He was enjoying the time with his nephew and Margret's family.

Einar curled his large hands under the fussing baby and scooped him from Margret's arms as she followed him to his brother. "Aron is so cute!" Einar cooed, handing the baby back to Olafur. "He looks hungry."

Aron opened his tiny mouth and sucked at the air. Margret laughed. "He's looking for a nipple!" she exclaimed.

Olafur took his son and handed him to his wife. "He's a good baby," Olafur said. "But he's constantly hungry! He won't leave his mother alone for too long!" He chuckled. "I want my wife back!"

Einar laughed. "If that's your only complaint, then count yourself as a lucky father."

"I am very lucky," Olafur replied, hugging Einar. "I have a beautiful wife, a beautiful son, and I finally get to see my brother again."

Einar hugged him back. "It's been too long since you left," Einar responded. "I missed you. Momma and Pappa have been getting older, but we are managing."

"I wish I could move back," Olafur replied. "But my wife's family lives here in Reykjavik, and we need all the help we can get with our growing family." He smiled broadly. "We plan on having five children, maybe more. You should expect a lot more nieces and nephews."

Margret beamed and patted Einar on the shoulder. "You're so lucky!"

Einar chuckled. "Yes, I am," he answered.

Magnus appeared suddenly behind Margret, pulling her into his arms protectively. She leaned her back against him and wondered if her future would hold many children as well. She looked back, smiling gayly and wondered why Magnus had a scowl on his face.

Margret frowned in confusion as Olafur's wife retreated to the back bedroom to breastfeed the baby. Margret caught Einar's glare as he stepped back a few feet from Magnus. She had no idea what had gotten into these two men, but she could feel an instant animosity between them. Margret shook her head, wiggled out of her lover's embrace and returned to the messy table.

"Johanna," Margret said politely. "Let me take that. I can clear the dishes." Margret piled the dishes onto one another and cleared the dinner table. Her aunt had cooked a wonderful meal of pan-fried cod and mussel stew with skyr yogurt for dessert. It was so delicious that Margret ate too much, and her stomach hurt a bit.

Magnus followed her, helping Margret take the plates back into the kitchen as Pappa chatted with Johanna about the fishing industry in Reykjavik. It was a busy time of year for fishing, and Johanna's late husband had left her a fledgling fishing company with many boats and employees. It kept her busy. She had learned how to fish and how to manage the family business. It took many years, but she was finally successful.

Margret was proud of her aunt and looked up to her. "She's a strong woman," Margret said. "I could only hope to grow up like her."

Magnus frowned. "Why?" he asked uncomfortably. "She's a widow. I would hope that's not what your future holds."

"No, I don't mean that," she argued. "I meant that she's so strong and capable. I could only hope to be the same one day."

"If you have a strong man by your side," he replied. "You won't need to be strong and capable." Magnus took more plates from the table and brought them into the kitchen.

Margret tilted her head to the side, wondering what had gotten into him. She was only stating the obvious about her beloved aunt. "She looks like my momma," she said.

"Your aunt?" Magnus said. "That's sweet. Was she close to you before your mother died?"

"Not really," she answered. "Aunt Johanna and her husband were always too busy with the fishing company. They had a lot of business catching, preparing and salting the fish."

Magnus nodded knowingly and kissed her on the forehead. Margret found herself a bit perturbed with his behaviour. She wanted to enjoy her long-lost family, and he just seemed to find everything negative about it.

"Do you have lots of relatives?" she asked.

"None," he said.

"None?"

"Nobody," he said firmly.

"Why? Don't you have cousins or aunts?" she said, curling her hair around her ears as she prepared the sink for the dishes.

"I have a few cousins in the northern part and an aunt here in town that I never see."

"Why don't you see your aunt?" she asked, clearly confused.

"You ask too many questions," Magnus responded firmly.

Margret frowned and started washing the dishes. She couldn't understand why he was becoming so rigid and confrontational.

He leaned over her and hugged her from behind. "I love you, Margret," he said. "Hopefully, one day, you'll see this and move here to Reykjavik. You'll see my home tomorrow. It's not great, but it has lots of potential."

❧

Einar watched Magnus putting his hands all over Margret, and it annoyed him. He didn't know why but it was angering him more and more. After seeing all these public displays of affection the entire night, Einar was at his limits of acceptance. He didn't like Magnus. He wasn't sure why but he just didn't trust the man.

Magnus returned to Johanna's early the next day and slipped his hand into Margret's.

"Pappa, I'm going to Magnus's property to see the home he inherited from his parents," she said comfortably. "We will be back later this afternoon. He doesn't live far from here."

"That is fine, dear," Pappa Jon said. "Just ensure that you are back early enough. We are preparing to leave tomorrow morning for our journey back home, so we will be awakening early in the morning. We need a good night's sleep; it will be a long day."

"I promise, Pappa."

Magnus curled his arm around her waist as he closed the porch door and linked his hand into hers as they both stepped onto the grass.

Margret felt unsettled and confused. They had made love yesterday in the park behind a bush! She blushed from the memory of their hurried lovemaking in public. It felt so wonderful and comfortable, like it was something she had wanted so badly for so long, and it had finally come true. Then it seemed Magnus had changed afterwards. She couldn't quite understand why but it definitely happened a few hours afterwards.

They had already argued once, and he had become quite authoritarian, shutting down all discussion and opinions from her. Maybe this was just how he viewed a woman's role in a husband's life. Margret thought about her out-of-wedlock liaison with Magnus yesterday, and she suddenly felt ashamed. She knew that she should have waited longer. Margret could have forced him to be a gentleman, move to Horn and marry her first. But he didn't seem interested in moving to her father's farm.

"What are you thinking about?" he asked. "I can see those wheels turning in your mind again."

Margret smiled meekly and looked ahead, squinting in the sun. Her eyes lacked focus on objects far away, which annoyed her greatly. She could see what looked like a barn in the distance. "Is that your house?"

Magnus frowned. "You didn't answer my question."

"I'd rather not discuss it, Magnus," she replied calmly.

"Discuss it!" he said firmly.

"I want you to move to Horn to be with me," Margret said firmly.

"No," Magnus replied. "There's no reason for me to abandon my house or sell my property to move all the way to the opposite side of Iceland."

"Then why did you have sex with me yesterday?" she asked, her anger rising.

"Because you're mine," he said simply.

Margret looked at him incredulously. "I'm yours?"

"Yes," Magnus answered. "You're mine. I don't want any other woman but you, and I'm certain you feel the same way about me."

Margret couldn't argue with that. She did feel like he was the only man she felt strongly about.

"I don't want to discuss it any further," Magnus stated. "You will love the house and change your mind hopefully one day. Who knows, maybe you'll even have my child in your belly already."

Margret's heart skipped a beat, and she faltered on a stone. Magnus caught her off balance and steadied her. "Are you okay?" he asked.

"I am fine, Magnus," she lied. "Let's see your house."

Einar crept outside in the sunny late morning. He felt puzzled and bewildered at his desire to protect Margret. She was clearly not in any danger, he told himself. There was no need to panic. But something in his gut told him to follow them.

His boots crunched on the rocky soil as he marched to the house on the hill. He was a far distance behind them, but he could see where they were heading because of the gradual uphill slope.

His thoughts jumbled in his mind. What would he say when he got there? Would he just knock on the door? How would he feel if they were making love? Einar grimaced at the thought. He was simply following his instinct, nothing more. Einar had protected Margret since she was a little girl, and he would just make sure she was okay.

A tiny voice inside his head told him that he was jealous and he should stay away. Einar argued with the voice, reasoning that it was okay to be there for her. He asked himself if he loved her.

The thought stopped him on the dirt path. He looked down at his boots and wondered if it might be true. Was his jealousy fuelled by his love for her that wasn't being returned? Einar looked up at the hill as they both entered the house. A light turned on. The door closed. He watched as the two shadows walked through the house, disappearing.

Einar walked closer and continued to the front yard. Everything looked fine. There wasn't any need to be worried. He asked himself again if he loved Margret. His heart thumped wildly in response. He couldn't imagine a life without her. The sobering thought hit his senses like a hammer. Einar blinked and doubted if she felt the same.

He turned his foot to leave and took two steps down the path. Then he heard a shout.

"We can raise a family together," Magnus said. "The house needs some work, and I will start on the repairs as soon as you move in."

Margret looked at him in astonishment. It was like he hadn't even heard her say that she wasn't moving to Reykjavik. She had told him again while they were walking to the house, and Magnus had pretended like she hadn't even said anything. Margret wondered if he had difficulty hearing, or maybe he was certain that she would eventually change her mind. She smiled politely and followed him through the house, looking at every room.

The front room was very large and in disrepair. The wood floor was cracked in several spots, and she could even see the grass below through one small hole. In the kitchen, there was a worn cupboard with mouse feces on the floor below the cutting board. The bedrooms had minimal furniture and felt very cold. The house was mostly freestanding, with only the very back built into the side of a small hill. The property occupied twenty acres, although Magnus had no sheep, so the fields were overgrown and in dire need of tending. She wondered how a man could live in such a dank, neglected property and still feel proud of it.

"You can sell this property and move to Horn," she said, thinking out loud. "The amount of work we'll need to put into bringing this property to a liveable state would just be too much for the two of us. My father and I have a stable sheep farm. We could find a house nearby and still help him with the sheep. We could maybe even start our own sheep farm." She smiled, knowing that this was the only rational solution. She loved Magnus but wondered why he wasn't more like Einar. That man would have fixed this house up, ship-shape! He would have even built a shed and a barn, purchasing all the animals, then sheering and breeding them. Margret wondered briefly how Einar would fit into her life if Magnus moved to Horn. She grimaced, knowing that he would slowly disappear. The thought of losing Einar filled her with an instant sadness.

"I can't believe you're saying this," Magnus shouted, his voice a bit too loud.

Margret took a step back. She had never been shouted at before. She felt a strange kind of fear dart up to her spine. She shivered. Had she said something wrong?

"You will move here," Magnus said calmly, his voice returning to normal. "As I said, the house needs some repairing, and the fields need to be tended, but I will do this. We will have a family here. I will make sure that it is a good family home."

Margret looked at him with astonishment. He wasn't even giving her a choice anymore. This was not being gentlemanly. She opened her mouth to protest and thought better of it. Margret would keep her mouth shut until he took her back to her aunt's place. Fear jumped into her heart. Her instincts told her to remove this man from her life. She wanted to run out of the house immediately. Her mind panicked with various solutions.

Magnus hugged her tightly. "Don't be so tense," he said. "I love you, and you love me. We will make it work. I can come back to Horn with you, talk to your father and help you pack your things." He kissed her forehead in deep thought. "We will be happy forever."

Margret didn't know what to say. Fear laced into her stomach; she felt crampy and nauseous. Her head swam, and her thoughts raced. She could not allow him to persuade her entire family with this plan too. "Magnus," she said softly. "I love you, but I cannot move to Reykjavik. I told you this before. I won't leave my father. You must move to Horn, or we will not be together anymore. Whatever we have will be over." She blinked, hoping that she did not say too much.

Magnus turned his head, looking away. He turned back and glared at her. Magnus grunted and grabbed her shoulders firmly. "Look at me," he said angrily. "You will not say such things. You will do what I say."

Margret looked into his eyes and realized that he was a mad man. She couldn't fathom never speaking her own thoughts and submitting to a man's wishes all her life. It seemed unnatural. She knew that many women did this, but she had always thought it was somehow wrong. She was human, after all. Margret had a brain of her own, and if God didn't want her to think for herself, then he wouldn't have given her intelligence. She was not a sheep. Margret had been raised to be wilful and strong because that was the only way to survive on this harsh island.

"I will do what is right for me," she said firmly, staring back into his eyes.

Magnus nodded condescendingly. "And what about our child," he said. "The one that may be in your womb right now. Did you ever think of what is right for him?"

"I am not certain that I am pregnant," she said, doubt filling her veins. She hadn't thought about that.

"Well, we can make it certain then," he said, unbuckling his belt.

Margret's eyes widened. "No!" she shouted and pushed his arms away, stumbling backwards.

Magnus frowned angrily and took two large steps towards her. Margret backed up and bolted to the side, sending Magnus crashing into the hallway table. She screamed, darted to the front door and pulled at it, but it was locked. She fumbled and unlocked it as Magnus straightened.

Margret looked back. "Don't touch me!" she yelled in a high-pitched screech.

Margret yanked open the door and almost slammed into Einar as he rushed in, barreling towards Magnus, knocking him backwards. Her mind couldn't quite register what exactly was happening or why, but she was immensely relieved that Einar had somehow been dropped down by heaven to save her.

She watched in bewilderment as Einar jumped onto Magnus, punching him wildly. Magnus scuffled across the floor, trying to get his bearings. "What? Why are you here?" Magnus shouted madly at Einar.

Einar rushed at him like a polar bear, slamming his fists into Magnus's stomach. Magnus grunted forcibly; the wind knocked out of his lungs, and he slumped onto the floor. Einar stepped back, looking at Magnus with fire in his eyes. He curled his fist up and shook it at Magnus, the anger pumping crazily through his head. "If you ever touch her again, I swear, I will kill you, then tear you apart to pieces and feed you to the sheep!" Einar took one large menacing leap at Magnus and waved his finger wildly. "Don't think I won't! You stay away from Margret! I will kill you, and I'll do it with my bare hands!"

"Einar!" Margret shouted.

Einar stopped, hearing her voice. He turned and was instantly calmed by her presence. Einar forgot for a moment that she was here, watching everything. He had lost his mind.

"Don't kill him," she said calmly.

Einar looked back at Magnus, clutching his abdomen, still curled in pain. Einar began to feel the anger in his body dissipate. "He was going to hurt you," Einar said.

"Yes, he was," she said calmly.

"I was just claiming what is mine," Magnus mumbled, attempting to stand up.

Einar felt the blood rush to his face upon hearing the domineering words. Einar lurched without thinking and punched him square in the nose, sending Magnus flying into the wall. Blood spurted in the air, and Magnus fell with a thud, sliding down the wall onto the floor, his bloodied head bobbing to the side.

"Oh my Lord!" Margret shouted, leaping towards him. "You've killed him!"

Einar put up his palm to stop her. He ran to Magnus, bent down and checked his pulse. Einar nodded his head reassuringly. "He's alive," he said. "The man deserved it for what he said!" His body vibrated from the testosterone surge. Finally, Einar looked down, shook his fingers painfully and inspected his knuckles. They felt bruised.

"Are you sure he's alive?" Margret asked.

"Yes," Einar said, straightening. "We can wait until he gains consciousness and make sure he's okay before I take you back home."

"I would appreciate that," Margret said, curling her arms around herself, shivering slightly.

Einar removed his jacket and wrapped it around her shoulders. "I'm sorry you had to witness that," he said softly. "I followed you both from Johanna's place. I felt something was wrong. I don't know why. I felt silly when I came to the house, and I turned to go back home when I heard you scream." Einar walked slowly towards her, wrapping his arms around her warmly. "I tried the door, and it was locked."

Margret felt the fear and anxiety dissolve from her body at his warm, loving touch. "Einar," she mumbled into his chest. "You don't have to apologize. You saved me. I don't know what I would have done without you." She kissed him soundlessly on his shirt. "Thank you."

They walked silently down the hill back to Johanna's house. Margret and Einar had stayed until Magnus awoke, groaning. Einar said some final words to him about getting his broken nose tended to. Then they left.

The sun was warm and high in the sky, providing a sweet warmth on their backs, although she kept Einar's jacket draped over her shoulders to stop the nervous shaking. "We don't have to tell Pappa," Margret said. "I don't want him to get angry too."

"I think he should know that someone attacked his daughter," Einar stated.

Margret thought about this and nodded. "You may be right," she replied. "Can we wait and tell him after we get back home?"

Einar dangled his swollen hand in the air as he walked and winced. "Alright."

"What's wrong with your hand?" she asked, concern streaking across her face.

"Nothing," he replied. "It's just swollen."

She stopped and pulled his arm. "Let me look at it," she said firmly.

He held out his right hand, and she inspected it, running her delicate fingers over his bones. "You've broken one of your bones," she said, pausing her fingers over the tender, swollen spot. "It looks like this one."

"Do you really think it's broken?"

"I think so," Margret replied. "Pappa broke his hand once from working, and it looks similar." She slid a gentle hand over his injury. "We will ask Johanna to send for a doctor before we leave."

"It's not urgent," he argued.

"It may need to be set," she replied. "We will tell Pappa you fell and broke your hand."

"Are you sure?"

"Yes," she said. "I don't want to witness Pappa trying to kill Magnus too. We'll tell him the truth when we get back."

CHAPTER 12

The earth was trembling again as they passed Mount Hekla. Margret could feel the awesome power of the active volcano. She shivered. It could destroy us all one day, she thought. Our problems would all be buried in a river of lava.

The horses' hooves clomped on the hard ground as the mountain loomed in the distance. "Why does it do that?" Margret asked. "Why does Iceland always have these earthquakes close to the volcanoes?"

Pappa Jon smiled. "Living with the volcanoes is part of being Icelandic. They do what they want with us."

"But Pappa," she persisted. "Isn't there a reason why?"

Einar spoke, "I believe it's the magma movement underground. The lava flows underneath the ground and creates shaking in the earth where we stand."

"That sounds reasonable," she replied. They trotted for a while across the vast empty landscape, void of animals or settlements. A few abandoned homes graced the countryside. She knew many farmers gave up on this part of the island due to the volcanic activity and the effect it was beginning to have on the land. The horses took them past Mount Hekla, and Margret noticed the ground calming down. She wondered if what Einar said about magma movement was true. She was beginning to realize that Einar was an intelligent man, contrary to his burly farm boy appearance.

They stopped to camp overnight, several hours away from the volcano.

Pappa Jon opened his pack and pulled out some salted fish while Einar started the fire. Margret watched the men busying with the small dinner. Her upset tummy grumbled, and she wondered if Magnus was recovering from the broken nose. She couldn't get him out of her mind completely. Margret thought she was going insane because he had treated her so badly after finally having sex with her. It proved to her that he needed a woman to be pregnant with his baby for her to stay. Otherwise, the moment Magnus became angry and possessive, his woman would leave without a trace. Maybe that's why he was so experienced with women; he could never keep them for long.

Einar intuitively noticed her discomfort. He draped his coat over her shoulders and sat next to Margret. Pappa Jon saw this but curiously didn't say anything.

"How are you feeling?" Einar asked.

"I'm doing much better, thank you," Margret replied, a feeling of warmth spreading along her skin.

Pappa Jon sat down wearily, watching the fish cook on the open fire. "It's been a long time travelling," he said tiredly.

Margret eyed him suspiciously. "You look tired, Pappa," she said. "You must relax as much as you can." She took the wood fire poker out of his hand. "I will tend to the fish. You rest."

"Okay, I think I will," Pappa said, lying down on his flat pillow.

The night slowly turned to dark as they finished cooking the salted fish. She turned to hand a piece to her father, and he was sound asleep. She tried rousing him but to no avail. He just grunted and rolled away.

Margret frowned worriedly. Pappa was normally very fit. To see him so tired was unusual.

Einar and Margret looked at each other with a mixed concern for Pappa. "He's just too tired from the journey," Einar said.

"I suppose," Margret said.

They arrived home several days later. Margret felt so delighted to be back home. She ran to her room excitedly and plopped onto her bed, smelling the familiar sheets. The sheep bayed in the fields, and everything felt wonderful. The journey was long and hard for Pappa, and she still felt worried. Her father was growing older every day. She would need to take care of him one day, and she accepted this with the clarity of a much more mature person.

"It feels so good to be home!" she shouted from the bedroom.

Einar chuckled. "Yes, it does," he shouted towards the back. Einar fixed his focus back to Pappa Jon. "If you are both settled, I will go home myself now. My parents are probably waiting impatiently."

"Wait!" Margret jumped off the bed and rushed through the house, hugging Einar fiercely. "Thank you, Einar. I mean it. We couldn't have done that trip without you."

Einar patted her hair. "It's my pleasure. I wanted to make sure that you both came back home safely."

She whispered in his ear. "We will tell him in a few days. Let him settle first."

"Certainly," Einar said quietly.

A few moments later, Einar had left and was closing the door behind him. Margret suddenly felt sad and alone. She realized that she had been living with Einar on their journey for close to two weeks now. Margret felt odd that he was leaving like somehow this was his home now. She shook her head and wondered what trickery was forming in her head.

Margret felt the urge to urinate again. She held herself between her legs as she ran to the outhouse. Margret felt like urinating all day now, and it was the strangest feeling. She collapsed her buttocks on the small seat and urinated satisfyingly.

Einar was supposed to come by today to begin building the emergency boat with Pappa. Margret was excited to see Einar again. She hurriedly wiped herself and stood, releasing her white dress back down. She slammed the door and rushed to the house to comb her hair, but she was too late. Einar was walking in the back door already. He was an early riser. It was 7 am.

"Einar!" Margret shouted happily. "How are your momma and pappa? I missed you!"

"They are happy to see me," Einar said, chuckling. "My parents are getting older, and I want to be there for them."

Margret chuckled. "I was thinking the same about my pappa," she said, smiling. "I want to be here with him. I can't leave him alone after losing momma."

"That's what any good daughter would do," Einar responded, grabbing the door and holding it open for her.

"Einar," Pappa Jon said immediately. "Good morning."

"Good morning, Pappa Jon," Einar replied swiftly. He could sense a peculiar change in Jon's tone of voice.

"I have something to talk to you both about," Pappa Jon stated firmly.

"Oh?" Margret replied, curling a lock of hair behind her ear. "What is it, Pappa?"

Pappa looked at his daughter, then glanced strongly at Einar.

Einar shuffled his feet, unsure what the problem was. Everything had been going great. Now, Pappa Jon's sudden change in demeanour was unsettling.

"My daughter has dark bruises on her arms," Pappa Jon stated firmly, grabbing Margret's arm and pushing up her sleeve. Two ugly bruises silhouetted against her fair skin. "Did you have anything to do with putting them there?"

Einar was shocked. He stammered briefly.

"No, Pappa, it wasn't Einar," Margret said, taking her arm back. "It was Magnus." She glanced at her shoes and then up again at her father, holding his gaze.

"Magnus," Pappa said menacingly. "What did he do? I knew I shouldn't have trusted that man."

"He, umm," Margret stammered. "He grabbed me. We argued at his house, and Einar came in to save me."

Pappa closed his eyes briefly, digesting the information. "Did he hit you?"

"No," she answered. "But he was threatening to hurt me."

Pappa sat down heavily in the armchair. "He was threatening to hit you?"

"No, he was threatening to impregnate me."

Pappa heaved and coughed harshly. He grabbed his chest suddenly and pinched his eyes together in pain.

"Pappa!" Margret shouted, running to his side. "I didn't want to tell you right away. I wanted to get home safely first. I'm sorry, Pappa. I didn't want you to worry."

"If I ever get my hands on Magnus, I will choke him to death with my own bare hands," Pappa said, his face turning slightly red and his hands shaking.

"Please don't get angry, Pappa," she said softly. "Einar was there. He saved me."

Pappa looked up at Einar appraisingly and nodded.

"Einar punched him a lot, Pappa," Margret said, reliving the gory fight scene. "He broke Magnus's nose. There was a lot of blood. Einar stopped hitting him when I shouted." Margret wrung her hands together nervously. "We stayed to make sure Magnus regained consciousness. Then we left. That's why we had to get a doctor to look at Einar's hand at Johanna's. He broke a knuckle in the fight."

"Oh, I understand now," Pappa said, releasing the frown from his brows. "I wondered about why he broke his hand in Reykjavik."

Einar stood still, wordless. He wasn't sure what to say.

"Thank you for protecting my daughter, Einar," Pappa said. "I owe you for that."

"No, you don't owe me anything," Einar said. "I care about Margret like she was my own family. I would never allow her to be hurt."

"Well, I appreciate that," Pappa replied. "If there's ever anything I can do to repay you."

"No," Einar said stubbornly. "It's nothing. I would do it a million times over for her."

Margret blinked and gazed back at Einar. She suddenly saw this man in an entirely different light, like somehow a truth had been discovered. She wondered if he loved her. Einar caught her eye briefly and held her gaze for a millisecond. In that millisecond, she knew.

"You're a good man," Pappa Jon said, shifting slightly in his chair.

Margret stood. "I will get you some fresh water, Pappa," she said, a frown of concern washing over her face.

"Einar," Pappa said, his breathing harsh. "Could you work on the emergency boat yourself today? I am a bit too weak to help this morning. I will join you later this afternoon when I recover my energy."

"Definitely," Einar said firmly. "I will go right now."

Margret turned to look at Einar leaving the house. "Thank you, Einar," she said. "Please come join us for dinner tonight. I would love to have you join us. You can invite your parents too. I will make a large dinner to replenish all the energy we lost on our journey."

"I would love that," Einar replied. "I will be back here at five o'clock."

Margret smiled and nodded. He was a good man with a big heart, she thought fondly.

CHAPTER 13

Everything went back to normal. Pappa and Einar had finished building the emergency boat before the winter winds began blowing. Margret felt more secure knowing there was an escape route. She wiped her brow and looked out over the landscape at the new boat and dock. They had used it to go out fishing several times already, and she enjoyed it. Margret knelt on her knees in the dirt, busying herself with harvesting all the last vegetables before the ground froze. She smiled to herself. Life had settled down into a comfortable routine, and Einar was a constant companion in her life now. Margret looked forward to seeing him every day, and she thought he felt the same way.

She straightened with a turnip in her hand, then rushed off to the outhouse in an urgent panic to urinate. Margret had been urinating an awful lot since returning from Reykjavik. She pondered why but couldn't find a suitable reason. Margret finished in the outhouse and slammed the door, running back to the vegetable garden to harvest more turnips and potatoes into her cart. She had turnips, some leeks and a few cabbage heads mixed in with the potatoes.

Margret laboured for several minutes, then felt another urge to urinate. She pinched her legs together and ran full speed to the outhouse again, exasperated with this frequent urination. Margret sat on the toilet inside the outhouse and wondered when her monthly curse would show up. She hadn't ever really kept track of it precisely but vowed to start counting the days since her last blood flow. Margret wiped herself and ran back to the garden. After pulling several potatoes, she was satisfied with the harvest. Margret harnessed the cart onto the horse and led her mare back to the house.

When she arrived at the house, she transferred the vegetables into wooden boxes and carried several into the house. She straightened for a fourth box and felt a sharp tug in her stomach. Margret pondered what sort of ailment would make her feel a tug in her abdomen. She concluded that it must be something she ate and carried on until she was done.

A sudden weariness overtook her, and Margret unexpectedly felt a swirl of dizziness. She stumbled into the house and flopped onto her bed, exhaustion overtaking her. Margret briefly wondered why she was so tired before her eyes fluttered closed. She fell asleep suddenly in the middle of the afternoon.

"Are you okay?" Pappa Jon asked at the dinner table.

"Yes, I'm fine," Margret lied.

"You seem tired, and you're acting funny," Pappa said. "Always running to the outhouse!" He chuckled.

Margret smiled meekly. She knew why she was so tired now. It had been a month of strange symptoms. Margret poked at her food as a wave of nausea swarmed her head. She maintained her composure and continued eating, trying to hide her discomfort. Margret didn't have a clue how she was going to tell her father that she was pregnant.

An entire week went by quickly. Margret awoke with a groggy head and looked out the window. She estimated it was just before sunrise. She had not told her pappa yet, and it was eating away at her conscience. Margret contemplated again how to tell him, but no pleasant conclusions came to her mind. She must tell him soon before her belly starts showing.

Margret was concerned for his health and didn't want to add any more stress. He was getting more of those pains in his chest. Margret urged him to call for a doctor, but he refused. She sat up in bed and looked around in the dark.

Something had awakened her, she realized. Margret wondered what it was. She heard something, a scratch or something scraping on the floor. Margret pulled her worn slippers on and wrapped the large robe around her small frame.

She padded across the room and into the hallway, walking towards the kitchen. The sound had stopped, and the house was eerily quiet and dark. Margret could barely see in the darkness. The sun had not risen yet, but the skies were beginning to brighten to a darkish purple, casting strange rays all over the sky. Usually, the rays looked beautiful and amazing, but today they looked dark and shadowy like someone had purposely drawn a painting with the intention to scare her.

She shifted her feet quietly into the kitchen and bumped into a wooden kitchen chair. Margret reached down and realized it was lying on its side. That was very odd, she thought. She picked up the chair and put it back in its place.

Then she heard a gasp.

Her throat constricted, and she felt the hairs on her head stand up.

"Pappa?" she cried into the dark.

Margret shuffled into the kitchen, feeling her way around until finally, her foot collided with something soft. She bent down, and in the bluish lightening dawn, she noticed her father on the floor.

"Pappa!" she yelled. "Are you okay?" Margret fell to her knees and grasped her father's head. He was very heavy and didn't move easily. She nudged him more and shook him.

Pappa Jon's right arm was clutching his chest. His fingers were gripping his nightshirt tightly.

"Oh my Lord!" Margret cried. "Pappa! What should I do?" She had no experience with heart attacks and had no idea what to do. She listened to his chest, and his heart was beating very slowly. She began to panic, and her heart raced as her mind fought to find a solution.

"Pappa! Can you hear me?" she yelled.

There was no response.

She laid a hand on his forehead, and he felt cold. Margret jumped up and grabbed a warm blanket from the sofa. She rushed over to his prone body on the floor and wrapped the blanket around him. Margret laid her head on his stomach and hugged him tightly, trying to transfer her energy through him to help him fight.

She couldn't lose her Pappa, Margret thought. It was not feasible. There wasn't any way she could survive without him. Even the simple thought of his death was ludicrous. Margret shook her head and hugged him more. The panic in her heart threatened to collapse her walls of strength. She breathed in silently and exhaled roughly. An abrupt calm fell over her as if a blanket had been draped over her shoulders by the spirit of her mother. She looked up, hoping to see her momma, but it was too dark. Margret knew what she needed to do now. It was urgent. She needed to talk to him. He needed to know some things from her. Pappa needed her reassurance, regardless of how panicked she felt at the moment. Her father needed her presence. "Whatever is happening to you right now, Pappa," she said warmly. "I want you to know that I love you so much, Pappa. I would never leave your side for anyone. You mean everything to me. You taught me so much, and you raised me to be a good person. I will always be grateful for this. Your future grandchildren will be strong men, just like you. Pappa, I have the first of your grandchildren in my belly right now. I am proud to have a baby, no matter how it was conceived. Pappa, I will raise my children as you have raised me, with strong values, love and integrity." She paused and exhaled, the tears freely streaming down her face. "I love you so much, Pappa. Don't worry about anything. I am here with you always."

Margret kissed his cheek and wrapped her arms around his shoulders, lightly lifting him in her arms. She swayed and rocked him as if she was the mother and he was the child. She cried profusely and let every tear run down her cheeks as she held her dying Pappa in her arms.

His body was heavy and large. Margret tried her best to hold him. She looked up and wished for her mother's spirit to be present and to reveal herself. But Margret could not see anything in the bluish-black night, only the sound of the wind howling against the house and the strong feeling that momma was here.

Margret shivered and held onto her pappa for dear life. She knew this was most likely the final moment she would have with her father. The thought kicked her in the gut so hard; she felt like the air had been knocked out of her lungs.

She clung onto him, rocking him. "I love you, Pappa," she said, repeating the phrase over and over again. "I love you, Pappa."

Margret didn't know how long she was on the floor with him, but she felt him gasp one last time, and she knew. His body went completely limp, and she struggled to keep holding him in her arms.

She began to cry heavily, and her hands shook as she rocked his lifeless body. The sobs heaved in her chest, and her eyes were so watered that Margret could no longer see.

She looked up to the ceiling and yelled bitterly. "Why?" Margret shouted at the heavens. "Why?" She collapsed onto the wall and pulled his body with her so she could rest. Margret would never let go of him. She couldn't.

CHAPTER 14

Einar found it quite odd that he hadn't seen Margret or Pappa Jon all day. No one had been out with the sheep except the younger farm hands today. He had just finished pulling in the dock and securing it for the winter, then returned to help Petr and Stephan with the animal feed. The two brothers had done a fantastic job keeping the sheep well fed during their trip to Reykjavik. The two men had tended the flock, and not one lamb was killed or stolen. They had many lambs this year, and Einar was delighted.

It was late afternoon, and Einar had a feeling that something was not quite right. He realized that he hadn't seen or spoken to Pappa Jon or Margret at all. Had it really been that busy? Einar wasn't sure, but he had wondered if maybe he was spending too much time with the Peterssons. He had many things to catch up on at his own home with his parents that it was truly overwhelming.

He stomped across the fields towards the Petersson's large house. Einar immediately noticed the same laundry from last week still billowing in the wind on the clothesline. He noticed a lady's shirt had blown off in the wind. Einar scrambled after it, chased it down the hill and finally grabbed the white frilly shirt satisfyingly in his hands. He turned to go back and noticed the curtains in the house were still drawn. This was very odd. Margret always opened the curtains every morning because she loved the warmth of the sunshine.

Einar quickened his step and widened his stride. In no time, he was at the door. He turned the knob, and it was unlocked. The door creaked open.

The entire house was dark. Light filtered in through the cracks in the curtains, sending strange rays of light across the dark house. He walked into the house and noticed someone on the floor of the kitchen.

He sensed not one person but two.

"Margret?" he called.

He heard a shuffle.

"Pappa Jon?" Einar called, his voice rising.

He walked up to the front windows and pulled the curtains aside to let the light in.

On the floor was Margret with her father in her arms.

"Oh my Lord," Einar shouted, running to them both. "Margret! Are you alright? Pappa Jon! What happened?"

Margret looked up with glazed eyes and a faraway gaze. She regarded Einar as if he was a ghost and said nothing.

"Margret!" Einar shouted, alarm filtering into his veins. A cold chill crept up his spine, and the hair on his arms rose.

Margret still gazed at him like she was looking right through him. Her gaze was disorientated. She didn't know what was going on.

Einar tried a gentler approach. He knelt beside them and cupped her chin in his hand. "Margret," he said softly. "Do you hear me?"

She nodded.

"Please answer me with a yes or no," he said calmly.

"Yes," she said, her voice cracking.

"You've been here for a long while, haven't you?"

"Yes," she answered.

Einar looked down at Pappa Jon in her arms. Jon's face was blue, and the man was dead. Einar rubbed her arms gently and spoke compassionately. "Your father has died, Margret," he said sympathetically. "I'm sorry."

"No," Margret said firmly. "I can't live without him."

He grimaced and held onto her arms. "Listen to me, Margret," Einar said softly. "I need you to stand up and drink some water. I will get you the water, and I will hold Pappa for you."

"You'll hold him for me?" she asked incredulously.

"Yes, I will," he said. "I'll make sure he doesn't fall. Hold on; I will get the water."

Margret watched as Einar returned with a cup of water for her. He placed it on the table and crouched back down beside her. "Okay, get up slowly, my dear," he said, grabbing ahold of Pappa Jon's body. "I've got him."

Margret slowly shuffled along the floor, watching Einar with concern as he lifted her father's body. "Be careful!" she yelled loudly.

"I am," he responded. "Please go drink that water."

Margret took a few strides to the table and sat down on the chair wearily. She grasped the cup, tilted it and let the cool liquid course down her throat. Margret realized that she was extremely thirsty. How long had she been sitting on the floor with Pappa? Margret drank all the water and stood up to get more, with Einar watching her every movement.

"How are you feeling now?" he asked with concern.

"I was very thirsty," Margret said slowly. "You were right."

"Good," he said. "Drink more until your body feels satisfied."

She swallowed the next cup of water and turned to face him. "I feel a bit shaky and weak, but I think I'm okay," Margret said quietly, almost to herself.

Einar nodded. He shifted his body uncomfortably under the heavy weight of her dead father. "Margret, listen to me," Einar said slowly. "Your father has died. I don't know from what, but I will need to call the Church for burial. I am going to lie him gently flat on the floor for now."

Margret watched him lay her father's body on the floor. He gently lowered her father's head and straightened. "Do you have a sheet?"

"Yes," she said. "I will get you the sheet from his bed." Margret ran to the back bedroom and returned with a bundle of white sheets. She helped Einar lay the sheet over the top of her father's body. Margret felt the tears begin to well in her eyes again but swallowed them back. After they were done, she sat back at the table. "He died of a heart attack," Margret said quietly. "Thank you, Einar, for helping me. I needed you today."

Einar pulled her to standing and hugged her tightly. "I will always be here for you, my sweetheart. Always."

She nuzzled her face into his shirt and sniffled. "I don't know what to do, Einar," she said.

"Don't worry, my dear," he said reassuringly. "We will deal with it together. Pappa Jon will have a proper burial at the churchyard."

She nodded into his shirt. "Yes," she mumbled. Margret whimpered lightly and suddenly grabbed onto him tightly, wrapping her small arms around him. She sobbed into his chest, letting the grief engulf her.

Einar wrapped his arms around her tightly, rocking her in a soothing rhythm. "It will all work out, my sweet," he said. "I'll help you with everything. You mean the world to me, Margret. I will always be here for you. I will take care of the farm as I always have, and we will do it together." He paused, thinking. "You are stronger than you think," Einar concluded.

She smiled. "Thank you," Margret said, her voice hoarse and the emotions spilling from her.

Einar kissed the top of her head. "Let it all out," he said repetitively, swaying with her gently in the small kitchen. "I'm here for you, my dear."

The small funeral was held, and all the local folk gathered to say goodbye to Pappa Jon. Margret held her head up strongly and grasped Einar's hand throughout the service. Einar went home with her; they ate and slept together. He didn't want to let her out of his sight. They didn't have sex; they just slept. Margret liked that he was patient with her and sensitive to her needs.

Einar held her tightly in bed every night, curled against her backside with his arm draped across her waist. His warmth felt so comforting for her soul. He sometimes murmured little sweet nothings in her ear, which made her smile. His love was the light guiding her from this bleak tunnel.

It was dark when she awoke, and Margret could feel his arm still draped around her. She didn't mean to awaken him, but he stirred regardless, in tune with her body.

"Are you okay?" he mumbled sleepily.

She felt a wave of nausea grasp her, and she clutched her belly. "I feel a bit sick," she said wearily.

"Maybe it was the funeral," he said. "Sometimes grief will make you feel physically sick."

"No," she said softly. "I'm pregnant, Einar," she paused uncomfortably. "It's Magnus's baby. I tried to tell Pappa that he would have a grandchild that night on the floor after his heart attack. I don't know if he heard me or not."

"Oh."

"No matter how the baby was conceived, I will love it with all my heart," she stated, pausing uncomfortably. "You dislike me now," Margret grimaced.

"No," Einar replied. "I love you, Margret."

Margret turned to face him. "Do you really love me?"

"Yes, I do," he replied. "I have loved you for a very long time. I will raise the baby as one of my own. Anything that comes from your body, I will love."

Margret felt tears of unconditional love and acceptance fall from her eyes. "Einar, you are a special man," she said. "I love you as well." Then she kissed him for the first time, and it felt like heaven had placed them on a cloud of true happiness.

CHAPTER 15

Things had finally begun to get better. The sheep were tended to. Einar was hardworking, sweet and tender. The heavy pain of loss was still like a cloud of grief, but Einar somehow made the cloud lighter. They were married quickly in the church with close friends and relatives. Her heart swelled with pride and love for her new husband. Her aunt Helga said that she wasn't surprised that Einar was the perfect husband for her.

Margret agreed. He was a devoted partner, almost doting on her. She felt spoiled and grateful. It was so different than the relationship she had with Magnus. She did not miss Magnus anymore. He had become a monster, someone she thought she knew but clearly did not. She was content to be with Einar. It felt like he was the man for her all along and all she had to do was open up the gates of love to allow him in. He took care of her, the farm and everything. They lived together at her house, and the first few weeks of marriage were wonderful, although the weather was not.

The winter was approaching swiftly. Iceland was becoming especially cruel and unforgiving. The winds were picking up with swirling fog and snow across the landscape. Icicles were already forming on the house. They had the sheep sheltered in the barn that Einar had fixed with the two farm hands last week. Margret stared out the window and mused about how much of a good man he was. She glanced down.

Her belly wasn't even showing yet, and nobody knew she was pregnant except for Einar. The nausea had stopped suddenly. She was happy about that. She munched on a flatkaka as she watched him secure the barn doors with Petr and Stephan. Her eyesight was still not good at distances, and she hoped that maybe she could afford some eyeglasses one day. Margret had heard that several doctors needed eyeglasses for seeing things close up. She hoped they would make eyeglasses for seeing in the distance one day.

She squinted but was able to discern which figure Einar was by his gait alone. He had a strong muscular way of holding his shoulders back, and his legs were large as well. Margret had grown quite fond of him in the past few weeks. She wondered why she hadn't seen him like this all these years, then suddenly, she understood, as if all the pieces of the puzzle were finally put together in front of her. Margret tried not to regret her relationship with Magnus and reconciled that it was all part of the plan. Einar had saved her, and they were brought together by an unfortunate series of events, although she was happy and thrilled to have it all work out in the end. Margret still grieved the death of her father immensely. Some days she would wake up in the middle of the night and walk into the kitchen, thinking he was still alive. The sudden reality would hit her hard, and she would sob on the floor where he had died. Some nights, Einar would find her asleep on the floor and carry her back to bed. That man really loved her like nothing else in this world, Margret thought.

She watched as Einar walked back from the barn, his figure coming more and more into focus as he got closer. Margret turned to the door when a sudden pain ripped through her belly. She gasped and clutched her abdomen. Her nose suddenly began bleeding. Margret rushed to the outhouse, slamming the door behind her. Einar spotted her from a distance and followed. Margret shuffled herself onto the toilet lid and felt a sudden gush of blood fall out of her vagina. The pain cramped inside her womb, and she keeled over, clutching herself.

"Margret?" Einar said breathlessly through the door. "Are you okay? It's a snowy day; please come back inside."

Margret shivered. "I'm bleeding, Einar." She whimpered softly, a tear escaping down her cheek. "I think I've lost the baby, sweetheart. I think the baby's gone." She wearily cleaned herself and pulled her aching body straight.

Einar stood motionless as the door swung open. Margret stood grasping the worn wooden frame with a terrible red stain of blood all over her dress.

"Oh my dear," he cried. "My sweet. Oh my." Einar immediately grasped her armpits and knees, lifting her light body into his arms and carried her back into the house, her red-stained beige dress billowing behind them in the snowy November wind.

"It's a miscarriage," the doctor said, packing up his things in his leather doctor's bag. "Nothing to be worried about. It happens." The doctor addressed Einar. "She is young, and everything looks fine now. You can start trying to have another child a month after the cramping subsides."

Einar looked stunned. "Oh, alright," he said slowly. He paid the doctor and showed him out.

They both sat silently for some time, processing the news, the good and the bad.

Margret spoke first. "Do you want to make a child with me?"

"Of course, I do."

"Okay," she said happily, the joy spreading throughout her. "Then we will start trying in a month's time."

CHAPTER 16

The bottle of aquavit passed from man to man around the fire. The strong drink was made from fermented pota-toes. It was flavoured with caraway and was commonly called brennivin by some folks in Iceland.

Magnus grabbed the bottle and took a quick gulp. The alcohol seared down his throat and stung his stomach. He wondered how many more nights of drinking it would take before he would forget about Margret. Maybe he never would. Perhaps they were just meant to be together, and somehow, miraculously, things would become right again.

"Don't hog it all!" his friend, Hans, said loudly, snatching the bottle roughly away from Magnus.

A gust of wind blew into the fire, almost extinguishing it as the group cowered with their hands over their heads. "It's too cold! Let's go inside!" Magnus shouted as he straightened unsteadily and stumbled into his home.

The house repairs had not been completed. He rarely had the motivation for such work. If he had Margret as his wife, he would have repaired the house. He reconciled that it was largely her fault and not his. She caused the breakdown of their relationship by being stubborn and wilful. In turn, she was also to blame for the miserable state of repairs at his house.

The group of four men stumbled through the door, cursing, as the winds howled in behind them. The snow swirled into the house as they slammed the door shut. "Cold as death out there!" Hans hollered, chuckling drunkenly.

"Yes, the December wind is blowing winter at us again," Magnus responded, slurring a few of the words.

"I can barely understand you," Hans joked. "You drank too much!"

The entire group of men broke into drunken laughter from the understatement. They were all very inebriated, banging into the door frame and stumbling.

"You need to get the wax out of your ears!" Magnus countered back.

Hans hollered raucously at the statement, slapping his knee, stumbling and then fell hard onto the sofa. A floorboard creaked underneath the sofa and cracked through, allowing the couch to shift into the crack.

"Watch out!" Magnus yelled. "That sofa is going to go right through the floor!"

"You should fix the floors!" Hans yelled back.

"No, I won't."

"Why?" Hans asked.

"You know why," Magnus said, rubbing his crooked nose. The fight with Einar had left him disfigured. He didn't mind, though; it looked good on him. The broken nose gave him a rough handsome look, but it also reminded him of what she had done to him. His heart hurt terribly inside his chest. He had been struggling with a mixed wreck of emotions. One day, he would be horribly angry and vengeful, then the next day, he was happy to be rid of her.

"Margret?" Hans said incredulously. "She didn't cause your floors to disintegrate!" Hans laughed loudly, spurring the other men into a cackling fit again.

Magnus felt his blood boil murderously. "She caused all of this! Her stubborn ways and her stupid wilfulness!" he shouted angrily. "She ruined everything."

"Forget about her, Magnus," Hans said, quieting down after noticing the vicious look on his friend's face. "I'm sorry," he apologized. "I know how much you loved her." Hans paused, patting Magnus on the back. "You need to let her go, my friend. She's of no use to you now."

"Maybe," Magnus said thoughtfully. "You might be right. Einar can have the wilful wench to ruin his life now."

"Exactly!" Hans said cheerfully, slapping his friend on the shoulder.

Magnus took another swig of the aquavit and smiled cruelly. His face changed suddenly as a sombre thought crossed his mind. Margret was the only woman he had ever loved. Magnus stared over his friend's head at an old painting on the wall and wavered unsteadily.

Hans looked at his friend worriedly. Magnus wasn't doing well. He hoped his friend would forget about this woman, but something told him that it wasn't over.

The morning wind was cold, and December was nearing. She could feel it in her bones. Margret stretched and sat up in bed. She had awakened early again.

"Sweetheart," Einar said lazily. "It is too early. Come back to sleep."

"I can't sleep," she replied.

"Your father's ghost?" he asked.

"No," Margret replied. "Not this time. I am not sure why. I'm just restless."

Einar leaned over and grasped her waist, pulling her back into the warm blankets. "Maybe you need some convincing," he said, kissing her bare back. "You're cold. I can warm you up, my sweet."

Margret smiled as a playful grin appeared on Einar's face. She loved it when he was like this. He really adored her. "I may be persuaded," she said, chuckling.

Einar's large hands grasped her thin body, pulling her roughly into the sheets. "You're mine then," he said triumphantly. "I will give you two good reasons to stay in bed."

Margret giggled. "And what are these two good reasons?"

"One," he replied. "I can keep you warm, very warm, right here." Einar pulled her hips into his warm body and spooned her easily, draping his arm and leg over her.

"And what's number two?" she asked, smiling.

"Oh," Einar replied. "That's a surprise. You'll have to beg for that."

Margret chuckled sweetly. "I have to beg?" she said, pulling his arm around her warm breasts. "Well, would this be sufficient?" Margret calmed her voice and lowered her tone sexily. "Mr. Olason, may I please see my second reason? Please," she said, drawing out the last syllable deliberately.

Einar pulled her chin towards his and kissed her lips softly. His hands roamed around her body freely, touching and arousing her. "Yes," he said. "You're a good girl. I like the way you beg. Say please again."

"Please, Mr. Olason, show me," she said, batting her lashes.

Einar flipped her on her back and mounted her, kneeling in-between her hips. He straightened and showed her his rigid penis. "Reason two, my wife," he said smiling.

"Oh my, yes," Margret pleaded.

Einar kissed her lips and leaned over her, engulfing her entire body. He was a large burly man, and Margret loved being smothered by his sheer size. Einar grasped his penis and positioned himself at her entrance. He stopped suddenly and asked, "Is everything okay? Has the cramping stopped?"

She smiled, warmed by his gentleness towards her body. "Yes, it's been a month, and the cramping stopped many weeks ago."

Einar kissed her again and slid easily into her wetness, feeling the world settle in the right place, making love to his wife for the first time.

"You are the most beautiful woman in the world," he said slowly, as he rocked his penis into her rhythmically, making sweet love to the best woman he's ever had.

CHAPTER 17

They made love almost every third day now. Margret felt insatiable in his arms, and he was a powerful aphrodisiac. He would stretch, moan or kiss her, and she would be physically ready for him in an instant. She loved the effect he had over her.

The men were in the fields today tending to the sheep. She watched outside her bedroom window as the winter winds faded slowly with the seasons. It was warming slightly this spring, and she couldn't wait for summer this year.

She looked down at her round belly. Not many people noticed because Margret was so thin, but she could see the bump. Margret ran her hands along her pregnant tummy. By her calculations, she would be five months pregnant soon with their first baby. She was thrilled beyond belief.

Margret watched as Einar prepared for the annual wool sheering. Einar had developed an influential contact that bought all the wool every year, picked it all up by boat, and eliminated the need for the annual trips to Reykjavik. But there was still much for them to do. Margret worried that she didn't know enough about sheep ranching to help. To compensate, she took control of the house, cleaning, cooking, doing laundry and even figuring out how to do minor repairs when necessary. Margret knew once the house filled with their children, things would get even busier. She accepted this fact, even relished in it. A big family was what she had always wanted. Margret would do whatever was required of her to make their home welcoming for a future happy family.

She worried if this baby would be a miscarriage too. Margret prayed that her baby would be born healthy and safe. This pregnancy was different, she mused. Margret could feel the baby kicking in her belly, and the nausea was so much worse than last time. She still felt like vomiting every morning, although it was slightly better if she munched on flatkaka and ate skyr yogurt often.

Margret sat down and slipped her feet into her favourite sheepskin boots. They had an inner woollen sock layer and laces to wrap around. She finished wrapping them and stood in the rare sunshine streaming through the window. Margret exhaled, grabbed a few items, opened the door and stepped out onto the frosty ground. It was still cold but not a January-type cold. Instead, this Icelandic spring coldness seeped right into your bones. The island was very humid, and it somehow made everything feel colder. Her fingers would freeze instantly, even with the sheepskin gloves on.

Margret hiked across the field with two buckets in her hands. It took her a good while before she even got close enough to be heard. Her family property was expansive, almost 20 acres. The sheep were near the barn today, which was much closer to the house. Her boots crunched on the snowy ground as she made her way toward the hardworking men.

Einar noticed her when she had left the house. The barn was on slightly higher ground than the house and provided a good vantage point. He glanced at Margret lovingly as she walked towards them. She looked absolutely stunning. Her blonde hair was shimmering in the sun, and her body was growing fuller from the pregnancy. Her breasts hung larger and her buttocks curved around her heavier thighs. He loved the effect pregnancy had on her, and he loved that she was carrying his child.

"Margret, my love," he said. "What have you brought us?"

Margret smiled sweetly. "I brought you some blood sausage with rye bread and some skyr with strawberries." She laid down the buckets and opened the flaps. "You men work so hard out here. The least I can do is make a good hearty lunch."

Einar hugged his wife and kissed her on the forehead. "Thank you, my love. It's most appreciated."

All three men grabbed sausages and rye bread, munching the nutritious noonday meal. The younger men said thank you and finished the yogurt as well. The food disappeared faster than it took to make it. Margret smiled satisfyingly as they ate every morsel.

Einar swallowed the last few bites. "Please go back in the house," he said softly. "I don't want you out here too long. The wind is terrible today. You can fill the stove with more coal and make sure the house is warm when we get back. I will bring a few sheep with us in the house to keep the warmth in." He looked up at the rare clear sky. "The sun will help with the heat, but this May is unseasonably cold." He kissed Margret and wrapped his right hand around her waist. "Please take care of my baby. That little one is just as precious as you are."

Margret giggled. "I will." She started walking back when a thought struck her about the coal heating. It was imported coal and quite expensive. They only used it on the coldest days, but since she was pregnant, Einar had been insisting they heat the house more often. The homestead was insulated, of course, but there must be another way to heat the homes, she thought. "Oh, Einar," Margret called back. "When you come back home, I have an idea of heating the home I'd like to discuss with you."

Einar looked up, perplexed. "Yes, darling, of course," he said. "I want to hear your ideas."

Margret nodded satisfyingly. "He's a good man," she whispered to herself. "Magnus never wanted to hear my thoughts." She hiked carefully back with the cold wind blowing in her face.

They ate a hearty lamb stew and drank water from the cooled ceramic water jug. Margret was lucky to have a crude pipe leading into the house for fresh water, although it was hot. Pappa had built the pipeline and installed it under the floor a few years back. It was his project for finding better ways to live in Iceland. The water source was a small hot spring on the hill, only fifty feet away. They had always used the small hot spring for bathing and dishwater. She remembered her mother bringing the water into the house in buckets every day.

Pappa had built the pipe into the floor as a convenience, so they didn't have to haul the water into the house anymore. It was a crude pipe that connected to the hot spring on the hill. Pappa built a tap and lever in the kitchen so they could turn it on and off. It leaked sometimes, but Einar was always keen on fixing it.

Margret finished cleaning the dishes and disappeared into the washroom, returning with the metal tub.

Einar immediately jumped up and helped her. "You want to take a bath, my love?" he asked.

"Yes, I would," she answered. "I haven't bathed for a week."

Einar opened the tap and filled the jug with water, then poured the hot water into the metal tub. He repeated this process multiple times until the metal tub was half full. Margret grabbed a washcloth and removed her clothes in the kitchen. They were lucky in Iceland. All the water was already at a perfect bathing temperature. Sometimes it was too hot! She tested the temperature by dipping her toes in. Then she cautiously stepped her entire foot in, then continued slowly immersing her leg into the tub. She gradually submerged into the hot bath and exhaled a sigh of contentment as Einar watched his naked wife bathe in the kitchen.

"You are beautiful, Marg," he said in a throaty voice.

Margret leaned forward and smiled at him. "You are very handsome as well," she replied. "I'm so proud to call you my husband." She soaked in the small metal tub, with her knees up and her back sitting upright. The tub was quite small, Einar could never fit in it, but she was only 5'2". Her pregnancy was changing her body rapidly, and she may no longer fit in the tub soon, she thought. Her hips were growing wider, and her buttocks had become noticeably larger. She was dismayed to see the changes in her body, but so far, Einar liked it. He almost relished in her new curvy body. She shook her head, unable to understand men and how they thought.

Einar sat back on the sofa, watching his lovely wife bathing. He sipped some brennivin. It still tasted quite strong to him, and he sipped it sparingly. He remembered something she had said earlier in the day and wondered why she didn't bring it up. She was usually somewhat strongminded and voiced her thoughts often. "You said earlier that you wanted to talk about heating," Einar said, opening the discussion. "Tell me your ideas."

Margret looked up, rolling her eyes. "Ah, it's nothing," she said timidly. "Just a silly thought that's probably not even possible."

"Silly or not, I'd like to hear your idea," Einar replied. "I think you're quite an intelligent woman. I like discussing things with you."

"Okay," she said, pausing to put her words in an intelligible phrase, so it somehow made sense. She had been thinking a lot about the hot water from the springs and the pipe her father had built. There just seemed to be something more they could do with it. "I'm not sure how to do any of this because I am not good with tools and lifting heavy things, but I've been thinking about the hot water from the spring."

Einar cocked his head to the side. "Go on," he said.

"Well," Margret said slowly. "If it's so hot all the time because the volcanic magma heats the underground water constantly, then couldn't we somehow use that to our advantage and stop relying on expensive coal to heat the house."

Einar rubbed his thin beard. He was turning twenty-two years old, but his beard still hadn't grown in fully. He developed a habit of rubbing at the dark blonde scruff in hopes of making it grow. "Interesting!" Einar exclaimed. "So, do you suggest heating the house with hot water instead?"

"I'm not sure," she said. "Either using the hot water or the magma heat from underground somehow."

"Well, the magma heat would be too hot to build a pipe in."

"I was thinking maybe the radiant heat of the magma," Margret stated simply.

"Oh, I see," Einar replied thoughtfully. "That may be difficult. But I like the idea of heating the house with hot water. It may be an easier solution."

"Do you really think so?" Margret asked incredulously.

"I think it is possible, yes," Einar said.

Margret smiled. "You're not just joking and trying to make me feel good about myself?"

"No, no, my sweet," Einar said. "I like the idea. It would save us so much money on heating. We wouldn't have to buy any more coal. It would be free heating." He rubbed his beard in deep thought again. "The hot spring we use for the hot water isn't too far away either."

"It's only fifty feet away!" she replied.

"It is very close," he confirmed.

"Yes, it is," Margret said excitedly. "Pappa built the pipe because it was so close."

"Let me see what I can come up with then," Einar said quietly. "You may be onto something that could help us for the long term future."

"You really think so?" she beamed.

Einar stood up, walked over to the tub and knelt down beside her. "Yes, I think you've come up with a marvellous idea in that beautiful little mind of yours." He leaned over and kissed her lips slowly, lingering with his mouth on hers for a few suspended moments. Einar looked down into the tub at his wife's naked body. "And after your bath, I'd like to make love to you. Slow and easy."

Margret felt the heat rush into her cheeks and a tingle in her vagina. She kissed him back. "I love you, Einar."

CHAPTER 18

The baby was born on a Monday in the first week of August. It was a girl, and they named her Emma. Their daughter was most likely born prematurely. Based on Margret's calculations, the baby should have been born in late August or September. Regardless, Emma was a healthy baby, small and a bit underweight at 4 pounds and 10 ounces, but otherwise healthy. Margret cuddled the baby girl day and night. She breastfed the infant and even offered the baby to Einar once in a while so he could hold her. He seemed unsure of handling such a small infant but soon became accustomed to it. Einar began to enjoy being a father. He rocked the baby when Margret was busy cooking and found that he could stick his thumb in Emma's mouth when she cried, and she would surprisingly suck heartily at it.

The baby was already six months old and learning to crawl. Einar had tried to rush the project of heating the house with hot water before the winter so Emma could crawl on the floor without the animals. But ultimately, he had failed. The property, sheep and wool season typically took up much of his time. Now, the extra attention necessary for the baby outweighed all other priorities. It was fascinating how quickly their lives were turned upside down from one tiny baby being born.

It was February, and the winds were terrible today. They all stayed inside. Luckily, they had sold so much wool in the summer that they had plenty of coal. But it still gnawed at the back of his mind. If they could somehow manage to build a system to heat the house with hot water, then they would be much better off.

Einar rolled over and hugged Margret, spooning her backside with his warm body. She murmured and awoke sleepily.

"I'm sorry, my love," he said. "I didn't mean to wake you."

"No, no," she replied. "I love waking up in your arms."

His hands smoothed along her curves and grasped a heavy breast. She moaned. He kissed her shoulder, and she moved her hips backward into his groin. He didn't need any further invitation. He slipped his naked penis into her aroused vagina and made sweet love to her in the early dawn morning.

The hot pool was just up the hill, and Einar was determined to find a way to heat the house with the hot water. He stomped through the snowy landscape, looking for a clue, something he could work with. The morning rays of the northern lights greeted him with green and purple hues streaking across the dark morning sky. It was 7 am, but winter nighttime lasted forever in Iceland. Similar to the midnight sun in the summer, it was the exact opposite in the winter. It was dark for most of the day, and sometimes only four to six hours of sunlight would grace the island.

The green and purple hues danced along the skyline like long ropes of shimmering colours, waving in between each other. Einar stood momentarily mesmerized by the natural display of art. He smiled and instantly felt grateful for the beauty around him, his wife and his family. The wind blew forcefully in his face, but it didn't bother him; he was accustomed to being indestructible.

Einar smiled and continued walking. He looked down to the ground to make sure he placed his feet properly on the snow-crusted earth. He walked farther up the hill until he reached the hot pool. Pappa Jon had lined the pool with rocks, stacking them up as a fence, so the sheep didn't fall in. The steam rose majestically in the frigid morning, creating a large cloud of mist over the small pool. He stepped away from the pool, scratching his beard thoughtfully as he watched the steam lift into the sky.

He had an idea.

Einar walked back to the pool and knelt down over the small rock wall stretching his arm over the steam. It was very warm.

Einar stood up and chuckled. "That's it!" he said exuberantly. "We will heat the house with the steam! Not the water! Just the steam!"

He searched the ground for the buried pipe which led into the house. He couldn't see the pipeline, but he could see the mound that led toward the house. Einar deliberated for several moments, then decided that he would hire two workers to help him build a larger pipe for the steam, and he would also cover the entire pool to trap the heat. But this idea posed some problems, the pool was fifty feet away, and it was higher than the house. He knew that heat rose, and it would be impossible to get the steam to rise downhill.

Einar pulled on the tip of his beard thoughtfully and hiked back to the house. He searched the frozen ground for a clue. He walked past the front of the house on a low hill in another direction along the slope. Einar had felt the ground magma rumble in this area on occasion. He hiked faster, the wind blowing harder in the unobstructed landscape. Einar wrapped his head with a scarf and walked farther down the hill, almost directly in front of the house. He squinted in the dark morning.

He saw something in the snow.

Einar ran towards it.

His breath came out in foggy streams until he arrived at the tiny spot. He knelt down and inspected it. He took his glove off and inserted his hand in the snow.

It was wet.

He put the glove back on and dug with his hands into the snow a bit further. There was a layer of ice under the wet area.

Einar had an idea and ran to the barn, getting his ice pick out. He ran to the house and grabbed some hot coals.

"What are you doing?" Margret asked.

"I think I've found the solution to your heating idea!" he shouted happily as he raced out of the house to the wet, snowy spot.

Einar dumped the hot coals on the frozen ground and stepped back as the ice quickly melted. Suddenly, a thin fountain of steam rose. He laughed loudly. "Yes!"

Einar rushed back and slammed the ice pick into the snowy spot. It submerged into water! He hollered. "I did it!" Einar worked tirelessly for over an hour, picking at the sides of the ice until finally, a small pool formed.

He ran excitedly back to the house to tell Margret. This was the hot pool that would heat their home! It was fifty feet away, but it was perfect.

Margret hugged Einar with pride. He was a wise man. He had discovered a way to heat the house with the steam heat. It may or may not work, but Margret thought his idea was sound. He had hired two men to start the work in May, waiting until warmer weather.

She hoped it would work. Constantly filling the stove with coal was exhausting with a baby in her arms.

Margret sat down heavily on the kitchen chair.

"Are you alright?" Einar asked, concerned.

"I just feel a bit dizzy," she said, feeling confused. She didn't get dizzy too often.

"Did you miss your monthly curse?" he asked.

"I never did get it again after Emma was born," she said softly. "The midwife said it was normal when breastfeeding."

"Could you be pregnant again?" he asked.

"I don't think so," Margret answered. "The midwife said it was difficult to get pregnant while breastfeeding." Margret thought about it and remembered that she did have some light bleeding a couple of months ago. "But I guess anything is possible."

"Please rest, my love," Einar said. "Just in case."

"Okay," she said. "I will."

A beer bottle rolled onto the floor. Magnus looked up at his friend's prone body lying splayed out on the cold floor. They had been drinking all night, and the morning dawn was approaching. He pushed Hans over onto his side. Magnus sat up.

He felt his stomach rumble and realized he hadn't eaten all night.

Magnus crouched and pulled himself up from the floor, stumbling towards the kitchen. He opened the cupboards looking for something to eat. There was barely anything. He found some old hard flatkaka and a few slices of dried meat. Magnus stuffed the food in his mouth and chewed ravenously. He grimaced. It tasted awful! Magnus forced himself to chew and swallow. He would have to get some food from the town merchants soon, although he had little money.

Magnus looked around the house, searching for something he could sell for food. The entire house was bare. He had already sold most of his tools and furniture. Magnus leaned against the cupboard. What was he going to do? His eyes searched everything, and he couldn't find anything worth value.

He stomped angrily into the washroom, a tiny room no bigger than a large closet. It had a washbasin bowl, a water jug, a small table and a mirror. He poured water into the basin from the pitcher. Magnus bent over and washed his face, splashing the cool water over his face and beard. He groaned from the pleasant feeling of water on his skin.

After several minutes, Magnus dried his face with a small towel and assessed himself in the mirror. His beard was overgrown, and his face no longer looked handsome. He looked tired, drunk and ragged. To make matters worse, his nose was swollen, red from overdrinking and slightly crooked.

Magnus stared at his broken nose in the mirror, remembering the woman who caused this disfigurement. His fragmented heart still seethed with anger and resentment. Margret was supposed to be his wife! Life was not supposed to work out this way.

Magnus hung his head over the basin, holding onto the small table. His eyes moistened, and he could feel tears threatening to escape from his eyes. His heart beat widely in his chest from his rising emotions.

Magnus straightened suddenly and kicked the table angrily. He was not going to cry.

He glanced in the mirror again, looking at his reflection. Magnus mused over the events that had led him to where he was. He spoke to his reflection. "You didn't get your nose broken for nothing, Magnus."

He pushed himself away from the table and walked lazily to the front room, stepping over Hans on the floor.

Magnus stepped over the rotting floorboard in the middle of the living room and stopped. He had an epiphany.

This old house was always a big nuisance. It needed endless repairs and was always a pain in his backside.

But the house and property were worth a lot of money.

Magnus smiled, looking up to the ceiling. He would sell it and be rid of this crumbling reminder of his failures in life.

He kicked the bottle across the room and stepped to the front door. It creaked when he opened it, further strengthening his resolve to sell the property.

Magnus stepped out into the lightening skies and exhaled. He would find someone to buy his property in Reykjavik today.

Chapter 19

Margret rolled onto her side and felt a strange tug. She had been experiencing a peculiar burn in her throat every time she ate and didn't quite understand what was going on. She still had occasional dizziness and now headaches.

Margret rose up out of bed and realized Einar was already out working in the front yard on the steam heating. She stood and felt a wave of dizziness. Margret grasped onto the door and made her way to the outhouse to urinate. She wrapped her mother's old red shawl around her and opened the door to the July sun. The land was warm and flooded in sunshine all day and night. She slipped on her wooden sandals and made her way to the outhouse. Margret grasped the wooden door and a strange feeling streaked across her abdomen.

She looked down at her tummy and placed her hands on her stomach. Then she felt it again. She looked down, astonished. Margret knew that feeling. She was excited, confused and bewildered all at the same time.

The strange pain was a baby kicking.

Margret smoothed her hands along her belly and smiled.

Einar hugged her, clearly overjoyed. "Another baby!" he shouted exuberantly, swinging her up into his arms.

"Be careful!" she shouted, laughing. "I am most likely three or four months pregnant already!"

"What?" Einar shouted back.

"I didn't know!" Margret said, chuckling. "I thought I couldn't get pregnant while breastfeeding. But I just felt the baby kick, Einar! That means it is past the first three months." She smiled down at her slightly rounded belly. "I didn't feel any kicking until four months with Emma."

"Oh my Lord!" Einar said, smiling broadly. He kissed her roughly. "So we will have another baby in five or six months?"

"Yes, I suppose that's correct," Margret replied, chuckling.

"Well, my dear," Einar said excitedly. "I love you!" He placed her down and held her chin, kissing her again. "We are going to be parents again!"

Margret laughed and kissed him back. "I'm so glad you are happy."

"Of course I am!" he shouted.

"Stop shouting!" Margret yelled.

They both burst into laughter and hugged.

Einar peered over her shoulder, eyeing the landscape outside. They faced the open oceans, and the hot spring he had unearthed was in the front of the property. The rich green grass was coating the meadow.

A thought crossed his mind.

The structure over the hot spring to capture the steam was only partially finished. If they were having another baby, he didn't want his wife putting coal in the stove anymore.

Einar released her and held her at arm's length, looking into her eyes. "I love you, my dear. I must get this steam heating finished before the baby comes!" He kissed her roughly and disappeared out the front door, whistling for his helpers to come.

Margret giggled. Men are so funny sometimes, she thought.

The house and twenty acres sold quickly, leaving Magnus with mixed emotions. He was happy, sad and disappointed at the same time. This was his parent's dream house, and he wasn't responsible enough to keep it in good shape or repair it. One woman had caused his downfall. It was all because of her. If he had married Margret and had babies, then they would be living happily ever after. But instead, he fell into despair and uselessness.

Magnus walked up to a vendor at the market and bought some salted fish.

"I remember you," the old man said. "You used to bring some good fish to me. What happened? Did you stop fishing?"

"I lost my wife to another man," Magnus said sadly, trying to gain sympathy.

"You mean Margret Olason?"

"Yes, her," he said solemnly.

"I know you loved her, but you have to let some people go," the man said. "I saw her new husband, Einar, this summer with some helpers. They were buying housing materials in the northern part of the island."

"Oh?"

"Yes," the old man said. "I know Einar. He had Margret and his small daughter with him. A cute baby."

"She has a baby daughter?" Magnus asked, astonished.

"Yes," the old man replied. "The babe looks like a year old, maybe older. A cute little thing."

Magnus stood in shock. No words came to his mouth.

"Are you okay, son?"

Magnus blinked. "I'm fine," he said, swiping his longish hair to the side. "I knew they most likely married, but I didn't know they had a child so quickly."

"I'm sorry to be the one to break the news," the old man said. "Don't worry; you will find another woman. Maybe you should start fishing again. Bring me some fish every day. I will pay you."

Magnus stood rooted to the spot. He straightened. "Yes," he said. "Maybe I will do that. Thank you, my friend."

Margret stood around the steam pool structure with the men and her daughter. Since becoming a parent herself, she returned to the Icelandic names of mamma and pabbi for her children's sake. It seemed fitting because Margret lovingly reserved the English names of pappa and momma for her own mother and father. Now that they were deceased and Margret was also a mother, the world seemed a completely different place.

The ground often trembled in this area, and Margret was vigilant like any new parent would be. Emma ran around the stone structure and shouted happily as Margret kept an eye on the rambunctious girl. They were all admiring the structure they had built and discussing which would be the best way to pipe the hot steam into the house.

Margret was immensely proud of her husband for devising the plans to make this work. Nobody else in any surrounding farmlands had thought of any such idea. When they were at the northern market visiting Aunt Helga, they were discussing the plans with market owners after purchasing the wood, corrugated sheet metal and nails. The sheet metal was something very new that the British traders were just beginning to import into Iceland. There were discussions of it being used to build houses instead of wood, which was scarce and cumbersome.

They had purchased enough sheet metal to construct a rectangular metal vent that would carry the rising hot steam into the house.

"Won't the vent freeze so much that it cools the trapped air in the winter?" Stephan asked, scratching his head.

"I have an idea for that," Einar said, pointing up the hill. "We will insulate the vent like a coat does for us."

"We can't put coats on the vents!" Petr exclaimed.

"Of course not," Einar chuckled. "We will use the earth, just like we do for our homes. We will dig a shallow trench and build the pipes into the trench, covering it with packed earth."

Margret smiled. "That's a clever idea!" she replied instantly, supporting her husband. She had thought of insulating the vents too. Margret was glad they thought alike. "How does the air get pushed into our home, though?"

Einar shook his head. "That I haven't completely figured out," he replied honestly. "I was hoping that, because heat rises, the warm air would naturally come up the hill to the house. If we don't get enough air, I will devise a fan of some sort to push the air."

Emma suddenly crashed into his legs and fell onto her butt, hitting her head on his shin.

"Oh my Lord, girl!" Margret shouted, grasping the troublesome girl and lifting her up. The toddler cried as if wounded fatally. Margret shushed the girl and inspected her head. Everything looked fine, just a scratch on her arm.

Emma screamed louder as the men watched with sympathy. "Is she alright?" Einar asked.

"She's fine," Margret responded with an exasperated inhale. "Emma likes to attract attention and then hurts herself in the process. She just has a scratch."

Emma hollered louder. Margret held her head and kissed it multiple times. "Mamma kissed it better," Margret cooed. "It's alright, sweetheart. I know it hurts. Don't go running everywhere, my baby girl."

Emma sniffled and buried her face shyly into her mother's bosom. Margret looked at her husband. "I should go back to the house," she said. "I think she needs a nap."

"I will carry her back to the house," Einar said thoughtfully. "You are too pregnant. Your belly has grown quite a lot in the past two months. It looks like you're carrying an elephant in there!"

"Definitely not an elephant, but it might be a boy," Margret responded sweetly, handing the toddler over to her father. "Thank you, sweetheart."

"I will be right back, men!" Einar shouted over his shoulder as he cradled the screaming toddler back to the house. Emma didn't always like it when her father held her. She was definitely a mamma's girl.

Margret walked behind them both, waddling through the late summer grass, watching her husband's muscular backside. She smiled. He was a strong, capable man, and she couldn't be happier.

If the girl was just over a year old, then it could be very likely that the child was his daughter and not Einar's. Magnus pulled his long beard in the mirror and cut it with a pair of rusted scissors. It didn't cut through the coarse hair very easily, so he had to isolate smaller tufts of hair, pull and then cut.

He looked in the mirror and smiled. He was beginning to look more like himself. His nose was permanently crooked, but his hair was short now, and his beard was disappearing.

Magnus wondered if the daughter was from his loins. His heart lifted at the possibility of having a daughter. He mentally calculated back the months that he had made love to Margret. It was very close. Magnus didn't know exactly what month the girl was born, but the pregnancy's timing and resulting child lined up.

He nodded in the mirror. The same handsome face smiled back. He was intent on repairing his life, with or without a woman. Magnus was fishing five days a week, selling the catches to the market vendor and renting a small house with Hans. Things were beginning to look up, and he could feel the tides of change happening in his heart.

Margret might even be missing him, especially if she kept it a secret from her husband.

He creamed a lye solution over his face, grasped the straight razor steadily in his hand and began to shave. He cut himself once, seething and cursing as he applied pressure to the blood oozing out. Magnus finished shaving and put down the razor, splashing cold water on his face. He thought about Margret, relishing in the thought that she might miss him.

He dried his face in the mirror and smiled.

Well, it was her fault everything fell apart anyway. She deserved a life of misery.

Einar smiled proudly at the vent in the house. Margret hugged his waist and kissed him on her tiptoes. "You've done it, my love!" she exclaimed.

He grasped her lovingly and put her hand towards the vent. "Do you feel that?" he asked. "It's warm air, free warm air."

"Yes, it is!" she exclaimed happily. "I can't believe it. You've done it! You've figured out a way to heat our house with the power of the hot springs."

"It is not perfect," Einar said thoughtfully. "I may still have to devise some sort of fan that pushes the air faster into the house. But so far, the venting gives us some extra heat."

Margret kissed him squarely on the lips, holding his bearded face in her hands. Her small tongue slipped into his mouth, and they kissed in the kitchen for several moments before Einar led her to the bedroom. Einar's hands slid expertly down the sides of her breasts as they entered the bedroom. Margret felt her temperature rise as she began to kiss him urgently. There was something about a capable man that excited her sexually. Einar pulled her down to the bed, and they cuddled into each other's arms, Einar spooning behind her to allow room for her pregnant belly.

Suddenly, Emma came running into the bedroom, knocking down a set of books. Margret looked up at her daughter with a mixture of frustration and love. Emma looked shocked and curious as if she somehow knew she had interrupted something.

Einar pulled away slightly from Margret, sat up and summoned Emma into his lap. The little girl bolted happily and jumped nimbly onto his thighs. He hugged her fiercely and kissed the top of her head. Emma giggled and squirmed in his grasp, looking at her mamma's huge round belly.

"Baba?" Emma squealed happily, laying a hand on her mamma's pregnant abdomen.

"Yes, it's a baby," Margret replied, holding her hand onto her round belly. "You're going to have a baby brother or sister soon."

Einar smiled and tickled Emma. "You hear that?" he cried. "Emma is going to have a baby brother."

Margret caught his mistake. "It could be a baby sister too."

"It will be one huge girl then!" he said joyfully. "Have you looked at your belly?"

Margret laughed. "Yes, he's a big baby."

Emma squirmed as Einar began to tickle the little girl. She squealed in delight and twisted to escape but to no avail. Einar tickled her armpits and had the girl laughing hysterically.

"Okay, you two!" Margret chimed. "Time for Emma's nap time."

Einar scooped the little girl into his arms as they both walked towards the nursery room. Margret kissed his shoulder gently. "Another time, I guess," she said softly.

"We will have another opportunity, my sweetheart," Einar whispered. "Soon."

Einar was true to his word, and he made wonderful love to Margret that night. She felt his seed release in her vagina again. The feeling was so exquisite. It set her loins on fire and made her legs tremble. She stretched contently and swung her legs over the bed, wishing for the baby to come out faster this time.

It was a large, heavy baby and was becoming harder to continue carrying.

She grasped onto the bedroom dresser and stood slowly, her large belly extended out in front of her.

A sharp cramping pain shot through her lower abdomen. She instinctively grasped her belly and cried out. Margret exhaled in short breaths and squinted her eyes, trying to get over the pain. She knew this pain; it was the contractions of forthcoming childbirth.

Margret held onto the dresser securely and walked carefully to the kitchen wishing her husband would come back early for lunch. She wouldn't be able to make it to the barn. The mid-wife, Anne, was not due to arrive until next week. They were going to prepare for the childbirth and discuss arrangements for her to stay with them to help with Emma too.

Einar and Margret had become successful with sheep and wool farming. The price of wool had increased, and their flock had produced many offspring last spring. The flock numbers were higher than ever before. Einar had begun selling off some of the herd and culled an animal or two for meat. The vegetable gardens had flourished as well; they had grown many root vege-tables as well as a strawberry garden. They had enough garden food to last the winter. They also milked the sheep, and a local cheese farmer was buying the raw milk. They had enough money to pay a midwife, she knew. Anne was also Aunt Helga's cousin, so that helped immensely.

Margret clutched the bottom of her belly with both hands and walked gingerly to the kitchen. All the money in the world wouldn't matter right now, though, when she didn't have any way of contacting Anne to come sooner. Margret grasped the water jug and poured herself a cup, drinking it immediately. Her thirst surprised her. She drank another glass and settled into a chair, the contractions easing off. Margret exhaled a sigh of relief. Maybe it was just the beginning, and it would take another week of these contractions, she mused.

She sat contently at the kitchen table, drinking the fresh water until the contractions stopped. Margret thanked the heavens. She didn't want to have the baby without the midwife here. She wasn't even sure what they would do. When Emma was born, the farm hand's sister had cut the cord and delivered the baby. They were lucky she was a good midwife, but she had since moved to Reykjavik, and now there was nobody in the area of Horn to deliver babies.

Margret moved to the couch slowly and laid down on her side, holding her large belly. She gazed at the quiet house around her and was amazed at how her life had improved and changed so quickly. Einar was a pivotal moment in her life, and she couldn't be happier.

Emma's voice sounded from the hallway. "Mamma," she mumbled sleepily.

"Come here, sweetheart," Margret shouted. "Mamma's on the sofa. The baby is kicking, and I need to rest."

Margret could hear blankets shuffling and the little girl's light footsteps padding along the floor. Emma appeared in the hallway, her hair messy and piled up on top of her head.

"Looks like you are finished your nap, sweetie," Margret said lovingly. "Come here and lay with Mamma for a bit."

Emma padded softly down the hall, through the kitchen and curled into her mother's arms on the sofa.

"I love you, sweetheart," Margret said, kissing Emma's forehead.

Einar returned for lunch, finding his wife and daughter sleeping peacefully on the sofa. Margret's belly was incredibly large now, and he began to worry. She was often tired and looked weary.

He laid his hand on her head and smoothed her hair. "Margret, my love," he said softly.

She awoke instantly and smiled. "Sweetheart," Margret said. "I will get up and put on some soup. I put it all together last night. I just need to boil it. I had some contractions this morning and couldn't walk to tell you."

"My dear," Einar responded. "You stay right where you are. I'll cook the soup. Then afterwards, I will send Stephan to summon Anne to come right away."

"Are you sure?" Margret said. "It may just be contractions that come and go for another week."

"Yes, I'm sure," he said, running his fingers over her hair. "I want you to be as comfortable as possible." Einar kissed the top of her head and straightened, looking for where the soup contents were.

She pointed to the far left corner of the kitchen. "It's there in the bowl," Margret said. "All the potatoes, vegetables and broth are chopped together in the bowl. The meat is in the ground cooler."

Einar picked up the bowl, dumped it into a pot, then shuffled to the ground cooler where they kept all the meat. It was a small area dug out into the ground, a bit smaller than a closet but big enough to hold a large amount of food. He opened the latch and felt the cool air rise from the cooler. He stepped down the small ladder and found the cut-up sheep meat in a cloth bag. He closed the latch and returned to the kitchen. Margret had fallen back asleep.

Emma rushed to him and grabbed his legs. He dumped the meat into the pot, poured hot water over the mixture, and then placed it on the stove.

He grasped Emma under her arms and lifted her high onto his shoulders. "You go up here, and then you can see everything, my baby girl!"

Emma squealed in delight as Einar threw some coal into the stove and lighted it. He mused over the problem of heating the stove with hot water. It was a much tougher conundrum than simply heating the house. He knew that some kind of machinery would have to be devised to convert the hot water into blowing heat strong enough to heat the stove, but this was beyond his knowledge or understanding. For now, they would continue to rely on coal for cooking.

He stirred the mutton stew and spiced it with whatever he could find. Emma watched in fascination from his shoulders as he cooked lunch. Einar looked towards the sofa, and Margret was still asleep. He would wake her when the soup was ready and ensure she was fed before locating Stephan out in the fields. Einar would tell him to board a boat to Aunt Helga's house and bring Anne to Horn right away.

Magnus walked to the fish vendor with Hans, holding several large nets of fish. He had been mulling over Margret and her daughter, almost obsessing about it. Every morning Magnus awoke, wondering if he was a father. And every night, he seethed with anger at the injustice of being denied knowledge of his daughter. Magnus was angry at the world but understood he had to work with others to get anything done. A plan had begun forming in his mind to set things straight in his life.

Magnus handed one of the nets to Hans. "Thanks for helping me out today," Magnus shouted over his shoulder. "I caught a bit too much today!" Magnus said, still deep in thought.

Hans nodded. "Anything for you, my friend," he said. "I'm glad that things have been getting better for you. The house was such a burden."

"It was a burden!" Magnus said. "I turned a corner to a better life when I left that old house behind. Now I have a regular fishing income and can provide for a family soon."

"You have a woman?" Hans said incredulously. "You never told me!"

"Oh, no, I don't have a woman," Magnus replied happily. "I just meant for one day in the future."

"Oh!" Hans responded, agreeing. "Yes, work towards a better future, always."

They walked the remainder in silence to the fish vendor. The old man purchased all the fish graciously and paid Magnus in coins.

Magnus pocketed the money and left to go back home with Hans.

Hans pulled away slightly and started walking in a different direction. "I need to go back to work!" he shouted. "I'll be back at dusk. It's been extremely busy at work building houses. Lots of people are moving to the city."

"Oh, alright," Magnus shouted back. "Before you go, I have a question."

"What's your question?" Hans asked, stopping suddenly.

"It's nothing really," Magnus said slowly, trying to word it correctly. "I just wanted to know if you'd be there with me when I needed your help, similar to today, but for anything, I mean."

"Of course, Magnus!" Hans exclaimed. "I've always got your back. We're like brothers."

Magnus smiled. "I was hoping you'd say that," he said. "Yes, we're like brothers. Always!" Magnus rushed over and slapped him on the back. "I'll let you be. Get back to work, brother!"

CHAPTER 20

Anne arrived two days later. Margret was relieved. The contractions had multiplied, sometimes five during the day, and now they were coming at night too. She felt the baby drop into her lower hips, and Margret knew the childbirth was imminent.

But the only problem was the childbirth process wouldn't start. Every time Margret thought the baby was coming, the contractions would get stronger, then taper off slowly. Margret could feel the baby's head lodged in between her hips, making it difficult to walk. She rolled over and moaned, her belly feeling enormous.

Einar awoke instinctively. "Are you alright, my love?" he asked worriedly.

Margret ground her cheek into the flat pillow. "I want this baby out," she said. "He's too big."

"Do you really think it's a boy?"

"Yes," she replied. "Emma didn't feel like this, and besides, what baby girl would be this big?"

Einar leaned over, kissing her belly. "Take it easy on your mamma, boy," he said to her swollen abdomen.

Margret chuckled. "Listen to your father," she added.

"Have we agreed on the child's names?"

"I think so," she said. "We've been arguing about it for months. The only name we both agree upon is Nathanael. You were strongly against Jon and Elias!"

"Jon is too common!" Einar protested indignantly. "I know it's your father's name, but everyone has that name in Iceland. And Elias is too close to my name; we'll get it confused."

"Then Nathanael it is," she stated decisively.

"If it's a girl, we are calling her Eva," Einar said. "That's it, no fighting over that one."

"I like Eva," Margret stated.

"I love you," Einar said, kissing her lips gently.

Margret kissed him back and then curled into his open arms. "I love you too," she murmured into his chest. "Make this baby come out, please."

"I can't do that, my love," he said, hugging her warmly. "All we can do is wait."

Margret exhaled and melted into her husband's arms. Einar rocked her gently and began to hum a childhood lullaby. Margret listened to the soothing song and felt the world's troubles fall away. Her husband was with her, and he'd take care of her as he always has. She felt loved and treasured. It was the most wonderful feeling in the world.

She wasn't sure how long they had laid in each other's arms, but he had drifted back to sleep in the late morning darkness. It was January, and the sun didn't stay around for very long, nor did it heat up the earth. It was frigid, and they remained mostly indoors now, waiting for the baby to come. She nuzzled her chin into her husband's chest, smelling his musky male scent, with hints of wool and a woody smell. It was a pleasant smell, not rancid or pungent, just calming and lovely, like the feeling of a warm blanket wrapped around her shoulders. She loved the way her husband smelled; it was so much a part of her routine that she sometimes forgot how much she loved this man. Margret could smell him on her pillow, on her clothes and on her skin after making love. This was the man she was spending the rest of her life with, and she felt blessed to have such a good man.

The afternoon arrived quickly, and Margret curled out of his embrace, leaving him napping. She looked over at his sleeping face. He was so tired lately. Margret felt guilty. He was doing everything for the house, milking the sheep and trying to exhaust Emma's excess energy. Anne was thankfully cooking and cleaning as well as taking care of Emma regularly. It was the best thing for the small family right now.

Margret padded quietly into the kitchen, finding Anne preparing a sheep's head. Emma sat on the counter with Anne, staring wide-eyed at the dinner being spiced and oiled.

"Is it a monster?" Emma asked curiously.

Margret giggled as she sat down at the table. "Silly girl," she said.

Anne swung around. "Margret," she said, surprised. "You are up! How are you feeling?"

"Not that well," Margret replied. "I wish this baby would come out soon. It's been three weeks already."

Emma tilted her head to the side as she peered into the pot. "Monster!" she squealed. "It got one eye!" Her language skills were improving rapidly. She was a bright girl.

Anne scooped the little girl up and placed her down on the floor. "Go see your mamma," she said, chuckling.

Emma ran across the kitchen to her mother. Margret mussed her daughter's hair and kissed her on the forehead. "It's sheep's head," Margret stated knowingly. "You'll love it. It's very yummy. Pabbi gets to eat the eye, though."

"Ew!" Emma exclaimed in disgust.

"I have only eaten it once before," Anne said. "It was good, though."

"I have only eaten it once too, but it was tasty," Margret said, looking around the kitchen for the spices. "I can help, Anne. I will get you some spices."

"No, don't bother, Margret," Anne argued. "Please rest and lie down."

"It's alright," Margret said, stretching up to the top rack of the spice cabinet. She rummaged through the spices, finding three containers and turned to bring them back when a sharp pain seared across her abdomen. She dropped the spices and cried out, clutching her belly.

Emma cried, "Mamma!"

Anne rushed to Margret. "Sit down," she said soothingly. "Just right here on the floor. It will be fine. Trust me."

Anne grabbed her elbow and helped Margret down to the floor, propping her back against the wall. "Breathe," she said. "Exhale in short, strong breaths. Focus on breathing through the pain."

Margret nodded and followed her instructions.

"Can I feel the baby's position?" Anne asked.

"Yes," Margret said between heavy breaths.

Anne ran her hands along Margret's lower abdomen, expertly feeling and massaging the baby. She pressed here and there, positioning the baby for optimum delivery. "His head is down, so that's good," she said. "But his shoulders feel wide and may be stuck. I will try to mould his shoulders in so he can come out. It may feel uncomfortable, but it will aid the delivery. This may be why he's not coming out. He's too big."

Margret huffed and exhaled rapidly as Anne prodded her belly. She positioned her hands on both sides of her abdomen and pushed with her palms. "This may feel odd," she warned as she pressed the baby's shoulders through Margret's abdomen. Anne could feel the baby's upper body slightly turn inward, by only a fraction. Anne nodded worriedly. The baby's shoulders would need to be pressed on harder, she knew. Anne frowned, then proceeded to examine Margret's vaginal opening. Anne lifted her head under Margret's dress. "Your opening is getting larger," she said in astonishment. "The baby's coming."

"Einar!" Margret shouted suddenly as another contraction ripped through her abdomen.

"Breathe!" Anne shouted.

Several books fell to the floor in the bedroom as Einar came rushing out into the hallway. "Marg!" he yelled, seeing the two women on the floor. "Are you alright?"

"The baby's coming!" Anne said excitedly. "Grab some cloths, blankets and warm water."

Einar stood paralyzed for several seconds, then went running for where he knew the blankets and cloths to be. He remembered from Emma's birth that a lot of blood came out, so Einar also grabbed his wife's menstrual cotton rags. He felt the panic rising in his throat and attempted to calm himself down. He took two deep breaths and returned to the kitchen floor.

He bent down with the rags, blankets and cloths, placing them at Margret's bottom. Einar rushed to the kitchen tap and ran hot water in a washbowl and water jug. He cooled it with some cold water from the counter.

Einar brought the washbowl and jug to Anne. He glanced at his wife and was alarmed to see her sweating profusely. He rushed over to her head and cradled it, tracing his fingertips along her cheek and forehead. "It'll be alright, my love," Einar said, his voice firm and reassuring. "Be strong."

Margret exhaled roughly in short bursts and then suddenly was bearing down, grunting with all her might.

"Push!" Anne said loudly. "You're doing good. Don't forget to breathe." Anne positioned herself behind Margret's widespread legs, the dress forming a tent. She spread Margret's legs wider, trying to accommodate the larger baby. "Keep your legs wide, my dear."

Margret pushed with all her energy, screeching with a guttural cry.

"Okay, we're close," Anne said confidently, feeling Margret's lower abdomen. "The baby is still stuck. I'm going to press hard on the baby's shoulders. It may hurt, Margret. I will be pressing hard on your belly." Anne looked into Margret's eye. "You ready?"

"Yes!" Margret responded, shifting her buttocks slightly.

"Einar, bring the blanket!" Anne instructed.

Einar placed the blanket under his wife's bottom and laid it out past her vaginal opening for the baby to land on.

"Perfect," Anne stated, nodding her head. She washed her hands in the washbowl and dried them on a cloth. She knelt over Margret, positioned her hands and pushed down hard on several lower abdomen spots.

Margret groaned heavily, absorbing the pressure of Anne's hands.

"Not much longer," Anne said. "I think I've got his shoulder bent inwards. Let's try again."

"I have to push!" Margret said suddenly as a contraction gripped her entire body. She pushed madly, her face turning red.

"Keep pushing!" Anne yelled. "Breathe out between each push." She watched as Margret exhaled heavily, then started pushing again. "That's right. Keep breathing and pushing. Don't stop until I tell you."

Einar shifted onto the floor, pulling himself behind Margret. He grabbed his wife up against his legs and supported her back from behind. He wanted his wife to get through the delivery alive. Einar's heart shuddered, and his mind went blank. Einar gripped her warmly and tried to hide the fear rising in his heart.

Anne caught the look of fear in his eyes and looked down at Margret. "It will be alright!" she said confidently. "This baby will be born soon, and everything will be better. Come on, son, it's time to come out into the world." Anne spoke to Margret's belly. She applied pressure on the baby again, pushing downwards on Margret's belly, prompting another round of contractions.

Margret groaned and pushed instinctively, bearing down with all her might. She clutched Einar's arms with her nails, unaware that she was hurting him. A sudden pain seared through her vagina, like a knife searing her entrance. Margret screamed. "He's coming!" she cried.

Anne poked her head under the dress and held onto Margret's shaking legs. A bloody round ball of hair began poking out. "I see the head!" Anne yelled. "One last big push, Margret! You can do this! You need to get his shoulders out. Push hard!"

Margret roared as she pushed like never before. Her face was slicked with sweat, and her hair was matted against her head. The searing pain increased violently as the shoulders passed through the birth canal. Margret screamed at the top of her lungs.

"You're almost there!" Anne shouted. "I know it hurts, but you must get the baby out. You have to keep pushing until his shoulders are through. Hold onto Einar's arms tight as you push! Do everything you need to do; the baby is going to be stuck! You must do this!"

Margret dug her nails painfully into Einar's arms and clenched her teeth as she pushed harder than ever before, trying to focus on getting the baby out and ignoring the searing pain.

"Push! Margret! Push!" Einar said loudly, holding onto her tight.

Margret growled, bearing down and suddenly felt the baby move.

"His shoulders!" Anne said loudly. "His shoulders are through! Okay, no more hard pushing. A gentle push, Margret. Gentle. He's coming out. Your baby's being born. Gentle. Here he comes. I got him." The baby slipped out into Anne's hands. She laid him briefly on the blanket as she cleared his mouth.

A guttural cry filled the room.

Margret laughed, and her eyes opened, searching around her dress for a peek at her baby. Einar smiled and tried to see, but the dress was obscuring everyone's view.

"I just have to cut the cord," Anne said. "You have a healthy baby boy, Mr. and Mrs. Olason!"

Anne worked expertly cutting the cord and handed the bloodied infant to Margret. Anne wetted a cloth with warm water and gently washed the blood from the baby as Margret cradled her large newborn son.

"He needs to be fed," Anne said softly, wiping more blood from his face. She positioned the baby at one of Margret's breasts, and he latched on. Anne took another warm cloth and wiped Margret's sweaty face, gently cleaning the exertion from her face. "You did well, Margret. You can feed him, but I will need you to push one more time to get the afterbirth out. I will get a bowl. It can be quite a lot."

Margret nodded and smiled at their baby. Einar kissed her on the forehead and then kissed the baby's head. "Hello, Nathanael," Margret said softly.

"Welcome home, Nathanael, our son," Einar said, joining in the surreal moment.

Anne returned with a bowl and ducked under the dress. There was a lot of blood. She was alarmed but didn't want to upset the new parents yet. They needed their moment of newborn happiness. She positioned the bowl. "Okay, Margret, please push one last time, fairly hard, a good push so we can get that afterbirth out."

Margret grunted another push and bore down onto the blanket. She felt a gush of fluid release.

"Perfect, yes," Anne said. "There it is; push it all out. It's almost over, dear. Almost over. Push all of it out." Anne grasped the bowl as the afterbirth plopped out in a bloody mess. Some of it missed the bowl, but the majority was captured. "Good! Relax, Margret. You've done it. You have a brand new baby boy."

Margret slept for four hours, exhausted and depleted. She drank a lot of water, trying to quench a terrible thirst. The baby awoke her, crying out to be fed. She cuddled him and positioned his mouth at her nipple. The baby opened his mouth, searching for the nipple, then finally latched on.

Anne came into the room. "How are you feeling?" she asked, a concerned look clouding her face.

"Very thirsty still," Margret said wearily. "And very tired."

Anne looked at Margret worriedly. "You were bleeding quite a lot, Margret. I can put some stitches in or just leave it to heal on its own. I don't want you to worry."

"How much blood?" Margret asked tiredly.

"More blood than I'm used to seeing," Anne said slowly. It was the most she's ever seen, but she didn't want to alarm Margret. "I need you to rest. I have brought some raspberry leaf and lemon herb drink. I need you to drink as much of it as possible. We need the bleeding to decrease."

Einar awoke beside her, overhearing parts of the conversation. "I will make sure she drinks the herb drink."

"I have kept it in the cupboard on the right," Anne said slowly. "Just pour some hot water into a cup and add a spoonful of the herb mixture. Please get Margret to drink it all, even the pieces, ensure she consumes those too."

"I will," Einar stated decisively. "Please stay a bit longer, Anne. I will pay you. Margret is too weak, and I need your expertise to help me take care of her and the new baby."

"Yes, I was thinking the same," Anne replied softly. She didn't want them to know how worried she was. "I will stay another few weeks."

"Thank you, Anne. I appreciate this." Einar cupped his wife's arms as she fell asleep feeding the infant. He gazed at her face and noticed that she looked very pale. He darted a glance at Anne. "Is it normal for her to look so pale?"

Anne grimaced and rubbed her brow. "I need to be honest, Einar," she said. "I'm very worried about her. She has lost too much blood, and I want to check to see how much blood she is continuing to lose." She rubbed Margret's leg as the new mother slept. "I will wait until she awakens, and we will see."

"Is there anything we can do?" Einar said.

"Only the raspberry leaf and lemon will slow down the flow," she said.

"Okay," Einar responded. "How many times a day?"

"Four times per day," Anne replied decisively.

"Done."

Anne worked in the kitchen, washing the newborn in a small washbasin. She lathered the baby with a special soap made with oils and lye. Anne cleaned the baby with the oily soap, lifting the delivery debris gently off the sleepy infant. He was a large baby, she mused. She estimated he weighed 9 pounds. Anne smiled and kissed the baby on the head. "Do you know how much trouble it was getting you into this world?" she asked teasingly. "Well, if you knew, you'd be very grateful."

Baby Nath stared at her, then fluttered his eyes closed, enjoying the warm bath.

"Yes, you sleep, my dear," Anne cooed softly, washing his bloodied hair. She circled her soapy hands along his entire body, cleaning even his toes. Anne was enjoying bathing the baby just as much as the infant was. She lathered the soap into his sparse hair and scrubbed his scalp lightly. Anne cooed at him constantly, reassuring him that he was a lovely baby and everything would be alright.

Finally, she lifted the boy from the water and wrapped him in a towel, bundling his legs and arms into a small tight bundle. He was fully asleep now. Anne smiled and cradled the baby, singing softly.

She heard some blankets shuffling in the bedroom down the hallway and someone moving on the bed. Suddenly a rush of blankets and mumbling occurred, raising her awareness.

Einar was saying something, and she couldn't make it out. He was talking to his wife. Anne filtered out the noise thinking they needed privacy.

The noises and voices continued to grow until finally, Margret shrieked.

Anne came running with Nath in her arms. She walked quickly down the hall and turned into the bedroom.

The blankets were thrown to the side as Einar stood holding the coverings. His face was grave, and his eyes were panicked. Margret lay prone on her back on the bed. Underneath her buttocks was a large red stain spreading all over the sheets. Some of the blood was down her legs, and Margret tried crouching forward to inspect the mess. Exhausted, she laid back down and clutched her abdomen.

"Oh my Lord, Margret!" Anne said. "Have you been bleeding like this all night?"

"I don't know," Margret said tiredly. "My rags. It soaked through my rags."

Anne handed the infant to Einar and ran into the kitchen for another washbasin. She grabbed the soap and cloths. Anne rushed back and began to wash Margret's body in the bed, cleaning her buttocks and shifting Margret onto her side as she worked, then pulling the sheets off. "Einar!" she said urgently. "Please get me some clean sheets for the bed. Thankfully the cotton pad I placed underneath her absorbed most of the blood. So at least it's not on the bed underneath." Anne cleaned the inside of Margret's legs and her vagina, inspecting the flow. It was heavier than she thought. She touched her vagina lightly. The injuries were healing on their own. It wasn't the minor damage to her opening that was responsible for all the blood, she thought alarmingly. Margret was hemorrhaging from inside.

Anne fixed a clean rag onto Margret's bottom and clasped the side clips. "Listen to me, Margret," Anne said expertly. "You are hemorrhaging. There is too much blood, and we must stop the flow of blood. I am going to insert some packing, and then we need to hydrate you with an abundance of raspberry leaf tea and lemon."

Margret nodded. "Whatever you say," she said tiredly, her hair slicked to her head.

Einar returned with the sheets, placing them on the bed. Anne nodded her thanks and began shifting Margret's body around as she attempted to change the bedding.

Einar watched with a heavy heart, then realized he needed to get some medicine into her body. "I will make the herb drink right now," Einar said, abruptly leaving to the kitchen with Nath. The baby began to cry.

"Make sure it's very strong!" Anne shouted to his back.

"I will!" Einar replied. A dark panic crept up his throat while he walked to the kitchen. The anxiety threatened his sanity. He tried to force it down, but his heart beat wildly, and his mouth went dry. He could not lose his wife. It was unfathomable. Margret was his everything, his life, his family, his reason for living. He must do everything in his power to keep her alive and well. Einar hurriedly shuffled through the cupboard, finding the raspberry leaf and a cup, pouring hot water in it. He stirred the hot medicine drink and added honey, swirling the mixture together. He poured drops of the concentrated lemon juice into the cup, along with three more raspberry leaves and dried lemon bits. He sipped it and added a bit more honey. It was a bitter, sour drink.

Einar stirred the finished warm drink while Nathan's crying rose to a crescendo. He put the infant on his shoulder and patted his back repeatedly. "It's alright, son," Einar said softly.

"Your mamma needs help." Einar continued with the patting until, finally, the baby burped. "My good little man!" Einar said happily. "Now, let's go help your mamma."

Einar grabbed the drink carefully and held Nathanael in his other arm. He balanced the two, walking swiftly back into the bedroom.

Anne had cleaned up the majority of the blood and was in the process of changing the sheets.

Margret looked up at him, pale as a ghost and put out her hand for him to grasp.

Einar put the tea on the dresser and held her hand. "It will be alright, dear," he said slowly, his voice cracking. "I simply cannot lose you. You mean everything to me." Einar paused, trying to quell the moisture from his eyes. "I must do everything in my power to help you, my love. We will make it through this together, as we always have with any hard times. I will always be here for you." Tears formed in his eyes as he squeezed his wife's hand and shifted the baby to his lap. "All of us are here. We're here together."

Margret smiled as tears flowed freely down her pale cheeks. She had never seen her husband cry before, and the rare emotion moved her like nothing else. In this special moment, Margret saw how deeply her husband loved her. She flashed back to all the years they had spent as youngsters and how he always protected her and ensured her safety. Margret remembered when he journeyed with them to Reykjavik, cuddling her on the streets of the vendor stalls and finally, when he saved her from Magnus in Reykjavik.

Margret couldn't contain her emotions, the tears spilled out, and she sobbed for him. She cried for everyone, for her children and the little girl who she used to be. Margret remembered how tough it was growing up without her momma. A chill crept up her spine. She could not allow that to happen to her daughter, husband and her son. Margret prayed that history would not repeat itself today, tomorrow or twenty years from now. She must be strong and recover.

Anne shifted Margret to her side and tucked the last corner of the bed under the thin mattress. Margret rolled back, then carefully lifted her back up onto the pillows. She gripped her husband's hand faintly. "I must be stronger than I have ever been," Margret whispered loudly. Her voice cracked as she fought a wave of dizziness. "I will not allow my children to grow up without a mother." Margret sniffled the tears back, straightening her chest. "Our history will be better than our parents. Our history will be something they write in the books that children will learn. We will always persevere, and I will muster whatever strength I have left so I can grow old and grey with you all." Margret smiled weakly with tears running down her face, wondering if she had any strength left to recover. Her pale face belied her conviction.

Einar hugged her tightly with the baby sandwiched between them. Einar wiped the moisture from his eyes and handed her the hot drink, holding it to her lips. "Drink it all, my love," Einar said. "It is bitter, but I put honey in it for you. I will keep bringing you this medicine every hour if I have to. I will take care of you, my beautiful." He watched as she took the cup in her hands and drank the hot drink. "We will persevere, and yes, we will grow old and grey together."

Margret sipped at first, then finally tipped the cup up, drinking the last dredges of tea.

"Eat the leaves too," Anne instructed. "We must get this bleeding under control."

Margret dipped her fingers in the cup, pulled out the leaves and placed them in her mouth, chewing on the wet leaves.

Einar ran his hands over her hair and curled a strand behind her ear. He kissed her head and watched as baby Nath squirmed towards her breasts. Einar lifted the infant to her left breast as Margret cradled the baby. Little Nathan searched with his mouth until he found a nipple and sucked happily. "We will persevere, my love," Einar repeated worriedly, holding Margret's pale hand as he watched her tired body slump back into the pillows.

She awoke to her legs stiffening. Margret could barely move. She was alarmed but didn't want to cause a panic. Margret shook Einar gently in the darkness. "Sweetheart," she whispered. "I'm very thirsty. I need some water."

Einar stirred from his slumber, then awoke suddenly. "Are you okay?" he asked worriedly.

"I feel weak," Margret answered honestly.

"I will get you water," Einar said, getting out of bed slowly. "Don't move. I will get you some herb drink too."

Einar patted her hip and stood, walking to the kitchen. His heart thumped in his chest as he fumbled in the dark for the raspberry leaf mixture. He spooned the herb medicine into the cup and poured hot water on top. Einar grabbed the dried lemon bits and sprinkled them into the cup as his hands shook.

He stopped and pressed his hands onto the counter. He was afraid. Einar realized that he had never been afraid of anything in his life before. Now, the fear of losing his wife felt like a stick lodged in his heart. The hairs on his head stood up as he thought of a future without her. Einar gazed out into the darkness of the kitchen. He must do everything in his power to help her heal.

He cannot live without Margret.

Einar grabbed the two cups and returned to the bedroom. He placed them on the dresser and sat down on the edge of the bed. Margret was sitting up. He grabbed the water and held it out to her. "Drink this first. The raspberry leaf is still too hot."

Margret wrapped her fingers around the cup as Einar held her other hand. She peered over the rim and could see the concern washing over his face. Margret drank the water and handed the empty cup back. "Thank you," she said weakly.

Einar hugged her suddenly, squeezing her tight. "Don't leave me, Margret," he said softly.

Margret sniffled back her tears. "I won't, my sweet," she replied. "I'm still here. I'm still fighting."

Einar turned briefly, grasped the raspberry drink and helped her drink it. He watched as she sipped the hot liquid slowly until it was empty. Einar took the empty cup and kissed her on the head. "Promise me," he said. "Don't ever give up." He gazed deeply into her face in the dark.

"I promise you, my love," Margret said, her pale face glowing in the night.

Einar began sobbing and fell onto her lap.

Margret shuffled herself over him and smoothed his hair. He kissed her legs repeatedly as his tears wet the blankets. Margret's heart melted with love for her husband.

They both lay together in this moment of suspended time until sleep overtook them, and the night consoled them both.

The bleeding became heavier on the third day. Margret had woken up with bloodied sheets again. Einar and Anne had changed the sheets and maintained a constant supply of the hot medicine drink. Her menstrual flow began to decrease slowly. The medicine was starting to work. A harsh cramping began in the evening, and even though Anne told her that it was necessary to stop the bleeding, the pain was excruciating. Margret clutched herself as Einar rocked her to sleep, trying his best to comfort her and take the edge of the pain away.

His strong arms encircled her body, holding her warmly in his embrace. Margret's nose touched the hairs on his arms, and she breathed in his masculine scent. It was one of her favourite scents in the world. It soothed her body and her soul.

She prayed silently that she would recover completely soon. Her eyes opened and blinked slowly as another cramp assaulted her. Margret squeezed her eyes tight and ground her teeth against the pain. She curled her legs up and grasped onto his arm, exhaling through the cramping. Margret didn't want to awaken him again.

Margret feared that she would die regardless of how much she fought to stay alive. She was terrified that her children would grow up without a mother. Margret shivered at the thought. She had never felt so weak and ill in her life. At least the fever had subsided, Margret thought. Some things were improving; she reminded herself. It was difficult to keep her mind positive when her body hurt so much.

The cramping started anew, searing throughout her abdomen and stealing her breath away. Margret gasped and held onto Einar's arm fiercely. She tried to focus on things other than the pain. Her eyes began to moisten from the sharp contraction. Margret ground her teeth against the agonizing cramp and prayed silently.

After several excruciating minutes, the cramping finally eased, and she let out a heavy sigh of relief. Her fingers relaxed on his arm, and hope fluttered in her chest. Margret nudged her nose against his sleeping arm and thanked God for her husband.

CHAPTER 21

It had been a long week. The cramping continued for the remainder of the week until finally, it lessened in intensity on day seven. Anne worked on her abdomen every day, gently pushing and massaging the muscles.

"Your body is shrinking your womb back to its original size," Anne said. "I know it can be very painful, but it is necessary. And it aids with the bleeding." Anne placed her hands again on Margret's naked abdomen and gently massaged the muscles.

Margret laid back with her eyes closed as Anne worked her magic on her belly. A sharp pain seared through her abdomen, and Anne stood aside, waiting for the contraction to cease. Margret pinched her eyes shut and willed the pain away. "It is getting better," Margret said, exhaling out. "It is not as painful as it was several days ago."

"We have been successful, Margret," Anne smiled. "I will continue to massage your abdomen until all the contractions have ceased. This means your womb will have returned to its original size. He was a big baby. Your body has a lot of work to do yet. I will stay until things have returned to normal and you are able to care for your baby on your own."

"You are truly a lifesaver," Margret said. "Thank you."

Magnus watched the storm clouds rolling in and wondered how it would feel having a baby in his arms. His face flushed with fatherly love, and he thought he might enjoy being a father quite a lot. He would take care of the baby and nurture it just like any mother. Magnus pulled on his beard, contemplating how it would change his life. He knew it would be a positive change, and he needed that more than anything right now. He wondered briefly what his daughter looked like. He imagined she had his dark hair and the same charismatic smile.

"Hey," Hans called out. "Hand me the next plank."

Magnus snapped out of his reverie and reached over to the used woodpile.

Hans had begun expanding his construction business and desperately needed a new shed to store more tools and equipment. Magnus had agreed to help, but Hans wanted it finished this weekend. Magnus thought it was a lot of work for little reward, although he knew he needed his friend for something important very soon.

Magnus pulled on the wood plank from the ruined boat and pried it loose. The plank sounded with a crack as it pulled off. Magnus hefted the wood board over to Hans. His friend grabbed it, positioned it into place and nailed it onto the partially completed structure.

"When did you want this finished?" Magnus asked, scrutinizing the incoming clouds.

"Today," Hans stated. "I have some large projects planned with the builder. I need the extra space for the tools I will be buying at the market tomorrow."

"That quickly?" Magnus said incredulously.

Hans lowered his arms heavily, the hammer and wood still in his hands. "I have a good business, Magnus," he said gently. "I don't want to be unprepared when it gets busy."

Magnus sighed, "I understand." He stared across the field, losing his focus briefly.

Hans grimaced and hammered the nails into the wood. He realized how hard it had been on Magnus recently. He could tell Magnus was regretting selling his house. His friend had lost his home and his woman. It seemed something had recently snapped inside Magnus's emotions, and Hans was worried for his friend. "I know it's been tough for you right now," Hans said, expressing his empathy for Magnus's situation. "You need to forget about that woman."

"I will not," Magnus said firmly.

"Why?" Hans asked, hammering in another board.

Magnus waited until he was finished hammering. "Because she has my daughter," Magnus answered.

Hans stopped and stared at Magnus in shock. "What?" he exclaimed in surprise.

"You heard me," Magnus said slowly. "I found out she gave birth to my child."

"Are you sure?"

"I'm positive," Magnus answered firmly. "The child is over a year old now."

"I'm sorry that she did that to you," Hans said. "That's not right."

"Margret is the reason for all this negativity in my life," Magnus said. "If it weren't for her, I would still have my house. I would have a family and be working."

"You can work for me anytime," Hans offered. "I have lots of work coming up."

"Thanks," Magnus replied, pondering the offer. "I am happy fishing for now. It's easy work." He looked up at the threatening clouds. "We have to finish this shed soon before the weather forces us to stop."

"Hand me some nails," Hans said. Magnus handed him a pail full of nails. Hans grabbed a handful, positioned the board thoughtfully and nailed it in. Hans wondered if it was true that Magnus had a child.

"This is decent wood I found for your shed," Magnus said, changing the subject. "It is rare to find such good wood. Buying the imported wood is so costly now that few people can afford it."

"True," Hans replied slowly. "I am grateful for that."

"I am here for you," Magnus said. "I hope you know that."

"Of course I do," Hans replied. "We are like brothers, remember."

Magnus nodded and cleaned up some of the remaining wood, sanding the grime and mould off. A few of the pieces he discarded because they were not salvageable. A pile of broken wood pieces sat haphazardly behind the shed. "We can burn those when they dry," Magnus stated, throwing another short plank onto the pile.

Hans finished nailing in another wood plank and stood back admiring his handiwork. "It's coming along!" he exclaimed. "Let's hurry to get as much done as we can. Thank you for helping me. It means a lot to me."

"You're welcome, and as long as the weather holds up, I will finish building it with you," Magnus answered, sighing. Hans worked too hard. Magnus didn't agree with spending his life working all the time. He wanted to spend more time having fun rather than working. They didn't always agree on everything, but he needed his best friend in his life. Magnus didn't have many friends left since he sold the house. He briefly pondered if that was Margret's fault as well.

"Hold this piece for the roof while I crawl up the hill and attach it from above," Hans shouted, walking around the snowy ground above the shed where they were building the roof. He laid down on his stomach and gripped the hammer tightly in his hand, sweat forming on his brow even in the cold winter.

Magnus held the reinforced wood as his friend nailed it in from above. "What kind of building work do you do during the winter anyway?" Magnus asked as the first flakes of snow started falling.

"Mostly roof repairs and interior rooms," Hans replied. "It is February now, so many of the spring projects are being planned, and they're only accepting workers that have the available tools and equipment." Hans rose and crouched onto his knees, looking down. "And I know of a vendor selling tools this Saturday. It's much cheaper to buy these items when it is out of season rather than wait for everybody to start buying tools at the same time in April. It's Iceland; imported stuff is going to be costly."

Magnus understood now why the shed must be built. "That makes sense," he said, mulling it over. Magnus had to ask Hans for his help soon, and he wondered how to bring it up.

Hans stretched out his arm, waiting for the next board. "Position it on the opposite side of the roof, forming a point," Hans instructed.

Magnus grabbed another wood plank and held it over his head, positioning it slowly into place. The boards were heavy and sweat beaded on his forehead, regardless of the cold weather. The winds were picking up. It wasn't a good day for working outside, he mused.

Hans concentrated on the exact placement and then hammered it in from above. Magnus watched as the nail pierced through the board and into the supporting frame. He needed to ask for his friend's help soon. An urgency to address things in his life consumed his mind. Magnus desperately needed a trusted ally.

Both men worked tirelessly into the cold dark evening. The snow began falling more and more as they worked against the clock and the weather. By 6 pm, the darkness had completely engulfed them. The shed was mostly finished. The only extra thing was to add dirt and grass on the roof in the summer and secure the hinges on the door. Hans positioned the built wood door on the opening, leaning it against the frame.

"It'll have to wait until tomorrow," Magnus said. "It's too dark, and the snowstorm is upon us."

"You're right," Hans answered, packing up the hammer and nails in the blistery swirls of snow.

"Let me take some of that," Magnus said, grabbing the wooden toolbox as the winds started whipping into his face.

Hans nodded, squinting against the falling snow, as they rushed across the hilly yard to the house.

Magnus followed as the storm clouds settled over their heads, releasing a dump of snow. Magnus ran with Hans towards the house, running from the snowstorm. "I need some help next week with something I've been planning," Magnus shouted against the wind. "Will you be able to help? It might take a week or so."

"Yes, of course! I won't be busy for another month and a half," Hans replied. "I'm here for you. Whatever it is, we'll get it done together!"

"You're certain?" Magnus asked, stumbling to open the door as the snow progressed into a dangerous blizzard.

"Definitely!" Hans said confidently, struggling to open the door as the weather chased them inside. "Anything for my brother."

"Good," Magnus said, nodding decisively as they entered the house, slamming the door behind them. Magnus smiled. Things were going to start getting better. He'll show everyone what kind of man he was. Magnus looked down at his hands and wondered what Margret and his daughter would think of his strength when he takes back his life. His hands began shaking with emotion from the hurt buried deep in his heart. Magnus looked up and inhaled deeply, trying to dispel the anxiety. He would do this right. He would take back his life, and nobody would stop him.

Chapter 22

The ground rumbled as Einar walked out to the sheep. The tremors seemed to get heavier in intensity in certain years, then die away for months or even years. Einar shrugged and stomped towards the barn. It was just another one of the normal everyday things about Iceland that others found unusual. When he bought wood or steel from the import vendors, they always told him how different Iceland was from everywhere else. Einar just told them it's the only place he has ever known. Iceland was normal for him.

Einar could see the flock below. He stopped to count. It was easier to do from a distance. He counted carefully in groups to avoid getting confused. Einar pointed his finger in the air as if counting on a board. Finally, he arrived at a final calculation. There were sixty-eight sheep! He couldn't believe it. They had done so well! Plenty of lambs were born last year, and that was certainly good luck. They had sold so much wool in the previous year that it wasn't necessary to sell any sheep. So they kept them all to increase the size of the flock.

He peered farther into the flock, trying to select the best sheep to cull for the household. They had been running low on stored meat for several weeks. It was time. Einar held the rifle slung across his back as he trudged along the barren snowy landscape. The winds had calmed down significantly today, and he was glad. The winds were strong all week but became unusually calm this afternoon. Einar was relieved. The winds were a nuisance, always blowing directly in his face forcing him to squint in the wind.

Margret still squinted a lot when looking in the distance, even on a sunny warm day. They both knew her eyesight wasn't the greatest. Einar vowed to find her a pair of eyeglasses so she could see better. It was a problem, though, because the only eyeglasses invented were made to see things close up. He would have to enlist the help of an eye doctor to find a solution. He wanted the best for his wife. If she could see better, it definitely would make a difference in her life. He loved Margret so much.

Einar walked across the hilly countryside, his boots crunching on the hard-packed snow. He arrived at the sheep meadow in no time, browsing the sheep for the best one to cull. He patted their heads and spoke calmly to the sheep. They responded with bleats and sheep calls, some from the lambs, some from the ewes and the rams. He patted an older ram on the head. He was a trusted stud, producing many offspring, but he was getting old, so they used him primarily for wool.

"Good morning," Einar said to the ram calmly, patting his hand along the ram's entire back. His wool was thick and heavy. Einar would need to sheer the wool on this large animal before culling. He deliberated and picked another male who didn't reproduce as much. His coat was thinner, and he weighed less. Einar walked to an old ewe and patted her head. "Betty," he cooed. "You haven't produced any lambs at all last year." He patted her heavy wool coat and smoothed it down her back. She was a good choice too. Einar mused as he stood amongst the sheep, deciding which animal would be the best to cull.

It most likely would be an old female or an older male. Einar pulled the breech-loading rifle off his back and checked the weapon. He had cleaned it last night. It was a newer rifle Einar had purchased a few years back when he lived with his parents. Many Icelanders owned guns, mostly for hunting and farming. He had hunted with his father many times as a youngster and had culled many animals for Mr. Petersson before his untimely death. Einar looked across the field, and the enormity of the world fell onto his shoulders. He now owned this land with his wife. His parents were ill and old. Einar took care of them as much as possible, hiring a caregiver to live full time with them.

The wind blew a sudden gust of cold air into his face.

He pinched his brows.

He was a lucky man. God had somehow blessed him for all his hard work.

Einar grabbed the old ewe and put a collar on her, leading her away from the flock. She bleated warmly, following her master dutifully.

"Betty," he said calmly. "I hate to do this, but everyone's time comes sooner or later. We have to eat. You've been a good mamma for all the time I've known you." He patted her shoulders and then petted her head affectionately. "All the lambs you've produced in past years are now having lambs of their own. You've had a good long life. I will make it quick for you. I promise."

Einar led Betty inside the barn, away from the main flock. She bleated at him. "My wife just had a baby," he said calmly. "She needs meat to recover her lost blood. It's been a month, and she's feeling much better, but she's still weak and dizzy every day. We will make more blood sausage and sheep's stew to get her feeling better."

Betty bleated as if to answer.

Einar pulled the rifle from his back and pulled a bullet from his hunting belt. He loaded the bullet in the breech and closed it.

Since Betty was a ewe, she didn't have any horns, so he positioned the end of the rifle on the top of her head. She was too tall for the rifle's length, so he sat down and pulled her down with him. Betty laid down on the ground with her head on his lap. He petted her head affectionately. Einar stopped and laid down the loaded rifle carefully. He had almost forgotten. Einar chastised himself and pulled out the shears from his bag. "That could have been a costly bloody mistake," he mumbled to himself.

He patiently sheared the wool from her back and sides expertly. She seemed to enjoy the attention and calmly allowed Einar to continue removing her winter coat. A pile of wool gathered on the ground, and Einar stood up, bundling it into one of the large wool bags attached to the wall.

Betty stood up as soon as Einar did this. "Hey, hey," Einar cooed. Usually, he sheared and culled animals with one of his farm hands, but they were not available this weekend. Einar chose not to wait any longer because the children were sleepy, and Margret seemed to have enough energy to get about the house today.

Einar returned to the animal and sheared the remaining coat from the sheep's body. He had done this a thousand times over, so he was quicker than most farmers. He laid her down and sheared the other side as well, ensuring that the entire coat was removed and only her pink skin was visible. It was amazing how sheep looked so smaller once their coats were sheared.

Einar smiled, pleased with the job and gathered the wool again, depositing it in the wool bag. Again, Betty stood and followed him. Einar cooed at her, "Let's go back, now," he said, leading her back and pulling her down again. She laid down obediently. "I will make this quick."

Einar attached a leash onto the collar and stepped on the leather cord with his foot to keep her from standing up. Einar positioned the rifle onto the top of her head again. Perfect positioning this time, he thought.

He said a silent prayer of thankfulness and pulled the trigger.

The gunshot echoed throughout the barn and the countryside with a muffled bang. Some of the flock turned their heads but most ignored the loud, muffled noise from the barn.

Betty was killed instantly.

Einar remained in the barn, field dressing the animal, blood staining his shirt all the way up to his shoulders, his rifle slung across his back.

Margret awoke to find Einar gone. She cuddled into the cold spot he had left beside her in bed. She had become so accustomed to his constant presence in the house that Margret felt sad he was gone this morning.

She knew he was out to cull sheep today. He had mentioned several times they were getting low on meat. Margret had been eating ravenously since recovering from the birth. Breastfeeding her son was a chore in itself! The boy demanded milk every two hours, it seemed!

Margret stretched and heard baby Nathanael roll over in the wood rocker. She peered over and saw that he was still asleep. The house was unusually quiet. She assumed Emma was fast asleep as well.

Margret stood quietly, slipping on her favourite old grey dress. She immediately felt the room spin and grasped onto the dresser to keep herself from falling. The wave of dizziness gripped her senses as she fought to stay upright.

She had been feeling better, although the dizzy spells were still a challenge. Margret needed to be more aware of standing abruptly. She had lost so much blood in the past month, and it felt like her body was busy making new blood. Margret held the back of her hand to her head and waited for the light-headedness to pass.

She inhaled deeply, then exhaled as the vertigo lessened. Margret straightened firmly and padded gently into the kitchen. She was surprised to find Emma awake. Anne had left back to the north yesterday. It was time, Margret knew. She had resolved to begin tackling the household chores more and more. Margret's strength was returning every day, and Anne's presence was becoming less of a necessity. Einar, Margret and Anne had come to the collective decision last Friday. Saying goodbye to Anne was a tearful day. She had become such an essential part of their lives and family; Margret was going to miss her.

"An, na?" Emma asked in her adorable clipped toddler language.

Margret smiled sweetly and patted her daughter on the head. Her first words were mamma, da and Anna. "Did you wake up looking for Anna, my sweet?" Margret asked.

"Ya," Emma answered sweetly.

Margret grasped her daughter and lifted her up slowly. "She will visit someday, sweetheart," Margret said. "She has helped us so much with you and your baby brother."

Emma snuggled her head into her mother's shoulder.

Margret grasped the ceramic baby cup from the counter and filled it with sheep's milk. The cups were much more hygienic than the old ceramic spout bottles. Margret always found those too difficult to clean, and even Anne had warned the old bottles grew bacteria that were harmful to infants. It was hard teaching Emma to drink from a cup; she was only a sixteen-month toddler who had just started walking six months ago. Margret grasped the cup with her, trying to make sure she held the cup safely.

"Hold it like this, okay?" Margret instructed. Emma grasped it with her tiny fingers.

Margret sat Emma on the small wooden high chair and turned back to grab them both some yogurt for breakfast. She dug in the cold room and brought up some skyr, mixing it in with some partially frozen strawberries.

Margret turned around in shock when she heard the cup crash onto the floor. She went rushing to her daughter. "Emma!" Margret scolded. "I told you to hold onto it!" White ceramic pieces littered the floor everywhere. The tiny cup had shattered upon impact, and milk was all over the floor, obscuring the sharp pieces. "Look at what you've done!"

"Sorry, mamma," Emma said sadly.

"You need to be more careful," Margret scolded, bending down to pick up the larger pieces. Emma started to move out of the chair to help her mother. "No! You stay right there! You'll step in it!"

Emma's lips quivered, and she started crying.

"No, sweetheart," Margret said more softly. She knew Emma was just trying to help. "I'm sorry for shouting. I will clean this up. Stay right there." Margret fetched the broom and mop to clean up the mess when there was a sudden knock on the front door.

She looked up, bewildered. Who would be knocking on the door? Maybe Anne had come back for something she had left behind, Margret thought. She grabbed Emma, positioned the girl on her hip and rushed to the door. She would be delighted to see Anne again.

Margret flung open the door.

On the front door step stood Magnus with a scowl on his face.

She couldn't believe her eyes. Her brain didn't understand why she was looking at Magnus right now. He shouldn't be here. Why was he here? Mixed thoughts began to carousel through her mind. Margret didn't have any time to adjust to the reality of what was happening or even understand what was going on. But the hatred on his face seared through her soul. Then he looked over at Emma, and his face softened into an awkward smile.

"What are you doing here?" Margret said, more aggressively than she had intended.

His gaze settled back on her face as he spoke with a twitch in his right eye. "I'm here to take back what is rightfully mine," Magnus sneered.

A man appeared behind Magnus, mumbling something incomprehensible. Margret looked past Magnus and could tell by his stance that the friend was uncomfortable about their purpose being here.

"And what do you think is rightfully yours?" Margret spoke strongly, clutching onto her daughter protectively.

"My daughter," Magnus said stonily. "And my wife."

An evil tendril swam into the pit of her stomach as fear chilled her to the bone. For a moment, Margret was speechless, unable to respond to the absurdity of his statement. Then a curious calm overtook her. She wasn't fearful of her own safety.

No, not at all. It was her daughter that he had threatened. Her motherly instincts heightened dramatically, rising into her throat and shooting her anger up like a geyser. Margret had little control over the protective fight response that seized her entire being.

"Emma is not your daughter!" Margret shouted viciously into his face. "I aborted your daughter in a bloody miscarriage, you filthy slime!" Margret spat in his face. "Don't you dare show your face in my household!"

Hans's face dropped in surprise, and he pulled his friend's elbow back. "It's not your daughter!" he shouted anxiously, trying to motion for Magnus to return to the horses. They had been travelling for three days straight including the boat ride across the island. They were both weary and irritable.

Magnus calmly wiped the spit from his cheek. "Whore!" he yelled back. "You're a liar! You never told Einar! That daughter you're holding would be the exact same age. Lies!"

Hans pulled on his elbow again. "She might be telling the truth, Magnus," he warned.

Magnus roughly swung his arm out of his friend's grip. His heart hammered in his throat. They had not come all this way to learn that it wasn't his child. "Impossible!" Magnus shouted. "We travelled for three days straight to get what is mine, and we are taking it."

Hans stepped back uncomfortably. "Let's just go," he said. "It's a mistake."

"Go?" Magnus shouted. "I'm not going back without my daughter. I know lies when I hear them."

Margret knelt down and placed the baby girl down, whispering in her ear. "Go run to your bedroom and hide under the bed." She released the little girl.

Emma ran hard across the room, disappearing down the hall.

Magnus pushed his way inside to follow the girl. Margret felt raw anger sear through her soul, and the wrath was uncontainable. Her parental instincts erupted out of control. Margret screeched loudly and jumped at Magnus. She attacked his face, scratching at his eyes, her fingers poking into his nostrils and eye cavities.

Magnus was taken by surprise; he hadn't expected her to fight. He squinted his eyes closed protectively and struggled to get the situation under control. Magnus scuffled with Margret, trying to grab her hands, but she was like a possessed demon. Margret clawed at him, screaming in his ear. "Get out of my house!" she yelled ferociously.

Magnus was forced back into the doorway by her fury. She was like an animal stuck to his face. He couldn't see from the hail of fingers in his eyes. Margret screamed with a chilling screech that reverberated over the fields. Magnus was taken aback by her ferocity, tripping over the doorstep and falling back outside.

Hans stepped back and tried to urge Magnus to leave, but he knew his friend's ego was offended now. "Come on, Magnus," Hans said. "Let's get out of here. She's lost her mind."

Magnus wiped the snow from his pants and stood firmly, facing Margret as a baby started to cry within the house. He didn't quite understand at first, but it quickly became apparent that Margret had another baby in the house, and she was protecting them. Which also meant that Einar was not in the house, Magnus concluded. He smiled cruelly as blood coursed down his face from the scratches. "Your husband isn't here to save you," Magnus said with a sinister smile. "We will leave your other baby, don't worry, Margret. But you and my daughter are coming back to Reykjavik with me."

"She's not your daughter!" Margret screamed, lashing out violently in response. She kicked at him and flailed at his eyes again, but this time he was ready. He shielded his face as the flurry of fingers hailed down uselessly on his hands. Another child started screaming. It was his daughter.

"Go inside and get Emma!" Magnus shouted at Hans.

"She's not your daughter!" Hans shouted back.

Margret looked up, then kneed Magnus in the scrotum. He keeled over in pain, yelling.

Margret grabbed his hair, bent down and bit him on the ear, tearing a bit of flesh off. Then just as suddenly, the wave of anger weakened as a dangerous wave of dizziness attacked her senses. She was overexerting herself; her body was telling her. Margret fought to contain the vertigo and spat blood in his face angrily.

"Ow!" Magnus screamed in pain. "You witch!" He grabbed her arms and pulled her into his body, trying to restrain her. Margret kicked and flailed angrily, although he could sense her energy fading. She was hysterical, and he had to find a way to subdue her. His friend was not helping! Magnus searched his mind for a way to control the situation. What was her weakness? Magnus tried to think rationally as Margret hailed hell and fury on him. She just had a baby, he thought. But before he could think of a solution, Margret suddenly lost energy, going limp in his arms.

He looked down incredulously. Margret had fainted from overexertion and collapsed in his grasp. Magnus chuckled. He didn't even touch her! She just fainted. He snickered.

"There you go," Magnus said cruelly. "You crazy witch. You ran out of energy." Magnus laughed out loud, then looked at Hans. "What are you doing standing there? Go get my daughter!"

"I won't do any such thing," Hans replied stonily, watching the scene unfolding. Bile rose in his throat, and he felt disgusted.

"Something's wrong with you all! I'll do it myself then!" Magnus said, lifting Margret over his shoulder, carrying her to the horses. He tied her legs together and her arms with rope, slicing the ends with his hunting knife. When he was done, Magnus threw her onto one of the horses' backs. She began to awaken, and he felt a fear rise in his gut. Margret was much more ferocious than he had expected.

She looked up at him, glassy-eyed and confused. Then her eyes focused on him. "I will kill you if you touch my daughter!" she threatened.

Magnus stepped back. A chill ran up his spine. Margret was restrained, he told himself. He had nothing to fear. "Shut your mouth," he said softly and attempted to wrap a piece of cloth around her mouth. She bit his hand fiercely, drawing blood.

"Ow!" Magnus cried, shaking his hand. The horse whinnied, and he hushed the animal, trying to remain calm. "Fine, stay there, you crazy witch!" He threw the cloth at her and walked away.

In the back of his mind, he knew something was very wrong with the situation. Nothing had gone as planned, but he would not back down now. Another vital detail rushed through his mind urgently. An unseen danger, something he had prepared for diligently. Magnus had brought a hunting knife for the swine who had taken his wife away from him. Years of festering jealousy bubbled up like a volcano in his throat. Once Magnus had arrived at the homestead, his heightened state of vigilance had dissipated. Miraculously, the biggest threat, Einar, wasn't home. Magnus chuckled at his luck and returned to the house, entering the homestead. He looked to the right and saw the living room with nobody in it. Magnus crept down the hallway, absolutely certain that Einar wasn't home now. A baby cried mercilessly in a bassinet.

That must be her other baby, he thought.

Magnus ignored the baby and continued through the hallway.

Einar straightened when he heard the chilling screech. He halted and stood up from the carcass. He had been here for hours, and Einar finally had the carcass ready for the cold room. He was preparing to load it onto the sled for the horses when he heard the scream. A terrifying chill ran up his spine immediately. Maybe it was one of the sheep. They could screech when they were hurt. He peered out of the barn and gazed over the calm flock. Nothing was amiss there.

Einar shook his head. He was sure that he had heard a screech. It had to be loud enough for the sound to travel all the way to the barn, which didn't make sense. Nathanael's cries wouldn't be loud enough, Einar thought. Maybe Margret was hurt. The alarming thought seared through his veins, and he sprinted towards the house. The empty rifle flapped on his back as he ran. Margret must have fallen, or her bleeding had suddenly gotten worse. He knew in the pit of his stomach that something terrible was happening.

He looked up at the landscape and ran hard until he reached the far side of the hill. Einar slowed down when he saw the three horses. He tried to assimilate what was going on. His testosterone urged him to just rush into the house and attack. But common sense told him that there were three people and that it was most likely something else entirely. Einar couldn't fathom what or who it was, but his instincts told him to tread wisely. Einar exhaled slowly, attempting to make sense of what he was seeing. He heard a scuffle then a man appeared with Margret over his shoulder.

Einar took two large steps and stopped himself, crouching behind a bush. He wanted to rush the man like a bull but knew that was not the answer. He inhaled heavily and tried to assess the situation. There was another man standing beside the door. Einar stood frozen to the spot, covered in dried sheep blood from his shoulders to his arms. His hands shook with constrained anger as he watched the man tie his wife with rope and sling her over a horse like a carcass. When the man turned to go back into the house, he saw the glint of the hunting knife in his hand, but most of all, he saw the man's face. It was Magnus.

Einar felt murder in his heart. He wanted to kill the man instantly and cut him into pieces. But he had left his hunting knife at the barn. He looked to the barn and calculated that it was too far to go running back now. Then he remembered the rifle that was across his back. He slowly edged back to the crest of the hill and slid down onto the snow.

He rummaged in his belt and pulled out a bullet, loading it into the breech. He stood quietly, assessing the situation further. Magnus was gone, presumably in the house. The other man was standing facing the front door, his back to Einar. The man was standing strong, but he wasn't doing anything. He wasn't helping Margret, nor was he aiding Magnus. The man was just frozen to the spot watching the events unfold. Einar approached cautiously but quickly, all the while looking down the sight of his rifle.

Einar advanced closer to the man's back.

When he was ten feet away, Einar whispered loudly to the man. "Turn around slowly with your hands up," Einar instructed strongly. "I have a loaded rifle at your back. One swift move, and you will be dead."

Hans felt a shiver up his spine, and the hair stood up on his head. He didn't doubt there was an armed man behind him. Hans slowly raised his hands in defeat.

"That's right," Einar said, his voice quiet. "Raise those hands. Now turn around."

Hans turned slowly around, and Einar could see the knife in his belt. "You have a knife in your belt. You try to use it, and I will splatter your brains on my front door."

"I haven't done anything," Hans stated. "I won't be using my knife. This was all a big mistake."

"Is that so?" Einar replied stonily.

"Emma's not his daughter," Hans stated.

"What are you talking about?"

"Magnus convinced me to come here to get his daughter," Hans confessed.

"You're not innocent then," Einar stated angrily as he advanced closer, his rifle aimed at the man's head. "I want you to slowly, very slowly, take the knife from your belt, place it on the ground and back six feet away from it. If you try to fight, I will kill you. I won't even think twice."

"You can have the knife," Hans said. "I tried to convince Magnus to leave peacefully. He wouldn't. He's inside trying to find your daughter."

"Why does he want my daughter?" Einar asked, seething with anger. "Put the knife down now."

Hans slowly removed the knife and did as instructed. "Because he thinks Emma is his," he answered.

Einar swiftly picked up the knife and sheath, strapping it across his belt. "Magnus better pray he hasn't touched my daughter. Okay, go face the house. Hands behind your back!"

Hans obeyed and placed his hands behind his back. Einar picked up the loose rope on the ground and tied the man's hands tightly together. When he was done, Einar pushed the man down to the ground as he heard heavy footsteps and a girl crying in the house.

Einar aimed the rifle towards the door. Nothing. He heard a shuffle, but still, no one came to the door.

"Come here, little one," Magnus said, cursing as Emma bolted from her bedroom. She ran through his legs and down the hall, yelling for her mamma. Magnus looked around the small room as the little girl escaped. He didn't even see where she went. He swung around, confused and was stunned to be looking down the barrel of a gun.

"You have some nerve," Einar said. "I should kill you right now. You kidnapped my wife and are trying to take my daughter too. You deserve to die, Magnus."

Magnus stared at the gun and slowly raised his hands over his head, fear coursing through his veins at the bloodied man. He must have killed Hans already, Magnus thought. Einar was deranged. "I'm defenseless," Magnus said slowly. "You're not going to shoot me in cold blood while your daughter is watching."

"Give me one good reason why I shouldn't," Einar replied, his voice a low growl.

"Emma will be traumatized for the rest of her life," Magnus replied quickly. "She'd have witnessed a murder."

"Emma, sweetie," Einar said, keeping his eyes on the sights. "Go to Mommy's room."

The little girl ran frightfully into the nearest bedroom as Einar kept the rifle trained on Magnus. "Here's what's going to happen," Einar said. "I am going to back away, and you are going to move slowly towards the door, one careful step at a time. Any quick moves, and I will shoot you in the head. Don't doubt my intentions." Einar paused. "After all that has happened, killing you is exactly what I want to do right now."

Magnus slowly raised his foot to take one step forward as Einar took one step back. "That's right," Einar said, keeping him in his sights. "Each step very slow."

Einar took another step back as Magnus lifted his left foot and took another step forward. They continued this slow dance ten feet apart while Einar aimed the rifle at his head. Einar was boiling with anger and wanted Magnus dead. Although, Einar wasn't a murderer. He had never killed another human being, only sheep. Einar watched Magnus take cautious steps and wondered what his next move would be once they moved outside.

Magnus moved very slowly, very conscious of the deranged bloody Einar with hatred in his eyes. Magnus hated him too. The man had stolen his wife and raised his child. Margret had lied to Einar about the child, but it didn't matter. If Einar had never been in Margret's life, Magnus would be living with her as a family right now. Magnus had lived with so many months of jealousy festering, and the hurt was searing a hole through his heart. She had abandoned him for her silly ideas of what her life should be. Margret would pay for this one day, he thought.

Magnus stepped forward again slowly with his hands still above his head. He remembered the knife in his boot pocket. Magnus didn't come all this way to be defeated, he thought. Magnus continued walking forward slowly in tandem with Einar, wondering what his next move would be. He honestly didn't even know if he was afraid of dying. Magnus had lost his parents, his wife, his home and now his daughter. He didn't have much else to lose. The world looked at him as a failure. Magnus came back here to show Margret and his daughter that he was not a disappointment to society. He could not fail now.

Einar stepped near the threshold and halted. "You have to go through the door first," Einar said with a sharp nod. "I will move to the side and watch you go through."

Magnus nodded in agreement and moved several steps until he was under the front door threshold.

"Go on," Einar said, encouraging him.

Magnus stepped outside in the sun and snow. He looked to his right and noticed Hans was gone. Einar must have killed Hans before entering the house. But where was his body? This confused him. Magnus tried to figure out what had transpired and where his friend was. Had he gotten away in a bloody fight? Einar was covered in the man's blood. Magnus glanced ahead and saw Margret still slumped over the horse. He felt his anger boil up to the surface again. She had almost scratched his eyes out!

"Keep moving!" Einar shouted, a nervous obsession infiltrating his body. He trained the rifle on Magnus, looking down the sights and then suddenly, Magnus was gone. Einar looked up abruptly.

Magnus ducked, running to the side of the house away from the view of the doorway.

Einar cursed. "Come out, Magnus," he shouted. "I will shoot you without hesitation." Einar steadied the rifle to the entrance. He listened and heard a shuffle. Einar stepped quietly to the entrance, ready to shoot.

Another step.

Einar stepped outside and aimed to the left as Magnus jumped at him, slashing with his knife. Einar fired, the rifle recoiling then dislodging from his arms as Magnus leapt at him, his knife glinting. Einar quickly wielded Han's knife and slashed at Magnus, catching his arm coat and ripping it from his shoulder. Although Magnus was far more aggressive, stabbing out towards Einar.

Einar jumped to the side and stabbed forward. His knife connected with something solid, and Einar pulled it out roughly, holding onto his weapon. His hand was bloodied, and Magnus cursed.

Einar kicked forward, his foot connecting with Magnus's abdomen. Magnus crouched forward, exhaling with force and grabbed onto the offending foot, heaving on Einar's ankle.

Einar tried to balance and wavered, struggling to get his foot out of Magnus's grip. He pushed his foot forward forcibly into Magnus's stomach, trying to loosen the man's grip. Magnus lost balance, flying backwards and clutched his abdomen angrily. He was not going to lose this fight, Magnus thought.

Einar scuttled over to the rifle and fumbled in his belt, loading a bullet in the chamber. Magnus rushed at him, and before he could aim the gun, it clattered on the snowy ground again. Magnus stabbed out and his knife connected with Einar's upper left arm, blood spreading from the wound.

Einar slashed back at Magnus but felt the pain sting his arm sharply. His energy drained suddenly from his body, and Einar struggled to stand up, kneeling on the ground now. Magnus's eyes glinted with evil revenge.

Einar kicked out again ineffectively. He gripped the knife in his right hand and told himself to stay strong. Dizziness clouded his mind as he watched Margret shuffle off the horse.

Magnus hovered over him.

Someone hit Magnus from behind. Disorientated, Magnus turned.

Hans crashed into Magnus, stepping his legs over his looped hands and pulling them in front of his body for better leverage. The two men grappled clumsily. Hans clutched Magnus finally with his tied hands, dragging him backwards to the side of the house.

"Let me go!" Magnus yelled, trying to reach behind him. "What are you doing?"

Hans tightened the rope between his hands along Magnus's neck, the rope digging in. Magnus struggled, dropping his knife and began to fight fearfully from the strangulation attack, but Hans held him steady.

"You lied to me!" Hans yelled angrily. "You said that you were picking up your daughter and Margret. It's not even your daughter, you fool! And Margret doesn't love you anymore! You lied about everything!"

Magnus narrowed his eyes at the insulting words. Magnus kicked backwards, connecting with Han's shins.

Hans howled in pain and struck out with his elbows, dislodging his arms from around Magnus's neck. Magnus rushed at him as the gunfire sounded through the air. He didn't have time to turn around to see. The bullet slammed into his right shoulder, sending his body swinging around. Extreme pain seared down the right side of his body. Magnus yelled in agony and slumped down into the snow, leaving a trail of blood dotting the white landscape.

Einar pulled the rifle up and loaded another bullet.

"Don't shoot him again!" Hans shouted, standing in front. "I will take him back. We will leave in peace. He needs a doctor first." Hans looked down at his friend, and the amount of blood was quickly increasing. "He will die, Einar! Let me get him to a doctor, and then we'll leave."

Einar looked down the sights of his rifle as Margret limped to his side. "Are you okay, sweetheart?" he said.

"I'm sore, but I'll live," she answered, looking down at his left arm. "You are bleeding, my love." Her eyebrows bunched together with concern as she began examining the wound.

"We both need doctors," Einar said, lowering the rifle. He quickly cut the ropes around his wife's body, freeing her. She rubbed her arms as the ropes fell to the ground. Margret instantly began tending to his knife wound. She bent down, grabbed the knife and ripped a strip of cloth from the hem of her dress. Margret removed Einar's coat from his arm and wrapped the strip of fabric above the wound to slow the bleeding. Einar watched her as she lovingly attended to his wound. He rubbed the rope burns on her shoulders and kissed them gently.

Hans watched as the couple lovingly repaired each other, oblivious to the onlookers. He whispered to the semiconscious Magnus. "They really love each other, Magnus," Hans said. "It's time for us to go. We'll get a doctor, and I'll take you home."

Magnus mumbled something and groaned in anguish.

Hans looked across the snowy field past Einar's shoulder. "Can you send someone to get a doctor?" Hans asked loudly.

"Yes," Einar replied. "I will sound the bell, and my farm-hands will come. We will get Stephan and Petr to help. One of them can summon the doctor."

Margret patted his hand. "I'll do it," she said and rushed to the large bell, clanging it loudly. The sound reverberated across the fields as the injured parties all slumped tiredly in the snow.

Hans dragged Magnus a few feet away, sitting him up against the house. He bent down in front of him. "You're going to be okay," Hans said, pushing on the shoulder wound to slow the flow of blood. "A doctor is coming."

Magnus looked up, his eyes glazed over, and he lost consciousness.

Chapter 23

The summer sun was a welcome warmth on Margret's arms as she rocked Nathanael to sleep. The boy was seven months old and a little tyrant. He was always getting in trouble, even more so than Emma.

It had been a challenging year. Margret had finally healed fully from the difficult birth and hemorrhaging. Einar had stitches to close up the deep knife wound. He wasn't able to utilize his left arm for months until the wound had healed. Einar was in pain for some time; he clenched his teeth regularly and inhaled when it was too much.

Margret didn't have any injuries from the fight with Magnus other than a few ropes burns and bruises. Although, her energy was depleted so badly from the exertion. The bleeding started again soon after and had slowed her healing process. Margret had struggled along with her husband, but after a few months, the family was back on track.

Nathan fussed in her arms as she rocked him in the wooden chair outside. She covered him with a blanket and sang lightly to him. Margret had fed him, changed his soiled cloths and burped him. He still fussed, and Margret knew it was because he was tired. She rocked Nath rhythmically as he wiggled in her arms.

Margret looked out over the summer landscape. The green grass was so bright it looked like a meadow of greenery. It was a good start to the summer. They were all healed, and the past was behind them.

Magnus had returned back to Reykjavik, and Hans immediately turned him into the police. Magnus was charged with kidnapping and attempted murder. He was going to be in jail for a very long time.

Margret exhaled heavily. She was glad that chapter of her life had ended. She no longer had to be afraid of her first love. Einar had been the real love of her life, and it had taken this mountain of chaos to bring them together. They had an indestructible marriage now. Nobody could ever threaten that again. They were partners for life, and she was glad. Nothing could ever separate them, she thought.

Nathan's cries turned to grumbles, and he slowly quieted down in her arms. Margret gazed down at his sleepy eyes and felt a surge of motherly love overcome her. She loved her babies so much. Nath would be a big strong man one day, just like his father.

Margret kissed the top of his head and whispered. "I will raise you to be a good man," she said softly. "A man of integrity and passion. You'll one day be someone who will show others what it means to be a man." Margret kissed him again softly, with tears rolling down her cheeks. "Nathanael, you will pick up where others have failed. You will prove that integrity and kindness have a secure place in this world. Nathanael, I promise you this now, in this beautiful morning sun, that as your mother, I will do whatever it takes to raise you, feed you, inspire you and love you. Then the day you are a man, you will be set free to change this world and to help rid the evil that weaves into our lives, to stand up for what is right and to never back down. You will be a pillar of strength that others look up to and cherish. As your mother, I will do everything in my power to raise you right. This is my promise to you, Nathanael."

PART THREE

1873

CHAPTER 24

Nathanael looked up in the cold January wind. His mother had said that Iceland had changed a lot in the last fifteen years. The government was harsh on its citizens, putting restrictions on trade and punishing Icelanders who didn't work as hard as they thought they should. The Olasons still did well, which was a blessing in this ruinous government. But for how long, they didn't know. They had a healthy flock of sheep and a long-standing family sheep herding farm. For now, the country needed them. He knew some of his friends and neighbours weren't so lucky.

He could feel the ground rumbling again. There had been an unusual amount of magma activity in the ground lately. It was normal for Iceland, of course; he had been born and raised here in eastern Iceland, after all.

But even this much activity was unusual. It was January 3, and the wind was heavy with humidity and bone-chilling cold. Nathanael joined his father, Einar, in the fields. They were herding the sheep into the barns for shelter after allowing them out all day.

His father looked towards the south, shielding his eyes from the winds. "It seems like the magma ground activity is stronger towards the south. It's probably just Grimsvotn; that volcano won't stop tormenting us. It erupts more than anything else around here now."

Nathan gazed towards the southwest. "We should keep an eye out for it," he responded.

"Yes," Einar said confidently. "I'm not overly concerned, although it makes our daily lives difficult, it seems."

This wasn't an exaggeration, Nathan knew. Grimsvotn was a very active volcano, but it never caused massive destruction, so Icelanders were accustomed to its threats now.

"Still, Pabbi," Nathanael said. "It seems to be a bit more active than usual." Nathanael tapped a sheep with his staff lightly, herding the back of the flock into the large barn. Nathanael and Einar had built the larger barn to accommodate the expanded flock a few years back. They now had one hundred sheep and had even expanded their land to include Nathan's grandparent's farm to the north. Nathan's grandparents had passed away peacefully on a sad month in 1870. They were old and frail. First, Nathan's grandfather had passed from heart trouble. A few weeks later, his grandmother died of a broken heart. Nathan mourned their deaths heavily. They were the only family close enough for many miles, and he had loved them both dearly.

"Okay, son," Einar said loudly. "I think that's all of them. Let's get home and eat some lamb stew."

"I'm starving," Nathanael shouted as he closed the barn doors.

"You're always hungry!" Einar teased playfully. "Ever since you were born!"

Nathan chuckled. "I'm a growing man! Like mamma always says!"

"Yeah, your mamma spoils you," Einar said jokingly. "Ever since you were a baby!"

"No!" Nathan retorted, pulling his horse's reins. "She spoils Eva! She's the baby!"

"Yes," Einar nodded, mounting his horse, watching his son do the same. "Eva is the youngest. I was very surprised when we found out your mamma was pregnant again. We thought she couldn't have any more children after giving birth to you."

"Not that story again!" Nathan chided.

"That story!" Einar said. "You are lucky that your mamma is alive after delivering you. Be respectful or else." Einar shot a warning glance at his soon-to-be fifteen-year-old son.

Nathan grabbed the reins, looked down shamefully and mounted his horse. "Sorry, Pabbi," Nathan said quietly. "I love mamma. I know how much you both have been through."

"That's right," Einar said forcefully. "And don't you ever forget it."

Margret sat back and continued knitting the wool sweater. The old rocking chair creaked as she rocked back and forth. She no longer had any babies to mother, Margret chuckled. She missed the years when they were young! Emma was 16 already, Nathan was turning 15, and Eva was 12! She still couldn't believe where the time had gone.

Margret thought back to the ghastly past they had been through, and she was amazed at their strength as a family. They were one of the lucky families with a stable business. The wool industry took a few bad turns over the years, but it bounced back, and they were recovering now. The flock was back to a hundred sheep. She began knitting wool sweaters as a supplementary income five years ago. She sold the sweaters for a good price, and the wool was free. She dyed the wool with different colours and sold them to local merchants. Most of the sweaters were later sold at the Reykjavik market. She even noticed some people wearing the garments in the town of Horn.

The children started going to school at the age of six. The school was nothing more than a barn, really. The teachers were an unorganized collection of local mothers and grandfathers. Margret volunteered her time as well. All of her children were literate and well educated. She continually taught them everything she had learnt from Pappa so long ago. Margret was proud of her family and everything they had accomplished.

Magnus still remained behind bars. The justice system was rather severe in Iceland. Some had said he should have been executed for his crimes. Margret did not want to comment on such things. He wasn't in their lives anymore, and that's all that mattered. Hopefully, Magnus would be an old man when he gets out. She was content with this.

"Mamma!" Eva shouted from the bedrooms.

"What is it, my dear?" Margret responded.

"Nath says it felt like an earthquake in the fields yesterday!" Eva screeched overdramatically.

"We live in Iceland, dear," Margret said calmly.

"I know, Mamma," Eva said respectfully. "But he said it's been a lot lately."

Margret looked towards the front window. "Where is Nath? Are they still outside?"

"Yes," Eva responded. "He said it is worse near the barn."

"Oh my," Margret said. "Maybe one of you should go and tell them to return."

"I will go," Eva said, grabbing her coat and wrapping her boots on. As she reached for the door, a loud explosion sounded in the distance, rattling the house.

Margret stood in panic. "What was that?"

"I don't know!" Eva said anxiously, peering out the door. Nathan and Einar were running in a panic back to the house. "Something is going on!" she shouted.

Margret peered outside, dropping the wool sweater absent-mindedly. There was a plume of ash spreading rapidly from the southeast. "It must be Grimsvotn," Margret said. "Einar was warning us about that volcano."

Nath shouted from the field. "Get inside!"

Einar ran beside him and waved his arm towards the plume. "Grimsvotn is erupting! We felt the explosion. Get inside!"

Margret ushered them both in and closed the door. "Oh my Lord!"

Nath excitedly relayed the events. "We were slaughtering a sheep when all of a sudden, the ground started shaking!" Nath said breathlessly. "It felt like an earthquake!"

"I think it was an earthquake!" Einar interrupted.

"The fields actually heaved!" Nathan yelled.

"Now, I wouldn't say that," Einar countered.

"Yes," Nathan said. "They did! I saw. The ground moved, Pabbi!"

"Possibly an earthquake then," Einar said.

Margret locked the door as if that would somehow help them. She peered out the window and saw the cloud of ash coming toward them. "What do we do?" she asked.

"We stay inside until the eruption is over," Einar instructed.

"Is that wise?" Margret asked worriedly.

"We have no choice," Einar said.

Margret nodded. She knew he was referring to the old escape boat and dock that had fallen into disrepair. The emergency boat Einar had built with Pappa seventeen years ago was unusable, and the wood was rotting. "We need to prepare for this again," she said, nodding towards the ocean.

Nathanael looked towards the ocean. "Is that what that old ruined boat was for; our emergency escape?" he asked.

"Yes," Margret replied. "Your father built that with your grandpa Jon years before you were born. The magma activity of Hekla was the biggest concern back then." She waved her arms around to demonstrate the widespread activity. "It seems to have increased more and more over the years, and now it's Grimsvotn, which is much closer to us, and Askja is directly to the east."

"Askja hasn't erupted in hundreds of years," Einar pointed out.

"Yes, that's what Pappa Jon used to always say," Margret countered. "But you were always the one who was disputing that Askja could blow one day."

"Yes, but Askja always remained dormant," Einar answered. "My theories were wrong."

"Maybe they weren't," Margret said solemnly.

Nathanael listened to the exchange, worry blanketing his face. "Pabbi," he said. "I want to fix the emergency boat and dock tomorrow. Even if we have to buy some more wood, we must do this. We are surrounded by magma activity now."

"Yes," Margret said, nodding. "It is prudent to do so, my dear. We must provide a means of escape and maintain it, even if it is never used. We must make this a priority." She pointed at the window. "What is that?"

Everyone rushed to the window. "It looks like tiny tephra and ash," Einar said. "We are lucky it's not the large tephra."

"What's tephra?" Emma asked as she joined the commotion from the back.

"There's an eruption happening, my dear," Margret said worriedly, glancing quickly toward her daughter.

"Oh my Lord!" Emma said, rushing to the window. "What happened?"

"It's Grimsvotn," Nathan explained. "This is worse than any other eruptions we've seen."

Emma traced her finger on the glass. "That's ash," she stated.

"It is," Einar said solemnly. "It is light tephra. We're lucky."

"Will the house be okay?" Emma asked. "Will we be alright?"

"I think so," Nathan replied. "It is not large tephra, just the ash."

"Isn't it hot?"

"I suppose it is," Nathan replied. "Let's sit still inside, away from the windows. We should be protected; most of our home is built inside the hill, and the landscape is covered with cold snow."

"Okay," Emma said calmly. "It's still scary, Mamma."

"It is, Emma," Margret replied, her voice steady but worried. "It definitely is."

Chapter 25

Nathan hammered the long nails in as Einar pressed the wood together. They worked as a team, building the new boat. They had travelled to the north island and purchased nails and wood. It was a hefty price because of the government trading rules, but they had no choice. They couldn't make boats out of grass, he thought.

"I can see now why you never maintained the boat," Nathan said. "The wood is so expensive!"

"Iceland has been importing wood for centuries," Einar said as he concentrated on holding the next two pieces together. "It is one of the most expensive imports in this country. There are no trees left in Iceland to cut. It has been like this for centuries. The original settlers used all the natural wood long ago. This current government is not making it any easier by restricting trade."

"I heard of the trading changes," Nathan said, then his eyes brightened with an idea. "Maybe we could plant trees!"

"We can," Einar said, resting momentarily and flipping his longish hair to the side. "It's just some of the land is not suitable. Iceland is made from lava flow."

"Oh, yeah," Nathan said. "I never thought of that."

Nathan hammered the next nail in, then helped his father haul some more wood closer to the shoreline. They could not build the dock yet because it was still winter. They had dismantled the old dock pieces and the boat, reusing what wood they could. They worked tirelessly in the cold January winds, going back to the house every hour to warm up. The light snow lashed at their faces as they worked on the boat.

Einar looked up, standing back and examined the partially built boat. "I think this is good enough for today," he said. "We have gotten a lot done in only a week. This boat will be big enough for all of us and a few sheep."

Nathanael nodded, ready to return to the warmth of the house. They had been outside for over an hour, and the sun had already set, even though it was only mid-afternoon. Nathan wasn't a fan of the winter darkness. In January, there were only four hours of daylight. The sun rose just before noon and set in mid-afternoon. It left only a small window of workable hours.

Einar packed up the tools and headed to the shed with Nathanael in tow.

"We will get this done soon," Nathan said optimistically. "Tomorrow, we'll have another four daylight hours to work on it."

"By the end of January, we should have six hours of daylight," Einar said. "I'm hoping we have it done by then, and we can start working on the dock structure. We'll have to remove it every year, of course, and place it securely up the hill to prevent it from getting washed away in the winter ice flows. That is all we can do."

Nathan nodded and looked over the mountains at the already setting sun. "We should get back now."

"Yes, son," Einar said, patting Nathan's upper back. "I'm grateful to have you by my side, Nathan."

Nathanael smiled. "Of course, I'll always stand by you and mamma and my sisters."

"Your mamma raised you right," Einar replied, smiling.

Nathan nodded. "Hopefully, this boat will serve us well," Nath said. "Even if we don't ever use it for escape, we can always go fishing with it."

In early 1874, steam clouds were seen above Mount Askja. Nobody knew what was going on. The Olasons couldn't see the top of Askja from their property, but they all noticed a cloud above the horizon over the western sky.

In the autumn of 1874, things dramatically worsened with a series of earthquakes ripping through the northern part of the island, causing panic but not resulting in much damage.

Until December 1874, then the earthquakes grew in activity. A very dangerous situation started developing for the residents of northern Iceland. Margret had received an urgent message from Aunt Helga and Uncle Sig. Their town and their home were severely damaged by the earthquakes. The seismic activity had created a dike in the ground running from the northern part of the island up towards Mount Askja. There were several reports of ground deformation, and the situation was becoming dire in the north.

Margret reached up and fitted a wool hat onto Nath's head. "Be safe, my son," she said worriedly.

"I will, mamma," he replied calmly.

"You must return with your aunt and uncle," she said. "They are the only relatives we have left other than Johanna in Reykjavik. Your pabbi has to stay home this time. We need him here if another eruption happens. Make sure Stephan and Petr travel with you." She patted his arms and kissed him on the cheek. "Be strong and wise. Bring your aunt and uncle home to live with us. Make sure you have extra room in the boat for their belongings."

Nathan wrapped his arms around his mother, hugging her tight. "I will bring back Auntie and Uncle Sig. Don't worry, Mamma."

Margret looked worriedly into her son's eyes. "There may be more earthquakes. Be extremely vigilant once you arrive on land."

"I will, Mamma."

Travelling by boat was swift. Nathan and his helpers reached the small northern town in just a few hours. But when they arrived, they were unsure where the settlement was. Aunt Helga and Uncle Sig's village was destroyed entirely. The young men stopped and pulled the boat up onto the shore. There was rubble, debris and rocks everywhere. Nathan disembarked and sifted his hand through the black dirt. The land was deformed by the seismic activity. Ridges and dikes formed in straight and random lines, some connected, some not. Nathan looked up. The rubble did not look like a town or even a settlement. It looked like a war zone.

Nathan straightened and turned to Stephan. "We have to ask people where the survivors are being housed."

Stephan nodded and pointed towards the northeast, where fog clouds rose over the scattering of houses still intact. "Let's go there," he said. "It looks like there are residents over on the east side of the debris."

Nathan and his crew climbed across the debris towards the broken town. It was a laborious task, but they were young and fit. The group arrived at the town thirty minutes later, noticing that only a handful of people seemed to be the only ones alive. A chill ran up his spine. Was he too late to rescue his aunt and uncle?

Several people sat motionless on the front porch in disbelief from the earthquake's destruction. Nathan wanted to help them all, but he simply couldn't. They continued on until they reached a small group forming near a bakery shop.

Nathan asked the people calmly, "I am here to pick up my aunt and uncle Petersson. Does anyone know of them?"

"I heard some of the Peterssons fled eastward," a small woman replied.

A man spoke. "My wife is right. Several survivors have fled east, approximately two miles to a large homestead. They are staying there temporarily. You might want to try that. The homestead is the Kristjansson's, a large sheep farmer to the east. Keep going until you see the grey brick house and the red sign showing the Kristjansson sheep farm."

"Thank you, sir!" Nathan replied. He walked through the sparsely populated town until they again reached the countryside.

"This doesn't look good," Petr said, running to catch up to Nathan.

"You're right," Nathan said. "It looks like a major earthquake happened here. I hope they are both alright."

"I hope so too," Petr replied.

They hiked on for another hour until they saw the red sign in the distance. The cold wind blew in their faces as they hiked over debris towards the homestead. After several brutal minutes of walking against the fierce wind, they arrived near the large property. The men were tiring, Nathan knew.

"Let's go to the entrance," Nathan instructed as he hiked up the hill, his stomach burning from hunger. "We are almost there."

As they walked up the hill, seismic activity began, with the earth shaking lightly under their feet. Stephan and Petr glanced at Nathan. "It's okay," Nathan said. "Keep going until we are at the homestead. We are outdoors. It's safer than being in a house during an earthquake. Everything would be falling on our heads indoors. Just make sure to watch your step; I saw ground deformation."

Stephan and Petr nodded in agreement as they all cautiously hiked to the large homestead. The ground moved slightly beneath their feet, and all three men were alarmed. The house in front of them started shaking, and falling debris could be heard coming from the home.

"Hurry, we have to save the people inside!" Nathan shouted, running to the entrance. Stephan and Petr followed behind in a panic.

When Nathan reached the large home, several people ran out, yelling, their arms and shoulders bloodied. Nathan hollered into the crowd forming at the entrance. "Aunt Helga!" he shouted. A tight group of people pushed the mob out as several individuals fell outside over top of each other. Some people got up immediately and ran into the fields in a panic. Nathan scanned the crowd for his aunt and uncle. Disappointedly, he couldn't find them. He shouted again. "Uncle Sig! It's Nathan!"

A strong seismic movement seized them all, and Nathan fought to stay standing as several people toppled to the ground. It was chaotic as people clawed over others and then ran out shouting, "Earthquake!"

Nathan tried to stay clear of the panicked crowds, but he needed to get inside the house to find his aunt and uncle. He shouldered his way into the crowds against the momentum of people pushing outwards. Suddenly, a crack sounded overhead as a section of the outside wall broke. Nathan jumped back, narrowly missing the collapse of the entire front entrance. Several people lay underneath the rubble. Nathan stood squarely, trying to stay calm and looked behind him for the other two men. Stephan was helping Petr back up. One of them had a slight cut on the forehead. Nathan inspected himself, and he appeared to be fine.

He bent down and spoke to a fallen elder. "Are you okay?"

"My leg," the old man said.

Nathan bent down and wrapped the man's arm around his shoulder. "Hold on to me," he said as he led the man to safety. Nathan returned and dug in the rubble, throwing roof and wall sections off of the victims. Stephan rushed over to help as they freed many of the survivors. Some people stood on their own and walked away, but some, unfortunately, were motionless. Nathan swallowed hard and yelled again. "Anyone see my aunt Helga?"

"Helga?" a young girl answered. "Yes, there was a Helga in the kitchen."

"Is she still inside?" Nathan asked, his voice pitching.

"I don't see her out here!" the girl responded, glancing back as she ran towards the open fields.

Nathan removed several large pieces of building rubble with Stephan and Petr. They worked hard at clearing the debris for several minutes. The minutes turned into almost an hour before they could see the inside of the ruined homestead. Nathan surged into the house, squeezing through a narrow entrance of rubble. He looked right and then left. Several people were huddled, crying and screaming. Nathan looked straight ahead into the back kitchen.

"Nathan?" a voice shouted.

Nathan looked up and ran towards Aunt Helga, grasping her by the shoulder. She was limping with blood running down her left leg. "Aunt Helga!" Nathan yelled. "It's Nathan! Where's Uncle Sig?"

Helga pointed. "He was inside in the living area before the wall collapsed!" she shouted in a panic. "Find him, please, Nathan!"

"We will find him!" Nathan replied as Stephan and Petr rushed to the living area. "Don't worry! We will get him out too. Can you walk?"

"I think so," Helga said uncertainly, taking one step forward as her left leg buckled.

Nathan reached forward and grasped her by the armpits and knees. "I will lift you," he said. "Wrap your arms around my neck." Nathan shifted his weight steady to both his feet. He was a tall teenager, already six feet tall and his body was very slim, almost skinny. Although, he had lots of strength in his arms and legs. Nathan bit his lip and groaned, lifting aunt Helga out of the semi-collapsed house. People parted for him to exit. "Coming through! Make room! Have an injured person here. Out of the way!" Nathan shouted.

Nathan struggled to get out of the house, but finally, he stepped through the wider entrance that people had begun clearing. He placed Helga down on the ground as far away from the house as possible. "Are you okay?" he said, bending down to look into her eyes.

"I think I'm okay, except for my leg," she said, squinting through the pain. "Several support beams fell on me as I was helping cook."

"Let's see," Nathan said, ripping the layers of clothing from her leg. Aunt Helga's knee was cut and bloodied, but nothing looked broken. "I think you'll be alright. It looks like you bruised your knee. It will most likely be wobbly for some time until the joint heals."

"Thank you for coming, Nathan," she said suddenly.

Nathan smiled. "Of course, I am here to help," he said. "I love you both. You're family. We are here to take you home. Mamma said you'll be living with us. It's safer on the east side."

Helga hugged him fiercely. "Thank you!" she said, tears forming in her eyes. "We've been through so much. You have no idea how happy I am to see you."

"Where are your things?" Nathan asked. "I can go in and get them. We have made room in the boat for your luggage."

Helga wiped the tears from her eyes. "Nath, there's nothing left," she said solemnly. "We ran out of our house moments before it collapsed. It is a pile of rubble. We tried sifting through the rubble, but the earthquakes wouldn't stop. We had to run for our lives. The clothes we are wearing are all we have left."

Nathan grimaced. "I'm so sorry, Helga," he said.

"Nathan!" Stephan shouted.

Nathan spun around and saw Stephan and Petr helping Uncle Sig limp out of the house.

"Sig, my dear!" Helga yelled. "Oh my Lord, you're alive!"

Nathan rushed over to the group and hugged his uncle, taking over from Petr and wrapping his uncle's arm around his shoulder. "Are you okay, Uncle Sig?" he asked.

Sig coughed repeatedly from all the dust and debris. "Yes, I think I'm alright," he said. "I don't know. Your friends found me under the rubble. I could barely breathe!"

"You are safe now," Nathan said, saying a silent prayer of thanks in his head. "Good job, men!" he said to Stephan and Petr.

The brothers nodded. Stephan spoke first. "We should help others out before we leave," he said.

"I agree," Nathan replied. "Let's put Uncle Sig down on the ground near Helga, then go back in and help rescue more survivors."

Helga and Sig sat on the snow watching as Nathan, and a large group of young men hauled debris and helped survivors out. It took many hours, but finally, as the late afternoon darkness settled across the land, they had rescued over thirty people in total. Four people had died directly from the collapse. It was a somber day but one with hope for the future of the survivors.

Nathan was exhausted, and they all camped outside, eating sausages that all the rescuers had been given from the large Kristjansson sheep farm disaster.

"You are heroes," Helga said between bites of blood sausage.

"No," Nathan said. "We are just Icelanders helping others. I'm sure every single man and woman here would have done the same."

"True," Helga answered. "Well, Nathanael, I am so glad you are here and are taking us somewhere safe. It's been a horrible week."

"I know it has," Nathan said with empathy. "You've been through enough." Nathanael patted her arm and looked towards the oceanside. "We're taking you home. Our boat is a sturdy vessel. The seas are safer than this land lately."

CHAPTER 26

Margret couldn't sleep well for some reason. It was March 20, 1875, and she fidgeted in bed, anxiety wreaking havoc with her mind. She sat up and looked over at her sleeping husband. Margret loved him with all her heart, but he was a stubborn man. They had argued for weeks about leaving the area. He refused to give up the successful sheep farm. Margret had reasoned that they could sell all the sheep, move to another country and build a life in a geographically safer land.

He had said they wouldn't get anything for the land.

This was true, Margret thought. The seismic activity had made the northern parts of the island unlivable, and the eastern regions were constantly under threat from Mount Askja now.

The once sleepy giant had started erupting, and it sent a chill through Margret's entire body. As if her entire existence on this land, all the hard decisions she had made her entire life, led to these final decisions of staying or fleeing from this volcanic island.

In early January, several powerful earthquakes rocked northern Iceland again, then swiftly following, the seismic activity had caused an eruption at the top of Mount Askja. They had witnessed the huge eruption cloud and sought shelter immediately. As with Grimsvotn, ash fell down with little damage. The farm was over eighty miles from the peak of Mount Askja, but it was still too close for her liking.

Another eruption followed immediately, just north of Mount Askja at Fjarholahraun. Some people said they could see small areas of lava flow forming towards the northeastern villages. The earthquakes had already severely damaged northern Iceland.

Aunt Helga and Uncle Sig were eternally grateful for the rescue and for having a home to live in with Margret's family.

Margret loved her Aunt Helga, but she didn't seem to understand that their sheep farm was not situated safely on the eastern shore of Iceland. Nobody agreed with her except her son Nathanael. He had seen the severity of the earthquakes and had been standing on the ground while it was moving. Margret was grateful and proud of her son. He voiced his opinion in conjunction with his mother, although their words often fell upon deaf ears to the rest of the family.

Nathan was frustrated but always went out vigilantly to the boat every day to make sure it was maintained and ready when, or if, they needed it.

On February 18, things changed, and her husband started listening to her. A rift eruption occurred on the northern part of the island at the Sveinagja fissure, with lava flowing down onto the northern areas. The graben, an elongated block of the earth's crust that was lifted into a rift from the earthquakes, had three more rift eruptions in March, almost one every week. The lava was coating the northern island in liquid fire.

Margret padded into the kitchen and was surprised to find Uncle Sig and Nathan awake. She kissed Nathan on the cheek. "Good morning, sweetheart," she said.

"Good morning, Mamma," Nathan said stonily.

Margret eyed Uncle Sig suspiciously. She could sense the tension in the room.

Uncle Sig spoke first. "The eruptions of the northern areas aren't affecting the eastern regions," he argued.

Nathan pursed his lips in frustration. "Mamma," he said. "I won't argue with Uncle Sig any longer. He doesn't understand how dangerous Mount Askja is!"

"It's a dormant volcano!" Uncle Sig cried. "It has never done anything in recent history, except the small eruption we saw."

Nathan slammed his palm flat down on the table. "That is exactly why it is so dangerous!" Nathan said angrily. "I studied the magma activity and how Iceland's volcanoes have built and destroyed this island. The pressure underneath a sleeping giant is the greatest threat! Not the lava flows to the north!"

Uncle Sig stood up angrily, opened his mouth then stopped. He was staying with his niece's family by the grace of God, and Nathan was the man who had saved himself and Helga. He would respectfully remain silent. Sig frowned, then stomped down the hall without another word.

Margret watched her uncle retreat to his bedroom. When he was out of earshot, she spoke. "I agree with you," she said. "I think it is time we made plans to leave before we also lose our land and, God forbid, our lives."

Nathan sat down. "Where would we go?"

"I have heard good things about Canada," Margret explained. "The new country is seeking immigrants, and a large boat voyage for Icelanders is being discussed. An explorer named Sig Jonasson is already in Canada. I heard that he may be spearheading an immigration plan."

"Canada is so far!" Nathan exclaimed.

"I know," Margret said calmly, sitting at the table with her son. "I don't know if I want to leave either." She looked down at her hands folded delicately on her lap. She had aged beautifully, and her slim fingers laced together. "I have something to tell you that I never thought you would ever need to know, but I think it is time you understood our past. You will be a grown man soon."

"What is it?" Nathan asked.

"Before Emma was born," she explained slowly. "I dated a man named Magnus before I married your father. I've known your father all my life, but I was foolish, young, and I fell in love with a bad man."

Nathan looked at his mother with sympathy in his eyes. "Go on," he said.

"Magnus was kind and romantic in the beginning," she said. "I didn't know until later that he was a troubled man, and he tried to hurt me physically. Einar saved me and fought with him, knocking him unconscious."

"Way to go, Pabbi!" Nathan cried, laughing.

Margret shook her head. "No," she said. "It wasn't funny. I thought he had killed Magnus. But thankfully, he had not. Regardless, I left him and married your father." Margret paused, wondering how to explain the horrible parts of the story. "Well, Magnus came back the next year claiming that Emma was his daughter and tried to kidnap your sister and me."

"Mamma!" Nathan stood up in shock. "Why didn't you tell me?"

"There was no reason to," she said. "It was in the past, and you were a baby at the time."

Nathan paused and thought about something briefly. "Is Emma his daughter?" he asked incredulously. "Is she my half-sister?"

"No," Margret answered. "I miscarried, and then I became pregnant with Emma."

Nathan sat back down thoughtfully. "So if it doesn't matter because it is in the past," he asked. "Why are you telling me all this now?"

Margret shifted uncomfortably in the chair. "Well," she stated slowly. "I was told just recently that he is being released from prison on parole at the end of next year. The courts were rather harsh with his sentence, so he spent a long time in jail, but now it is nearing the time that he will be released tentatively."

Nathan looked into his mother's eyes. "This is why you want to leave," he stated.

Margret grimaced. "I want to leave because my island, my home, my only life, is exploding, and I don't want my children to die buried in a flow of liquid fire." She paused momentarily, curling an errant strand of hair behind her ear. "But I also don't want to be on this island when he gets out either." She stood and walked to the counter, pouring herself a cup of water. Margret drank the water, then turned, leaning against the counter. "Nathan, you must understand that decisions like this are made with a multitude of reasons. One reason is sometimes not good enough, but several together form one solid conclusion. It is the adult way of making decisions."

"I understand, Mamma," Nathan stood and walked over to his mother. He leaned over and hugged her gently. "I'm sorry that this all happened to you. I will never allow anyone to harm you again. I will always be by your side, Mamma. You are one of the smartest people I know."

Margret laced her arms around him, hugging him back. She felt hot tears roll down her cheeks. She was so grateful for her son. He was growing into a strong man with integrity and a kind heart. "Thank you, Nathanael," she said, her voice thick with emotion. "Always be the good man that you are growing into becoming. Don't ever change because somebody tells you who you shouldn't be. Deep down, your soul will always know what is right. Trust who you are inside, and don't hesitate to make it known to the world. I love you, son."

After a large sheep's head dinner, the entire family relaxed, discussing the current state of their beloved island. The discussion became heated again, but Einar was siding with Margret and Nathan now. He had sold many of the sheep after the rift explosions to a farmer in southern Iceland. The man had sent a team of herders last week and took the majority of the sheep. Einar had negotiated for him to leave ten sheep, just in case the family stayed and the volcanic activity settled down.

It was a matter of waiting to see what happened next.

On the evening of March 28, phreatic precursor activity started at Mount Askja, sending water clouds into the air. At 9 pm, a subplinian explosion occurred. The explosion was heard, and everyone rushed to the window. Margret was alarmed as she watched a rising column of gases, water and fragments extend into the sky above Mount Askja. A chill ran up her spine as she touched Einar's arm. "We must leave," she said quietly.

Einar glanced at his wife and knew in his heart that she was right. He looked back at the rising column and knew they didn't stand a chance of being buried under thick tephra. Just the gases themselves could kill them all instantly. He smoothed her hair and kissed the top of her head. "Pack the essentials and let's go now," he said solemnly. "We will leave by boat to Reykjavik. We can return once the volcanic activity is over. Maybe it won't be as bad as it seems, but we will leave for our own safety."

She kissed his shoulder. "Thank you for being the man that you are," Margret said. "I will tell the others."

The family rushed to pack one piece of luggage each, food rations for the boat trip and water. They spent hours preparing for the boat ride, some arguing about what to take and others not sure what to do.

Nathan felt the emergency chill his soul. He knew his mother was right. Somehow, she knew all along, and he was certain this was a race against time. Nathan pulled his small luggage of clothes to the front door, returning to grasp his sister's luggage containers as well. Emma and Eva were nervous and afraid. He hugged them both. "It'll be alright," he said. "We'll get out of here in time."

"Is it really that urgent?" Emma asked. "This has been going on for months."

"Yes, Emma," Nathan answered. "I believe it is time to leave. Dormant volcanoes are the most dangerous types. These old volcanoes have a cap on the top, but underneath, the magma is building stronger and stronger, creating a massive amount of pressure. We can't be anywhere near Mount Askja when it blows. No one will survive."

Emma blinked. "Okay," she said. "I believe you and mamma know what is best."

"Let's go," he said, gesturing for his sisters to go ahead of him.

Uncle Sig stood angrily at the kitchen table. "I am not going," Sig said. Aunt Helga stood beside him, uncertainty filling her demeanour.

Einar stopped and put down his luggage. "Look, it's almost midnight," he said. "If you want to stay, then that is your choice. Just know that we will be taking the only means of escape with us. If you choose to stay, there will be no escape, Uncle Sig." Einar stood firmly at the door. "None at all. You will be buried in ash and tephra. If you are right and nothing terrible happens, you can tell us when we return next month to survey the damage." Einar rushed to help Margret to pack a food container for them all. He turned his head towards Sig. "We are doing this for our own safety, our own lives. You both can choose what you wish to do with your lives. That is your right."

Helga sat down heavily on the kitchen chair. "I'm going with them, Sig," she said quietly. "I have experienced how this island can kill its inhabitants. I don't want to experience it one last time." She stood defiantly and rushed to her room to pack.

Uncle Sig slumped his shoulders. "Alright," he relented. "I will leave too." He walked slowly to the hall and disappeared into the back bedroom with Helga.

Once all the belongings were gathered at the front door, Margret draped her favourite wool coat over her shoulder and picked up her luggage. Nathan grabbed his belongings along with one of the food containers. Einar grabbed the other food container and his own bag. "Everyone needs to carry their own luggage to the boat," Einar said loudly. "We will stop to ensure the horses and sheep have enough feed, just in case. It's unfortunate, but we don't have room to take the animals with us. Nathan and I will open the fencing so the animals can flee to their own safety, if necessary. Otherwise, we will be back in a month's time."

The family nodded and proceeded out the door. The night was black, and the fields were barren with a mix of ice and earth showing. The spring season was abnormally warm, and the thaw was happening more quickly than usual. Maybe it was because of all the magma fires, Nathan thought. He hiked behind his mother and father, intent on making it to the boat as quickly as possible.

No one spoke. They all just accepted the grim conclusion of what they were doing. Light, moist ash was falling, and they all covered their heads as they stopped for the animals, opening the corrals. Some of the horses followed them to the boat, and a few sheep followed as well. Nathan patted his horse's neck. "You can't come," Nathan cooed. "I need you to take care of the farm, okay? Run if you need to." The horse's large dark eyes looked into Nathan's as if to answer.

Nathan turned and pulled the boat into the ocean with Einar. Slowly, they all embarked. At 3 am, they set sail for Reykjavik. The large swells of the North Atlantic Ocean propelled them and held promises of a dangerous journey. The water sloshed onto the boat, and it crested with every wave. Nathan struggled to steer the boat and made a mental note to go fishing more. By his calculations, they would arrive in Reykjavik sometime in the evening.

He had built the boat well. There didn't seem to be any leaks, and it fared better than most in the chaotic convergence of the Atlantic and Arctic Oceans. Everyone held onto the sides as the boat travelled south.

By 5:30 am, they had only travelled approximately 30 miles when they heard the large phreatoplinian explosion. They all turned in panic to stare at the catastrophic blast behind them.

The explosion lasted for almost an hour, spewing gases, water and fragments of tephra. They all stood fixated, watching in disbelief; it was the largest explosion any of them had ever seen. The column rose over 20 miles high and drifted over eastern Iceland, where they had just come from. The cloud grew larger and larger, encompassing a massive area over parts of the ocean. They steered the boat south, away from the expanding cloud of dangerous tephra and gases.

The ash was wet and sticky as it hit the mainland. The phreatic activity was most likely from the deep geothermal water. Pyroclastic flows began dangerously burying everything in its path. A caldera was left at the top of Mount Askja, the volcano losing its peak as it was blown to pieces and raining down onto the land and ocean. The grey whitish cloud of gases rolled into a larger and larger mass as Nathan steered the sails into the wind to gain speed. Luck was on their side, the winds were strong, and the sails billowed, racing the family to safety.

From the shelter of the south winds, they watched as the pyroclastic flows consumed their livelihoods, everything they had worked hard for, their animals were surely all dead, and their homestead buried. No one spoke a word. The sadness was too much to bear. They just stared at the ferocity of nature in disbelief and panic.

After a thirty-minute pause, another plinian explosion echoed across the island, releasing another cloud 20 miles into the air. This cloud was billowing in the same manner but released dry ash. Pyroclastic flows fountained from new rifts and vents, surging terror on anything in its way.

Margret hugged Einar, shivering. "We got out in time," she said, her words sending a chill through every single person on the boat.

"Thanks to you, my sweet," Einar said lovingly, kissing her on the forehead.

They arrived in Reykjavik at dusk. Several deckhands at the large fishery port grabbed the boat's rope and tied the vessel to the dock.

They saw the fear-stricken family and knew right away. News of the Mount Askja explosion had reached Reykjavik quickly. The locals weren't even sure that anyone had survived. The blast was heard from the south part of the island.

One young man spoke first. "You must be survivors of Mount Askja!" he exclaimed, hurriedly ushering them safely onto the dock.

"Yes," Nathan said. "Yes, we are."

"Do you all have somewhere to go?" the young man asked.

Einar nodded. "We need to find the Olasfsson fishery," Einar said. "My wife's aunt Johanna will take us in."

The young man laughed. "Well, you're in luck," he said. "I work for the Olasfsson fishery. I will take you to Johanna's. She lives only a few blocks away from the fishery."

Chapter 27

They had stayed in Reykjavik much longer than expected. It wasn't safe to return to the eastern parts of Iceland yet. The explosion had left two yards of thick ash in the caldera. Even ninety miles downwind, along the eastern shoreline areas, they were told that an inch of tephra had covered every living or dead thing. The Mount Askja eruptions had lasted a terrifying seventeen hours, sending a volcanic cloud of ash eastward all the way to Scandinavia. After the large explosion, volcanic eruptions continued from the Sveinagja fissure in April. Then only one smaller eruption from Mount Askja occurred in mid-May, and the land settled down somewhat.

During the last days of May, there was a booth set up near the Sunday market providing information for Icelanders regarding Canadian immigration. Margret, Einar and Nathan stood at the booth listening to the agents, learning about the details.

A boat would be leaving in a few weeks' time. The cost per person was exorbitantly high.

Einar stood back and shook his head. "We cannot afford this for all of us, Margret," he said.

"We sold all the sheep, except for the ten," Margret countered.

"Yes," Einar said. "But we cannot use all of our life savings on this trip!"

Margret squeezed his hand thoughtfully as they walked away. "But what shall we do here in Reykjavik? Nathan has started successfully fishing with the boat, but it's not enough money for all of us." She dropped her head in dismay. "Maybe we should make our decision after we move back to our homestead or whatever is left of it."

Nathan overheard the exchange and felt empathy for his parents. He was trying all he could to raise enough money for the family, but the prospect of moving to a different country intrigued him. They would no longer have to live in fear of nature. "I could go to Canada with Pabbi," Nathan offered. "We are strong men. We would save money that way and send for the rest of the family once we were all settled. If we failed, we could always return."

Both Margret and Einar mulled over his words in their heads as they walked back to the fishery.

Nathan walked faster to keep up with them. When he was alongside them, he spoke again. "If we never try, Pabbi, we'll never know what kind of life we could have had."

Einar nodded and kissed his wife's hand. "We'll see," he said noncommittally. "I'd like to see what is left of our property in Horn first. We can set sail tomorrow."

The group continued walking until they neared the fishery and Johanna's house. It was a short pleasant walk, and the sun was shining.

Nathan ran up ahead and opened the door to the large home.

"What took you so long coming back?" a young man asked, jumping off the sofa.

Nathan chuckled as his cousin, Kristjan, bounded strongly towards him. Johanna had remarried and had a son later in life. Kristjan was only a few years older than Nathan.

Another cousin, Viktor, stood up from the sofa with his brother, Aron. They were the sons of Olafur, his uncle. Nath enjoyed his father's stories about Aron when he was a tiny infant in Reykjavik. Apparently, his mamma couldn't put baby Aron down when she first saw him. Well, he was a very large man now, Nath chuckled. Aron was the tallest and heftiest of them all! Nathan was already six feet tall, and he had to look up to talk to Aron. He estimated the man was well over six feet, maybe even six foot four inches tall.

Nathan smiled inwardly. He enjoyed the closeness of family. Nath had grown quite warm to them all, and they had become some of his best friends. The cousins came to Horn sometimes, helping the family during the earlier years, and they all bonded well.

"Let's go fishing!" Viktor shouted. "I was waiting for you!"

"Okay, okay," Nathan replied, turning to his mamma. "We'll catch some fish for dinner. Don't worry, Mamma. I'll bring the boat back, and we'll leave in the morning to see what we have left of our farm."

Margret hugged Nathan. "Go spend time with your cousins," she said. "Hopefully, everything will work out in the end."

They left by boat to their old homestead the next Monday, choosing to spend some last moments with family before embarking on the journey back. The seas were just as rough as the first journey, but the boat was even stronger than before. Nathan had fixed it even better, installing a bench for sitting while fishing and places to secure the nets. They arrived in the early morning the following day.

Aunt Helga and Uncle Sig decided to settle on their own in a house in the city of Reykjavik. The only people on the boat were Margret, Einar, Nathan, Emma and Eva. They held hope in their hearts that their homestead was still livable.

As the boat neared the shoreline, their hearts sank. The land was covered in a thick blanket of ash, now hardened into the earth. It was a sickening greyish black colour. The green meadows were all gone.

They stepped out of the boat and pulled it onto the land that looked nothing like the homestead they once had.

Margret felt her eyes moisten, and she tried hard to stop the flow of tears, but it was hopeless. Einar wrapped his arm around her and squeezed her tight as the small family surveyed the damage.

They walked up the hillside onto the strange-looking new earth. They walked and walked but couldn't determine where the house once stood.

Einar stopped and held Margret as they scanned the strange fields. After quiet deliberation, they guessed where the house was buried and where the animals would most likely have perished.

Nathan hugged his sisters as they wept.

There was nothing left, nothing at all.

In mid-June, they had sold their land for almost nothing to the government and moved to a small settlement thirty miles south. It was a tiny house that they could barely afford with no running water and very little useable land. They bought three sheep, but the current government in Iceland made it incredibly difficult to prosper from nothing.

Margret cried as she held her husband for the last time in the morning. They had made sweet love the night before and held onto each other for dear life.

"You will be okay," Einar said. "We will send for you to come to Canada as soon as we are able. Don't worry, my love. The neighbours know us well. They know of the contributions we made to the economy in the past. They respect you."

Margret inhaled sharply. "I will miss you so much," she said, her eyes moistening again.

Einar kissed her gently and positioned himself over top of her. He ran his large hands over her abdomen and then slipped his penis into her one last time. She cried out in passion as her husband released his love inside her. They kissed, tears mixing with their saliva. Margret's heart thumped in her chest as she realized the full magnitude of what they were setting out to do.

"We're leaving our home in Iceland," she said sadly, whispering into his shoulder. "One day, we'll all be gone and living in a different country."

"Yes," Einar said, kissing her neck. "Don't worry. We will have a bright future. You must continue to believe that."

The large immigration ship sailed slowly towards the dock in the distance. Margret held her husband's hand. She turned and grasped her son's hand too. They walked bravely across the field to the dock, the entire family hand in hand. Emma and Eva were on either side of the family chain. Everyone had tears in their eyes, but something else was growing in their hearts. It was hope. An extraordinary warm feeling of optimism spread to each family member, through their bones and into their hearts. This was the beginning of a new life for all of them.

Margret knew it might take a while before she and her daughters could leave for Canada, but it was worth the risk. She would continue knitting the wool sweaters to support her family. They had enough extra money saved for one year, and then they'd have to leave to wherever Einar and Nath made their new home. There were rumours of a parcel of land called New Iceland, and Lord Dufferin, Governor-General of Canada, was naming it as such.

Margret was hopeful and fearful at the same time. Everything they had depended on and worked hard for in Iceland was gone. The Olasons had to take the risk for a chance at a better future. There was nothing left for them in Iceland.

The family reached the dock, and they all stood in line with the crowd of immigrants going to Canada. There were hundreds of men, women and children. Some of the wealthier families could afford to take every single family member. The Olasons decided that it would be better if the men set up homesteads in Canada first, then sent for the women later. They had little knowledge of the hardships they may endure in a new country. They expected it to be harsh. They somehow knew it wouldn't be easy.

The line moved up until finally, Nathan and Einar were next.

Emma hugged Nathan fiercely. "Don't you ever risk your life for anything!" she said worriedly. "You take extra good care of yourself and Pabbi! I want to see my brother in one piece when I get to Canada! And find us a future, Nathanael. We need it." She squeezed him tightly one last time, then released him. "I love you! I'm going to miss you."

"I love you too," Nathan said. "Don't worry."

Eva hugged him next, with tears in her eyes. "Make a good home for us there," she said softly.

Finally, Margret hugged him last. "Nathanael," she said. "Remember what I told you before. Be a good man. Always do what you think is right, even if the world is wrong. And never give up." Margret hugged Nathan tightly, sobbing on his shoulder.

Her wet tears dropped onto his coat as Nathan realized the full extent of the journey he was about to take. "Mamma," Nathan said confidently. "We are the Olasons. We are a strong bunch, and we'll always stay that way."

Margret kissed him on the cheek. "You're right, stay strong," she said, releasing him. "I love you dearly."

Nathan turned, waiting for his father.

Einar nodded and hugged his daughters, then stopped in front of his wife of seventeen years. Einar felt the reality of the situation heavily. He could not stop the tears from falling. His love for this woman had prevailed over anything else. She had been his rock and was now a part of his soul. Margret formed an integral part of his entire life. She was even a part of his teenage childhood. He had only ever loved this one woman, and she was his wife. Leaving the country without her was paramount to shredding his heart for the sake of future happiness. He gripped her tightly and swung her up in the air. Her feet lifted a foot off the ground as Einar embraced Margret fiercely. He buried his face into her neck so she couldn't see the tears. Einar could hear her crying into his shoulder and felt her ribs heave with the sobs. They stood there like this, suspended in time, not wanting to let go.

"Margret," Einar finally said, his voice muffled into her blouse. "You are the love of my life. You hold so much meaning to me, to my life and my future. I cannot even begin to imagine what it will be like living without you, even if it's for one year. It will certainly feel like an eternity."

Margret couldn't answer. Her body heaved with sobs as he gripped her tightly.

"Pabbi," Nathan said. "We're boarding. We have to go." Nathan clutched his father's arm. "We have to go now. The ship is leaving." Nathan peeled the two lovers apart, addressing his mother. "Mamma, we will make a new life. A better one. I promise."

THE END

Final Note to Reader

Before 1875, Mount Askja was a sleeping giant. The mountain had no volcanic activity in documented history for the inhabitants of Iceland. It was possible the Icelanders trivialized the dangers of the mountain and deemed it a dormant, harmless volcano.

Mount Askja is situated in the island's center, slightly to the east. The catastrophic explosion of Mount Askja in 1875 had started many years before the main event, with a growing rift that was forming between 1874 to 1875. It was a series of natural events the Icelanders only experienced as it developed and proved extremely difficult to predict.

I have included many references to possible predictions of Askja, although this is pure speculation about the conditions of Iceland at the time. Icelanders were accustomed to eruptions and lived their lives with this constant threat.

The first signs of trouble began in January 1873 when Grimsvotn, a volcano located to the south of Askja, exploded with a rather large eruption. Icelanders didn't think it was highly unusual because Grimsvotn erupted regularly, although this specific explosion was more powerful than usual. Some ash, or tephra, from Grimsvotn, had reached the top of Askja, forming a layer.

In early 1874, steam clouds were documented from the top of Askja. Since there were scarce inhabitants close to Mount Askja, farms were ten or more miles away; nobody really knew what had happened. Strong seismic activity began in August 1874, rocking isolated parts of the island and starting a series of unstable earthquakes, terrorizing the northern people of Iceland. The seismic movement increased in magnitude and continued until late December 1874, causing severe ground deformation. What nobody knew at the time was that a dike was maliciously forming underground from Askja to the north, causing the earthquakes and buckling the land into rifts. The pressure was building.

On January 2, 1875, the earthquakes became stronger and caused serious damage to farmhouses in the northern parts of Iceland, mostly near the Sveinagja and Veggjastyki grabens. Some reports were measurements of 6.5 magnitudes, although this was unclear at the time. Many properties were damaged, and people fled for their lives. The ground noticeably changed shape, and the grabens were visible. These grabens were depressed sections of the earth's crust with clear fault lines rising parallel on each side. The earth was opening up. Nobody realized that the earthquakes, located 30 miles north of Askja, were just the sideshow.

On January 2-3, the seismic activity climaxed with an eruption at Askja. There were no eyewitness reports other than the cloud atop Askja being spotted by farmers. It may have been a significant eruption producing a sizable crater, but nothing was confirmed at the time. Another eruption cloud a few miles north was also documented. Then a period of calm descended on the land after these two eruptions. The earthquakes diminishing in intensity possibly created a false sense of security before the catastrophe yet to come.

On February 16, there was intense hydrothermal activity documented at the top of Askja. Two days later, on February 18, 1875, a rift eruption tore through the ground deformation in the Sveinagja graben, where the earlier earthquakes of December and January were the strongest. The focus shifted once again to the north, causing panic. Within minutes, visible lava flows were erupting from the rifts.

A second, third and fourth rift eruption occurred in the Sveinagja graben on March 10th, 18th and 25th, respectively, scattering northern residents to flee. The continuous fissure did not produce one dominant cone but rather erupted along the entire ground depression in several smaller and shorter-lived craters, forming a line to Askja. A March 25th report totalled 40 craters in the Sveinagja graben. The magma underneath Sveinagja was desperately trying to find a weakness to the surface. Scientists have speculated that new magma had begun accumulating under Askja deep below the brittle crust. The December dike to the north began forming, looking for a way for the ground to ease the pressure through the rifts. The new magma was trapped underground, forcing it to start dangerously mixing with a shallow stale magma chamber underneath Askja. Since Mount Askja had been dormant for centuries, it had created a stagnant brittle magma chamber, which holds the magma in like a pressure cooker. This is why these types of volcanoes are the most dangerous.

On March 28, the rhyolite 1875 Mount Askja explosion started with a subplinian eruption, with phreatic (hydrothermal) precursor activity. A rising column with a large steam cloud was visible, and wet tephra had fallen as far as 30 miles away.

The town of Horn, where Margret and Einar's sheep farm was located, is 90 miles away from Askja, along the eastern shoreline of Iceland. Horn was the old original name of the new town that is now called Hofn. Sheep were, and still are today, a common food source for the Icelanders. The island of Iceland does not have many sources of food, so Icelanders brought sheep over in the early beginnings and struggled during the winters to keep their food rations. They resorted to utilizing every single part of the sheep, including the sheep's head, which is a common Icelandic delicacy today.

The scarceness of wood, which was mostly burned or used for building in the early years, made it difficult to build or heat Icelandic homes. Houses were built into the countryside, similar to Scandinavian houses, with grass roofs and only the front walls and doors made of wood. The earth provided the heat and insulation; often, body heat and sometimes animals were the only heat sources inside the homes. Although, coal was imported and used for heat in the stoves of the wealthier class families.

1908 marked the beginnings of geothermal heat in Iceland. As far back as the late 18th century, some countries had adopted geothermal heating, and in the late 19th century, some states in the USA had begun harnessing geothermal energy. Stefan B. Jonsson, an innovative farmer in southern Iceland, built pipelines in 1908 leading into his home from a nearby hot spring pool. This was the first documented case of geothermal heat in Iceland. It was a simple primitive system, but it worked. Several years later, many other farmers did the same, and it pioneered the birth of what is now called Reykjavik Energy, the country's geothermal heat and energy provider.

I would like to say that many historical characters appear in this book as the previous three books had done in this series, but sadly there are none. Lord Dufferin, the Governor-General of Canada and Sigtryggur Jonasson, the Icelandic entrepreneur and immigration agent to Canada, were both mentioned briefly in this novel, and these were the only historical individuals.

This book is about Icelanders, their heritage, their land and the biggest antagonist of them all, Mount Askja.

After the subplinian eruption, a rising cloud column was seen from 9 pm that evening until night cover. Whoever did not escape from the eastern Icelandic area between this time and the morning of March 29, 1875, perished.

At 5:30 am on March 29, a catastrophic phreatoplinian explosion rocked Mount Askja, blowing a crater off the top of the mountain. The dormant magma chamber exploded from the intense magma pressure underneath, releasing a column 20 miles high and lasted over an hour, burning and burying everything in its path. Six feet of tephra was deposited in the caldera, and an enormous ash cloud travelled across the North Atlantic Ocean, affecting countries as far away as Scandinavia. The ash from this explosion was wet and sticky. It burned and stuck to livestock, homes and people, burying everything in hot sticky tephra. Small rocks flew from the explosion like fireballs. Pyroclastic flows followed the explosion, making sure no one survived, obliterating the entire eastern side of Iceland. But Mount Askja wasn't done yet.

After a 30-minute brief cessation, another plinian explosion followed with dry tephra and another 20-mile columnar cloud. Along the eastern shorelines of Iceland, even 90 miles away, including the town of Horn, the ash was one inch thick.

After the eruption of March 28-29, the earthquake activity diminished, successfully finding Mount Askja as a source to relieve the pressure of the underground magma. Several smaller explosions along the Sveinagja rifts continued to occur during the year, and another smaller eruption from Askja in May 1875 occurred before things settled down completely in early 1876.

The volcanic explosion killed livestock, sheep farms and buried homesteads. The land was useless, and the survivors made a plan to emigrate to Canada. Mount Askja's explosion was not the only reason Icelanders wanted to leave. The government at the time was unstable, smothering imports and destabilizing the economy. Young people were dealt with quite harshly, and famine was rampant. Oppression was common among Icelanders, and collectively they searched for a way out. During the late 19th century, an estimated 15,000 people left Iceland, which amounted to approximately one-fifth of the population of Iceland at the time. Some moved to the USA and some to Canada.

Canada offered Icelandic people a tiny piece of land called New Iceland in what is now named Gimli, Manitoba. This is what started the series of The Olason Chronicles. A family saga of a strong group of hardy Icelanders who colonized parts of North America despite all the odds and later formed notable parts of the military and Navy during WWI and WWII.

In this final book of the series, the family saga ends by detailing the lives of these hardy Icelanders, the land they originated from, the mom who fought with all her might and the devastating volcano that forced them to flee for their lives.

Today, more than 200,000 descendants of these brave people claim Icelandic ancestry in Canada and the United States. God bless them.

I'd like to thank my family, cover designers, proofreaders, friends and all of my readers for allowing me to do what I love. Thank you from the bottom of my heart. Every single person in this world has a purpose, and so do you.

Never let your dreams die, and if you have to flee to find a better life, do it without hesitation.

ORDER THE ENTIRE 4 BOOK SERIES

THE OLASON CHRONICLES

Don't forget to leave a review

J. A. Boulet was born and raised in Western Canada. Her parents were both landed immigrants from Hungary, escaping during the 1956 Hungarian Revolution. Raised in a European refugee family, J. A. Boulet quickly grew into a strong emotional artist. She started writing poetry at the age of five and subsequently progressed to short stories and novels. Writing has always been a passionate dream throughout Ms. Boulet's entire life. She began to actively pursue her dreams of being a historical fiction author in 2020. J. A. Boulet published her first two books of The Olason Chronicles during the world-wide pandemic in 2020 and has been writing historical fiction ever since. She is currently working on a standalone book and another series, scheduled to be released from 2022 onward. Ms. Boulet still believes in true love and chasing your dreams. She currently lives in Ontario, Canada, with her two teenaged sons and a pet crested gecko named Mossio.

You can learn more on the
website: www.jaboulet.ca